Edelweiss
By Katriona E MacMillan

CW00853950

Cover Photography © 2016 Craig Anderson Photography, all
rights reserved.
Special thanks to Tammie Fairlie and Ross McMillan.

For (but by no means a reflection upon) my family.

Sorry mum.

K

Table of Contents

Foreword
Prologue
Chapter 1
Chapter 2
Chapter 3
Chapter 4
Chapter 5
Chapter 6
Chapter 7
Chapter 8
Chapter 9
Chapter 10
Chapter 11
Chapter 12
Chapter 13
Chapter 14
Chapter 15
Chapter 16
Chapter 17
Chapter 18
Part 2
Chapter 19
Chapter 20
Chapter 22
Chapter 23
Chapter 24
Chapter 25
Chapter 26
Chapter 27
Chapter 28
Chapter 29
Chapter 30
Chapter 31
Chapter 32
Chapter 33
Chapter 34
Chapter 35
Chapter 36
Chapter 37

Chapter 38
Chapter 39
Chapter 40
Chapter 41
Chapter 42
Chapter 43
Epilogue

{Bertram; found your man where you said he would be...and just as crazy as you warned. The story's a peach though, so read and revise. You know where to find me...

~J}

Foreword

My name is Juke Alwhenza; chief journalist in residence for the East Coast Press. Not four weeks hence I was sent a rather peculiar letter. The letter begged for our assistance in tracking down one Miss Abigail Jones. This book is addressed to her; at the request of an eccentric old man who lives in the wilderness and will label himself only as 'a friend.' The old man in question appeals for Miss Jones to get in touch through ourselves, or to approach the port town of Gaul, where he will be able to locate her for himself.

In return for our assistance the old man (who refuses-even after a month of living by his fire to tell me his name) has given us his story. A trifle, you may think...but in this day and age stories are as valuable as gold dust. I am a young man, born after the cataclysm – as many of us are nowadays. The few elders we have are dithering now, senile or damaged...deranged by all that they have lived to see...This old man is coherent, in spite of his eccentricities. His body functions as ours do, without the drooling, without the incontinence, without the terror that can be found in the eyes of those who lived through the great World Shift. This old man is the rarest of treasures... his story possibly the single living testament to the Time Before. I, Juke Alwhenza, commit it to paper in the dual hope that the old man can find some semblance of peace; and also so that we who remain have an account – for the first time ever – of how *exactly* the magic left our world.

J Alwhenza
East Coast Press

Prologue

(I arrived in the night and the old man gave me food and water. He said once I had eaten I had guest rights in his camp, and by the old ways that meant neither of us could harm the other. I have heard of such things before in the far east. He says he has no origins there. I spent a night sleeping under the stars in an average climate. He woke me late in the morning with a gentle toe prodded into my ribs. We ate a basic breakfast and he cleared his throat. I took that as indication of intent and fetched paper and ink. He has urged me to write his account word for word. From here on I shall do just that.)

The story you want from me both begins and ends with Abigail Jones. It begins on an island in the middle of a group of islands in the Circle Sea. The island was named Freisch once...now it is gone like the rest of them. Drowned in the Cataclysm that ended everything we once knew. I digress. Every story has a beginning and this one has many; but let me begin here, with an eight year old Abigail happily playing in her mothers high-heeled shoes and strutting around the manor in search of her parents to show them her achievement. She found them in the dining room; arguing in loud voices whilst Elena, the cook, set plates before them.

'There you are Abigail, it's time for lunch- are those my Leo Burtelli's? Take those off!' said Isabel DeLanois A.K.A. Jones at the sight of her. Samuel, her father, merely laughed, prompting further anger from Isabel's end of the table.

'Don't encourage her Sam for goodness sake! And don't think you are getting off so easily either. You are going nowhere. I don't care what the Guild said and I don't care what that Frank fellow said- you are staying here with your family. It's nearly harvest and there are fifty farmers out there who will need every spare hand they have.'

Across the table, Samuel grinned. Isabel stood, thumped both hands down as fists and turned her glare from her grinning husband to her grinning daughter. Rather than shout, she started to cry. Samuel was on his feet and around the table in an instant.

'Oh my love, don't cry, don't cry.' he said softly as he took her in his arms. 'It's a week at most and then I'm golden for a full year. No more conscription, no more Guild, no more Capital city. Just you me and the kid...we should go on holiday...Remember Port Skart..?' he soothed. His question brought a sly smile and an almost forgotten glow to her cheeks.

'Well we can't do *that* again if we have Abigail with us.' she told him, much to his delight.

'That's why we have Stephen.' he whispered in her ear. They shared a kiss before their daughter interrupted to tell them loudly that they were disgusting. The whole exchange ended with Isabel growling at her daughter to go and take off her expensive shoes before she destroyed them, and with them going on to spend the night together cosy in their perfect little family bubble...Their final night together in fact, albeit unbeknown to them at the time.

     The following morning Isabel and Abigail said goodbye to Samuel and watched him ride away with a small entourage of village guards as his escort – and with tears in their eyes. Years afterwards Abigail told me that her father was often gone. He was a research alchemist – and a good one; well known for his genius, his many small successes and, most of all, for his work in the field of disease control. Specifically, Dr Samuel H Jones was known for his advances in what was once known as 'dark science': a forgotten strand of alchemy that is no longer needed now that there is no magic to fuel it. In our time there were a hundred different wielders of magic – Abigail's mother in fact, was a healer in her own right – but many of those wielders used dark arts; spell-weavers intent on destruction and death. Dr Jones was a master at breaking these magic's apart; and reconstructing them into positive currents or of dissipating them altogether. As far as I am aware Samuel Jones had no inherent power of his own, save for his intellect and a reputable family name that carried both lowly title of Laird and lands of his own. Samuel Jones was a Doctor, a family man and a loyal subject. He was a hard working and beneficial member of the often-controversial-but-mostly-useful Guild of Alchemists. Understand stranger, the man was a pillar stone of the community...and like all pillar stones, the walls around him would eventually crumble into dust.

     Isabel and her daughter spent that first day together, clinging to each other like rafts lost at sea. They spent the morning in the library, where Isabel read to her daughter from her own favourite book; in *Spirits Wake*. In the afternoon they walked along the beach, not one hundred yards from their front door, and ended up in the Beeton village for afternoon tea with Grandma Rose. They finished a lovely, if somewhat empty, day by playing dress up with all of the expensive shoes and dresses from Isabel's wardrobe that Abigail wanted to try. When she tucked her daughter safely to sleep that night it was with rouge on her cheeks, purple-dyed eyelids and a wealth of pearls draped around her neck. She had to remove the high heeled shoes so that the child could sleep...and she tried desperately to ignore the wrinkles in her silk evening gown as her daughter dozed off in it. She went to bed thoroughly exhausted- to find that sleep escaped her. Around midnight she rose and went to Abigail's room, where a queer sense of motherly instinct made her lay her head finally for the night, and fall to eventual dreams alongside the soft sound of her daughters snores.

Stephen Laurence...now there was a man. He was the trustworthy sort, Stephen. He was the kind of man that you would meet once and trust to take care of your children whilst you went for a fortnights holiday. He was steady, and reliable, and at eighteen years old I imagine he was desperate for adventure and a change of circumstance. The truth is that all of this happened a long time before I ever met Stephen Laurence. The man I knew him to be was a leader...strong, and quietly confident...but in those days I tend to think of him as a scared young man who had destiny thrust upon him before he was ready. Said destiny came in the night, and in the form of his Laird; Dr Samuel H Jones, who rattled the door almost free from its hinges in his panicked attempt to wake him.

Stephen called to the unknown visitor to hush lest they waken his elderly father, asleep in the room upstairs. He pulled on plain black trousers on his way to the door, tripping all the way.

He answered the door still shirtless, and felt his blood pressure drop acutely upon sight of his Laird.
He gaped, luckily Samuel didn't give him time to talk.
'I need you to go to the town and evacuate the people. Get that hunter – the one with the voice – and ring the bells in the temple. Get everyone out.' his employer commanded and Stephen stopped in the act of pulling on a white butlers shirt.
'Mi'lord...what's happening?' he beseeched, his brown eyes showing the first traces of fear. Samuel pointed across the fields and towards the manor house, invisible in the darkness of the night.

'There's been a riot on Estora. One of the Lords has gone rogue. Get them out. I'm going for Isabel.' he answered in a rush. He gripped Stephen by the shoulder in a final moment of urgent severity. 'Get the people out of here, Stephen.' he said quietly. For the first time Stephen took in the blood on his face, the tares in his clothing, the way his other arm hung uselessly at his side.

'Laird...' he tried, but he was too late. Samuel was mounting his horse and waving him off from the saddle.

'Go.' said Samuel, his voice a fleck on the rising wind. Stephen nodded and watched him leave in a trance. He shook the last of the sleep from himself and dressed quickly. There was much to do and no time to do it in...and the hardest task of all lay behind him, and up the winding staircase.

'You have to.' Stephen tried for a fourth time.

'I told you. I am not leaving this house! Your mother and I started life here and this is where I'm going to finish it. You fetch me the crossbow from the barn-'

'Father.'

'-Fetch me the damned bow. Then go do whatever it is the Laird wants. There'll be none of those dirty Thieves coming into my house without a fight. Go. Get me the bow.' grumbled Stephen Laurence Snr. from his chair. Stephen squinted at his father hard, and then did as he was told. He thoroughly believed the house, the old man and the crossbow would all be in perfect working order upon his return...The old man could take care of himself, and besides, how bad would things need to get for his grouchy, institution of a father to succumb to defeat?

In the village Stephen began to suspect that he might be underestimating the severity of the situation. He fumbled in the dark until he reached Cobol's gate. Cobol was the local leather-worker as well as the chief hunter, and by sheer luck, happened to have the night off. The half-elf opened the door a fraction and narrowed green eyes at him. He heard a 'thunk' from inside; the noise of a sword being set aside. The glow from the solitary candle beyond seemed to light the whole path as the door swung inwards.

'What?' he grunted. Even through the gruffness of his tone the word shone beautifully, like a rough cut diamond. Words were an elf's stock in trade, they were enchanters all – whether they liked it or not. Cobol was of the second variety, who wanted nothing to do with his ancestry. He was also half human, which made controlling his ability easier for him. He saw the short sword at Stephens side before he answered and nodded.

'Who are we fighting?' he amended his question, words oozing honey. Stephen shook his head to clear it.

'The Laird says one of the Estorans went rogue-' he started. Cobol ushered him through the door and into his kitchen. He handed him a bow and arrows and selected a large model crossbow for himself.

'What're our orders?' he inquired as he worked.

'Evacuate.' answered Stephen. The elf gave a decisive grunt. He produced a backpack from nowhere and emptied the contents of a kitchen cupboard into it. As an afterthought he threw in a dagger and checked his water-skin was full.

'You can leave the sword, you won't get a chance to use it.' he explained. Something in Stephen's sudden stillness made him stop and raise an eyebrow. 'You've never fought a Thief before, have you?' he asked, carefully. Stephen unbuckled the useless weapon and set it on a tabletop.

'I've never fought anything before.' he admitted, embarrassed. He was the Lairds man, he didn't need to fight – that was why they had guards. Cobol tried not to judge him for it. It really wasn't his fault. 'They make eye contact with you, you're dead. That's all you need to know...That- and don't let them catch you.' said the half-elf in warning. On their way out the door he stopped for a second, and spun back to the butler. 'Come and see me some time next week, we'll start your training.' he said optimistically...but by the time they got outside the moon and stars had all but blinked out, and next week lengthened and stretched until it was more than a lifetime away

Samuel hurried his wife to the front door, having managed to stop her short of packing the kitchen sink. She had fretted over his broken arm, healed it quickly and with a great amount of fuss and questioned and badgered him the whole way. Abigail, on the other hand ,just thought they were playing some sort of game, and had happily changed into travelling clothes and packed away her favourite toys lovingly. With his hand on the door he turned to Isabel and kissed her; partly to shut up her whining and partly because the wrenching feeling in his gut wanted assuaged. The horse would take the three of them safely out of the path of danger. At the moment Estora lay directly to the north, straight across the water from the island of Porta; whose shores you could make out from the beach here on a clear day. They would head to Ronton Bay, in the south, where the army waited and where relatives might harbour them until this riot ran its course. He was unprepared for the hell that had descended outside their front door; and when he finally swung it outwards he stopped in his tracks and simply stared.

A ragged rumble of thunder rolled across the night sky and all but shook the beams from the joists in the ceiling. A spattering of stone dust jarred itself free and fell on Stephen before he dived through the open door. He had rung the bells for ten minutes whilst the hunter had gone door to door to drag people from their beds. The people of Beeton huddled around the temple doors in their nightclothes and rubbed bleary eyes. Some were missing, others had decided to stay and take their chances, a few were too old or infirm to be moved – but most of the village gathered, asking questions Stephen didn't have the answers to and trying to locate family members in the night. Stephen found Cobol in a cluster of hunters. He greeted him with a nod.

'We're moving now.' the half-elf told him in a lull. Stephen nodded and turned to the expectant crowd.

'We're evacuating.' he half-heartedly announced. There was a general murmur as people told him that they had already worked that much out for themselves, grumbled about missing family members or otherwise protested for one reason or another. Cobol cleared his throat and silence returned.

'The Estorans are fighting. As you can tell by the sky- they are approaching. They will come across the sea, so we must go through the forest and on to the Bay. Myself and the other hunters assure you that you have nothing to fear from the creatures of the night. We cannot guarantee your safety if you choose to stay here. The guards are gone and the enemy is coming. Make your decision. We leave now.' commanded the hunter, almost too quietly. The spell of his words fell upon rapt ears and worked their way into the minds of the crowd. He turned abruptly, and strode from the square and towards the tree line. Behind him and one by one the spell shattered, and the villagers started to follow.

About the same time as the bells stopped ringing the first bolt of lightning hit the manor house, scorching a trail down the white brickwork and sending the horse into a startled rear. It fled from

Samuel's grasp before he could recover himself and cleared the already open gate in one gigantic leap. Its foot caught at the last moment, and the poor animal writhed and twisted on the ground in fear before climbing onto unsteady legs and bolting towards the fields inland. Samuel swore, and then fumbled to raise his hood as the rain started to lash down on them. He turned to his family to find his wife and daughter several yards away and transfixed by the beach.

'Isabel.' he said flatly. 'We don't have ti-'

'Sam look.' she breathed in a faraway voice. She raised a trembling hand towards the water and Samuel peered after it through the rain. The waves washed steadily as always, hypnotically coming and going from the shore as the rain fell relentlessly about him– but those waves were ink black under the moonless sky and there, on the surface, a criss cross of shimmering blue light was forming even as he paused. In a bolt of light that echoed the storm above the blue light shot from the water and touched the land like tendrils of electricity and suddenly, all too suddenly, he saw what his wife was pointing at. There, amidst the waves, floated corpses; the pale, quiet faces of the dead bobbed in and out of view, dancing a macabre waltz as the waves rose and fell, rose and fell, with their lifeless limbs spread-eagled and their hair floating outwards from their heads...In the blackness of the night Samuel watched the first of the bodies touch the shores of his home. The corpse was once a young man, but now was no more than rags and bones. As it washed up he reached his arm out towards his wife and pulled her away from the sight. He was not quick enough. Before their very eyes the corpse twitched once, twice, three times. Samuel put himself between the corpse and his wife and backed slowly away as the creature got to its feet. Beneath its ragged, parted and decaying flesh the creature walked on a bed of blue sparks that zipped and zapped like an underground thunderstorm. The Estorans were the solitary known users of death magic; and here, facing them, was death magic in its purest form. Isabel screamed, Abigail clung to his legs and, at the sound of his beloved, the creature snapped its head in their direction. Its eyes bulged silver from protruding sockets as it saw them, opened its mouth to reveal a row of ragged, blackened, rotten teeth, and let out a guttural, clicking noise as if it were trying to talk in a voice long lost. As one the family dropped the bags Isabel had meticulously packed and fled for the cover of the forest.

They had made it into the forest safely- at least that part had gone well. Cobol had requested that everyone hold hands so they would not get separated, that had also worked well. In fact, everything had gone well up until the point where they reached the banks of the Green River, which flowed through the woods from north west to south east, consequently separating the forest into two parts. The party started wasting time, unsure of how to cross. 'We have to head north.' suggested one fisherman, 'The fjord is the safest place to cross unless we go right up to the bridge.' The bridge had been built across the northern edge of the island and a mile from the coast. It would be useless to them, too far north to do anything but lead them directly back into danger. It took a lot of persuasion but the majority finally agreed that the fjord was the safest option. And so the party regrouped and followed the river to the north west, noting the ever-increasing blackness as they went. There was a general feeling of nervousness within the townsfolk. With an hour left until dawn the sky should be lightening now, and yet it was as dark as any winter's eve. No stars shone, no moon lit their way, and it was all they could do not to panic. They had not even gone a mile when the little blue wisps and sparks sprung up around them, they hurried on with Cobol's soothing encouragement, heads down and scared, and single file down the narrow path that wound ever northwards.

Once they had finally reached the fjord and the rushing water was replaced with a calm trickle Cobol ordered that the torches be extinguished and wrapped in oil skin pouches to keep them dry whilst they crossed. Laurence went first, followed closely by the many women and children in the party whom he pulled up the brief embankment at the other side where years of water running underneath had worn away the soil to create a steep and muddy hillock. The people crossed the water, re-lighting their torches once they were safely uphill, wringing out their dampened clothes and wary of the blue flares which seemed to reach out to them from the soil. Twenty minutes later and the crossing was complete with the exception of the hunters and Cobol, who were forming a rearguard and still dry. Cobol spent the entire time looking over his shoulder and pacing the bank nervously until he heard the sound that he knew would come.

'Across, NOW! Don't fire, just go!' he yelled to the hunters, waiting until they were all crossing the river before leaping into the water himself. When he reached the other side Laurence grabbed him by the arm and hauled him up the embankment.

'What is it?' he asked. Cobol glanced at him briefly before turning his gaze back across the river. He scrambled up the hill and slammed a bolt into his crossbow.

'Howling.' he explained. 'They've set their bastard dogs on us. Get them to put out the torches again; the smell of the burning fat will attract them.' The last comment was directed to one of the hunters, a strong built, tower of a man who nodded sagely and hurried off to do just that.

'What do we do?' appealed Laurence. He felt lost- he had wanted adventure but he had not wanted to die - nor had he imagined a desperate flee in the middle of the night with hounds hot on his heels. He thought of his father, he thought of his Lord and Lady and of the child, and wondered if they were safe. He had no answers now, and Cobol was talking to him, he needed to concentrate.

'Go,' he was saying. 'Take them south.'

'You're not coming?' Laurence piped up, after a moment of misapprehension. The howling came again, closer this time, within hearing of the party (who looked to Cobol as if for instruction.) He gave them it.

'I'm staying here, I can fight them. Stephen will take you south.'

'No.' another hunter had spoken, and now he stepped forward. After a moment passed another three men, all without families to protect, all followed his lead. 'I have a better idea,' he continued. 'A group of us would be able to scatter them, confuse the scent. We'll stay with you.' The hunters around him mumbled their agreement; there was another howl, closer still than the last. The silenced townsfolk looked uncertainly from Cobol to Laurence, who sweated under their gaze. Laurence turned to the leather-worker, awestruck for a moment.

He offered his hand.

'Just go- don't look back.' warned Cobol as he shook it. There was a moment there, as they shook hands - two men, who had known each other for years- but who also knew that this might be the last time they met, just an extra heartbeat of respect and then it was gone again. The two men parted, each shouting orders to their own groups and heading off into the pitch black forest and towards whatever fate awaited them there.

It would be another full day before the exhausted townsfolk staggered into the safe haven of Ronton Bay, and in all the time they were there, and even although Laurence searched and searched, there was no trace of Cobol or the other hunters.

They simply never arrived.

Abigail heard her parents and she knew she should call out to them, she knew they would be angry with her but she couldn't help it. The trees were talking about her; they were watching her and whispering. Abigail was vaguely aware that trees weren't supposed to do that but the imagination of a child is a powerful thing, and the voices came frustratingly on the edge of hearing so that she couldn't make out what they said. A blue light illuminated her face as she made her way through the trees, through the mists and out onto the blackness of the clearing above the cliffs. The blue fairy stopped and turned to face the child, for a second she could make out the tiny veins in its wings, all of its tiny features- from its almost insectile legs to its minuscule little eyes - which glowed silver. The fairy smiled to reveal tiny pointed teeth before darting over to, and off of the cliff's edge, all at once it plunged towards the sea. The mists had cleared here, although the waves crashed violently against the rocks and created their own version of mist, a sea-spray which filled the air and landed on Abigail's cheeks and hair as she darted towards the cliff's edge, following the fairy.

'Don't go down there fairy- fairy come back! You'll drown in the water!' she screeched.

She hardly even noticed that her father grabbed her back from the edge- so intense was her grief. She was in a fit of tears, trying desperately to relate the story of the blue fairy's awful death to her relieved parents, but unable to stifle the little sobs which escaped her. She resorted to cuddling into her father as he carried her back towards the forest. After she had collected herself a little she took one last look over her fathers shoulder, wanting to fix into her memory forever the blue fairy's death (she would bring flowers here one day) and saw the outline of a man. She gasped, and tried to alert her parents to his presence; she urged them to look and pointed to him. The man did not seem to be really there, he looked like he was made caste in silver, and then veiled by a black cloak so that only some parts of his silver skin shone through it. He seemed to rise from the sea, before stepping rather too neatly onto the rocky ground at the cliff's top. Isabel and Samuel turned slowly, perhaps already knowing what they would find. As they turned the man faced Abigail, reaching out his hand towards her slowly. He uncurled his fist to reveal a patch of darkness which glowed with blue light. Abigail smiled, he had saved the fairy, and then the flash of blue was gone again and he was smiling directly at her, staring into her eyes. He whispered to her; and she knew it was meant to be *to her*, because even though the wind howled and the trees rustled and the sea crashed, even though he was too far away- she still heard him. 'Mine.' he had whispered. 'Mine.'

And just as she understood what he had said she also understood a lot of other things. One was that this night would change the course of her short life forever, and the other was that there had been a blue fairy, but that her parents would never have seen it because *they weren't able to*. She felt herself being pulled away, her father was running back through the trees and the spell was broken. She looked towards the shadow-man and saw other shapes rising over the cliff. She was scared, terrified even, but she was fascinated. She took one last look towards the edge before her father ducked her out of view, but the shadow had turned to face the sea. He was talking again, but this time she could neither make out the words nor understand what he was saying. The moment had passed.

And so the Jones family were on the run again, into the darkness- away from the darkness...over broken tree trunks and across misty ridges. They ran between trees and through clearings. They ran from the howling, from the blue sparks, from the shadow-man. Only when they had bolted out into a clearing to find that a pack of large, silver-eyed, dog-beasts blocked their escape did they stop running. Only when there was nowhere else to go. The dog shaped creatures began to circle the family and this, stranger, is when our tale becomes a grisly one. I would love to tell you that the good Dr Samuel H Jones managed to fight off all five of the grotesque beasts. I would love to tell you that the family, as one unit, survived the vicious attack and went on to live happily ever after- but this, my friend, is simply not the case. In actual fact the Lord Doctor Samuel H. Jones knew his own fate when he saw it. He drew his sword, determined not to go down without a fight, he told his wife he loved her and would do so forever. He took a step towards his daughter, who had been separated from the couple by a towering, circling beast. Fearful they meant to kill his daughter first Samuel took one step towards her, then another, he was met with a low growl. The growl became a snarl at his next step, and at his next, stopped abruptly. The dogs lips pulled back to reveal a jaw line that might snap a horses neck, these were not ordinary dogs, Samuel reflected, these were the kind found at home in nightmares.

Man and beast stared each other in the eyes. Seconds passed. Samuel had two options, he could attack, maybe throwing the dog off balance and reaching his daughter, or he could make a dash for the girl and risk loosing his arm. He hadn't thought about what he would do once he got to Abigail, he just knew he had to reach her. He hesitated a second after making his decision before diving to the defence of his child. The beast's first blow, which he was expecting, knocked him sideways so that he landed at her feet. The dog had managed to tare into his flesh on his left side, and the smell of blood was arousing the other creature's interest. He had barely landed but the dog was on him again; he swung his legs round and landed it a kick on the side of the head. The dog reeled back, and as it did so he followed it with his sword, the blade hit, but barely managed to wound the animal's leg. It was mad. It let out a howling, drool-drenched cry before levelling its head at Samuel, who didn't move. It made to leap, but stopped. Sam realised why too late, only when a whisper of air passed on the right of his face did he begin to turn. It was too late for Samuel Jones...A second animal pounced at him from behind, and as he turned it landed both of its massive front paws on his chest. He didn't make any noise as he fell to the ground. He didn't make any noise as the beast sunk its fangs into his neck. He would not go to his death screaming, he would not let his wife know what pain he was in...He would not show his agony, not when he lay at his daughters feet.

I shall spare the rest of the details, stranger, but Samuel Jones' death was not a pleasant one. He died in touching distance of his family, evil hounds with blooded faces growling at them until they backed away. The girl watched, totally helpless. She looked from her mother to her father's bloodied corpse. All thought had long since left her, gut instinct alone remained, and it told her to get to her mother. Her mother. It took a long time for Abigail to realise that her mother was screaming, over and over and over again, just screaming. It was a horrible noise, and Abigail knew that she would remember it forever. She determined to walk to her, to cuddle her and make her stop screaming. She took one step towards her and met with a snarl. The dog who had been circling her raised its head, its bloodied nose dripping as it looked at her. It freed itself from the feast and walked towards her, growling low in its throat. Abigail ignored the dog, thinking solely of her mother. They needed each other, mummy was still screaming. She half-saw the shadow-man out of the corner of her eyes and looked at him once more. He met her gaze and smiled...How could he smile now? The dog beasts dispersed on his arrival and the only sound in the little clearing was the frantic sobbing of her mother, whose voice had given up on her. He placed a finger on his mouth as if it was all a game, then he laid both hands on Isabel's shoulders.

Abigail did not watch her mother die. She turned away from it. She did not realise but what the shadow-man was doing was separating Isabel's soul from her body, he held it in his hands, a small, glowing silver-blue light that looked an awful lot like a blue fairy, and then folded it away into darkness. Abigail heard a whooshing noise, but still did not turn around. She spied the mauled and broken body of her father and turned back in fright. She raised her eyes to look at the shadow-man; sure enough he was looking at her. She tried to make herself as arrogant as possible. She was not scared of him; she knelt beside her mother and kissed her on the forehead.

'Touching.' said the man, there was no humour, no mocking in his voice. He lifted his hand and rested it on Abigail's cheek. She felt dizzy suddenly, and ached to sit down.

'Ah,' he began, talking softly, shaking his head slightly, 'But you know nothing, do you?' he sighed, and lowered his face to meet hers. 'Sleep.' he prompted, and before he'd even finished the word Abigail had hit the ground, the sheer power of his gift forcing her young and tired body to comply without question. Abigail slept, and never before, in all her short life or since, had sleep brought such blessed, sweet relief.

'So the story has begun stranger...friend; perhaps not the story you thought you were getting – but trust me...That one incident

– that one happening – was what started a chain of events that led to the changing of our world...of your world too, although none of you now are old enough to remember. Abigail Jones, that little girl with the green eyes and the red-brown hair- was never supposed to survive that night. Somehow she did. Somehow she escaped that vile creature, and the little girl that should never have existed, alongside the faithful butler who would not rest until he found her feverish and weak after the storm had passed: they grew up and changed the world...and that is where your story starts.'

'Fill the kettle if you will, whilst I decided how best to continue...'

Chapter 1

Abigail ran her fingers along the shelves and found her place. She slid the book back in and selected the next one along. She dropped into the leather easy chair and absent-mindedly set a stray finger to pushing the pendulum of the small golden clock on the desk. The clock made a comforting tick-tick noise as she ran a hand over the volume. *'Flowers and Folklore'* featured a silvery, snowflake shaped edelweiss flower on the cover and sported her fathers name as joint author. The fingers of her left hand shook as she opened it – the fingers of her left hand never stopped shaking. Elena said it was nerves but her aunt Catherine whacked her around the head whenever she saw it...it was unbecoming of a young lady, apparently. So was parricide, but that didn't stop her thinking about it twelve times a day. She lost all thoughts of her aunt in the crisp, fresh, undisturbed pages. Her father had written half of the books in the study, and Abigail was determined to plough her way through every one. Some of the words were too hard (she was still just fifteen, and Catherine had refused to send her to school...you guessed it: 'unbecoming') but Stephen, Elena and the other staff helped her where they were able. In a loose panel in the back of her wardrobe there was a notebook; and in that notebook was every word none of them had been able to figure out. Elena had told her about dictionaries in a very abstract way. To her understanding they were books of nothing but word-explanations, and Elena was appealing to a friend in the Bay for the procurement of one even as she sat at her father's desk that day, enjoying one of the few solitary moments she ever got.

A sharp rap on the window made her spring to her feet. She took a key from a pocket and ran to the door, clutching the book. At the last moment she remembered the clock was still ticking, and ran back to still it. She left the room, locked the door and deposited the book in a cabinet in the hallway. She ran the length of the corridor and slowed to a walk as she turned the corner into the entrance hall. Catherine was just arriving and she offered a curtsy as the maids relieved her aunt of her shopping bags and Abigail thanked her lucky stars for Stephen and his early warning system.

'Abigail, darling. We have guests for lunch. Take yourself upstairs and change out of those rags before they see you.' Catherine told her curtly. Without meeting her eye Abigail skirted her to the stairs. A cold hand on her arm made her stop and look up.

'Best behaviour. We will not have a repeat of last time.' she clipped her words icily. Abigail stared a moment, remembering the cold and the dark of the upstairs closet...She gave a borderline sulky nod. Keeping a neutral expression with Catherine was the key, but right now she was struggling to keep the hatred out of her eyes.

'Of course, aunt Catherine.' she responded quietly (and to the floor.) Once she was released she climbed the stairs without rushing, lifting her blue servants skirt so that she didn't trip, and closed the door to her bedroom quietly when she reached the top. She stood with her back flat to the door and caught her breath. A fifteen year old Abigail opened her wardrobe, and tried to decide which of her other rags might be better suited for company.

An hour later dessert had been served by a red faced and near-flustered Elena; who'd just had to make a full blown three course meal (for four) with ten minutes notice. The two guests, aunt and niece sat around the oversized dining room table and made small talk. Catherine did most of the chatting, Abigail pushed food around her plate and smiled sweetly whenever she was addressed. She tried not to talk; she always said something wrong when she spoke. The Lady Partridge was nice enough but her son kept talking about his prowess as a hunter and his successes in 'the field'. Abigail smiled her best smile and tried not to show any teeth. The boy was barely seventeen. She couldn't fathom what successes he might have had, given that during the last war he would have been eleven years old. She listened to his stories with feigned interest and laughed in all the right places. Over the years she had gotten quite good at that. Survival was one of the things she did best.

Dinner ended with coffee in the receiving room. Catherine played the piano and beamed at the praise she received. The boy, Iain, had a brandy whilst the ladies sipped sweet, black coffee from tiny china cups. It was late into the afternoon by the time the pair waved the guests away. Abigail watched them clamber into the black carriage that awaited them and trundle off down the cobblestoned path towards the village. Catherine swung the door closed and, to Abigail's surprise, offered the gathered staff a wide smile.

'You may attend your duties. Well done everyone. I expect the invitation will arrive within the week.' she announced, excitement evident in her eyes. The crowded staff dissipated back about their daily chores with dazed expressions whilst Abigail turned a frown upon her.

'Invitation?' she questioned, taking advantage of her aunt's momentary good mood to speak out of turn. Her aunt smiled down at her, she even raised a hand to pinch her on the cheek in a gesture that might, in some circles, have been considered 'affectionate.'

'And you my little flower, you did perfectly well today! I shouldn't think it would be much longer before we can convince him to marry you, and then it's off to start your new life! Aren't you excited?' she asked. Abigail stared and fought to keep her face blank. 'I'm excited. I think we can skip dinner this evening, it's a little late in the day, don't you think?' she finished. Abigail stared after her as she walked down the hallway to vanish around the corner. Only then did she visibly sag. Marriage? At fifteen? Stephen was the only one who noticed the fire in her eyes as she stomped upstairs (to pack.)

He tapped the door lightly and peeked around the side. In her haste she hadn't even bothered to close it. He stepped inside and clicked it shut behind him.

'If your aunt sees this you know what she'll do.' he warned quietly. She was across the room, taking clothing from her wardrobe and throwing it into an old carpet bag. She stopped in the act and flicked wary green eyes at him.

'I'm getting too old to let her push me around. I won't let her do it any more.' she decided, and got on with the packing. Tight-lipped, Stephen folded his arms across his chest.

'Don't forget to take a weapon.' he said slyly. She stopped again, and this time turned to him.

'Aren't you coming?' she queried blankly, as if the thought hadn't even crossed her mind.

'Course not. Why would I walk out on a decent wage and free rent?' he asked equally plainly. She frowned and lowered her chin so that her red curls bounced around to tickle her nose. She scratched it in annoyance.

'But you promised me you would look after me.' she pointed out, sulkily. It wasn't quite a plead; more a mix between statement of fact and a whine. He raised an eyebrow.

'I'm not the one that is leaving.' He let her ponder that for a moment, annoyed at himself because she was right. He had promised that...the day he found her in the clearing, head to toe in blood and soaked through from the rain. She was feverish, weak. Days had passed since the desperate flee in the night...he never found her parents...he never found his own father, come to think of it; just two rotting Estoran bodies and an abandoned crossbow...the crossbow...the single, lonely trace of Cobol he had ever found. He ran a hand over his face and worried that he found stubble there. Catherine would be pissed. He better shave.

When he started to pay attention again he realised Abigail was crying. She sat on the edge of the bed with her head in her hands and her little shoulders heaved up and down soundlessly.

'Hey...' he soothed softly, but she just kept crying. 'It's not that bad Abby.' he tried.

'I don't want to get married.' she half-whispered. 'I won't do it.'
Stephen had to stop a smile. He had known this moment would come for her whole life...she was a girl who lived in the present, dodging whatever trouble she was in at the moment and never thinking much farther ahead than breakfast time.

'You'll have to marry at some point...or else you might end up like Catherine.' he teased. She gave a mirthless laugh. 'Besides; you'll get out of here. Once you're out of here you will have your whole life...you'll be free. You don't need to run away. You just have to wait.' he explained gently. The poor kid, Catherine never sat her down and explained things to her. She stopped crying at his words and cuffed at her nose.

'And will you come with me? If I get married?' she considered hopefully. He clenched his jaw shut and shook his head.

'Maybe one day.' he said instead of what he should have. He thought she would cry again, but she didn't. She squared herself up instead, standing and beginning to sort out the mess she had made.

'Then I suppose I'm staying here.' she decided. Stephen smiled and gave her a pat on the shoulder.

'That's the spirit.' he said gently. She met his eyes with a lack of emotion that would have scared him, were he not entirely used to it by now.

'But I am *not* getting married.'

One week later the letter came. Both Abigail and Catherine were invited to Rapton, the Laird Partridge's home town, to attend a formal ball. Catherine responded at once to confirm their attendance. Abigail endured the dress fittings, the servants gossip and the excitement of her aunt Catherine for a whole week before they were ready to leave. They attended the ball as planned and everything went swimmingly...right up until the Laird Partridge announced his son's engagement to one soon-to-be Lady Abigail Jones, of Freisch. Abigail choked on her (watered down) wine and rose from her seat just long enough to tell the Laird exactly what she thought of his son. She blamed her aunt of course; who gives a fifteen year old wine? The words 'pompous' and 'arrogant' were used, and she most certainly recalled calling the boy a fool- Catherine pretended it was a 'joke in poor taste' and got her out of there before she said anything worse. Fortunately for Abigail they were more than fifty miles from home and had a boat trip to endure before they reached the manor. She hoped Catherine would have cooled off by the time they got home, but she grossly underestimated the simmering heat of her aunts anger...and the intensity with which it could burn.

The first sign to the household of the mistresses return was when Abigail came through the front door backwards. She fell over her dress and fought with the material to get back to her feet. Catherine took two strides into the room and hit her across the face with a riding crop that she had just liberated from the driver. Abigail backed away, the pretty, pink and white floral day-dress wrapping itself around her legs. She finally managed to free herself just in time for her aunt to slap her again. She spun, tripped and went over on her back and her aunt followed her down, slashing with the crop until she ran out of steam. Abigail used her hands to guard her face and waited. The blows stung; but her aunt had the stamina of a ninety year old, and she had long since learned that it was simply a matter of enduring and waiting till she was done.

'Lady Catherine. You're home early.' Stephen's voice, clipped short and tight, as if the words were hard to utter. Abigail risked opening an eye to look at him. She wondered what sight he could see, what the pair of 'ladies' must look like, brawling on the floor. Her aunt was a psychopath: interrupting her now was *not* a good idea.

'Get. Out.' Catherine muttered through gritted teeth. She paused to catch her breath then, enraged by the sight of her niece's open eye, she slashed down again with the riding crop. 'You, little, bitch!' She ground out, accompanying each word with a slap. Abigail bit into her lip to balance out the pain...she could still feel Stephen in the room. She waved a hand in the hopes that he would leave. Instead, he took a step forward.

'Stop it.' he said quietly – too quietly to hear. By now the staff were emerging, hanging around the top of the stairs or peering around the corner in the hallway. Catherine continued her assault, hitting another twice before pulling back for a third blow to find that Stephen had removed the crop from her fist.

'That's enough.' he said carefully. For the first time in anyone's memory his brown eyes had gone from soft to dangerous. Catherine turned to him in her anger, ready to wrestle the crop from his hands. When she met his borderline-terrible expression she changed tact. 'Very well. She can spend a night in the dark, and think about what she has done!' she spat into his face instead. She turned on Abigail once more and grabbed a handful of curls. Abigail finally yelled out when she started dragging her to the stairway. Stephen took another step forward and the servants at the top of the stairs scampered into hiding at the sight of a raging Catherine coming towards them. Abigail fought to prise her hair from her aunt's hands until she was halfway up the staircase. Suddenly the closet door loomed into view, and Abigail knew what she meant to do.

It is a trivial thing stranger: the darkness. It is a part of life. Everything in the world is light or dark, or a combination thereof. The darkness enables a primal fear in all of us; derived from a time where man lived in caves and had nothing but fire to keep away the creatures of the night. The darkness represents the unknown...and for a reason she could never fathom but that was perfectly obvious to everyone else; Abigail Jones was perpetually, illogically and irrevocably afraid of the dark. In fact, it was one of the very first things Catherine ever learned about the young niece who had destroyed her life by her mere existence. It was also something that she never failed to utilise as a punishment.

Abigail squirmed and struggled, she fought and clawed and bit – but Catherine was putting her in that damned cupboard whether she wanted to go or not. About three steps from the landing Abigail managed to break free and leapt away from her and back down the stairs.

'I'm not going in there again!' She shouted as she ran. Then something changed in her...the coldness crept into her. Stephen could see it fall over her like a shroud. Her shoulders relaxed, her hands went from her bleeding face to her sides. She flicked her hair out of her face with a confident toss of her head. She picked up a poker nestled by the door and walked slowly back to the stairs. 'Abigail!' whispered Stephen. There was no response. She climbed the stairs methodically back to her aunt and the household held its breath. She stopped the step below her and held out the poker, handle first, towards her.

'Just kill me then. I'm not marrying that idiot and I'm not going back in the closet. So just kill me. I can't live like this.' said Abigail in an empty voice. Catherine eyed her wildly, unsure of whether or not it was a trick. Then she grabbed the heavy iron poker from her unresisting hand and swiped it across the side of her mocking niece's head in a blow that might well have killed her. Abigail crumpled from the knees and slid down the stairs on her way down. The pain didn't compute, not really. The last thing she saw before she rolled to a halt was Stephen leaping over her and catching her aunt's arm just before she could go in for the final swing.

Chapter 2

There were flames, lots and lots of flames. There was an arm in the dirt at her feet. Most of an arm anyway. It was just lying there, a gold ring glinting on a finger...hardly any blood on it at all. She wondered where all the blood had gone. Then she wondered who the arm belonged too. She hoped they were alright; though with a wound like that she very much doubted it. A healer might survive it though...a healer like mum.

The man in black raised her chin with a finger. His lips curled into a smile. There was silver in his eyes. She blinked.

'And now we will see what you are made of.' said a hundred voices together. The voices came from the man's mouth.

'What?' she asked, obviously confused. There was, after-all, an arm in the dirt.

'I am not healing this child.' spoke the man again. She squinted up at him.

'Speak sense.' she mumbled on the table. When she opened her eyes Stephen looked down on her with a worry that had aged him ten years. Her head swam when she tried to sit.

'Are you OK? You probably shouldn't get up-' he tried, but she was already sitting.

'Doctor Swaness.' she all but whispered, greeting the middle-aged healer with as close to a smile as she could manage. 'Arghhh she hit me...' she remembered with a groan. Her brain thumped against the side of her skull in a futile effort to escape.

'You told her to.' said Stephen.

'Did I? That was stupid.' she answered.

'You think?' scorned Stephen, with an unusual flash of anger. Abigail focused on him.

'Where's Catherine?' she asked slowly. Stephen looked blindly out of the window. He sighed.

'She's in the cupboard.' he admitted, a touch of colour in his cheeks. He was annoyed and mainly at himself. He had lost his temper – but no wonder – and now he had no job, no home, and a terrible feeling that he was about to kidnap a fifteen year old.

He wasn't expecting her to laugh in glee and throw her arms around his neck.

'That's wonderful, honestly, wonderful! So...fitting.' she joked as she parted from him. Another thought occurred to her, even better than the last. 'You know what this means don't you?' she asked, suddenly bubbling over with excitement. Stephen nodded grimly.

'It means I'm sacked.' he said flatly. She laughed again and slapped him on the back. He couldn't recall ever having seen her this happy.

'I'm homeless Abby, it's not funny.'

'Oh but it is! Don't you see? This is what we've been waiting for Stephen. Let's go! Let's do it! Let's just run-'

'She'll be onto us already Abby, she'll send the hunters. We won't even make Placton.' he said with a shudder at the thought of being hunted. Then again at the thought of Placton; a horrible dive of a town where they were equally as likely to get robbed and left to die in the cold as they were to be found by Illion Marks and his crew.

'Oh don't worry about that, I've had an escape route planned for years.' Abigail sang out happily. He turned to her, a single eyebrow raised.

'Oh really?' he asked patiently.

'Really.' she replied, and tapped the side of her nose. He watched her a moment longer, then finally allowed himself a smile.

'It's just as well I packed you a bag then, isn't it kid?' he answered...and was still totally unprepared for it when she rugby tackled him with another hug.

          Ten minutes later they were hiding around the side of farmer Brain's stable and scoping out the security. Abigail watched the stable boy hang up a saddle and go inside to the sound of the lunch bell.

'Right on time.' she whispered, and checked the position of the sun. Stephen resisted the urge to put his head in his hands by rolling his eyes instead. His young accomplice had read too many books.

'Hey! Why do I have to do it?' he asked uncertainly.

'Because you are the one doing the kidnapping.' she explained.

'Oh.' he answered.

'I'll meet you on the trail.' she said (before he had a chance to protest) and disappeared from sight. Stephen sighed, then firmed his resolve. He was an outlaw now after all, and outlaws stole things, that's what they did best. He straightened his black butlers jacket and strode straight on in to the stable.

Inside, none of the four horses there were saddled – just his luck. The lowly stable stank of manure and rotted hay. A group of fat, black flies buzzed in the air and he batted them away in disgust. A white beast in a stall whinnied at him and scuffed at the ground a couple of times. He patted it on the nose and it nuzzled back. This was the one then. He was in the process of trying to work out how one attached the saddle to the horse when a door slammed shut off to his left.

'Shit.' he swore. He looked from the horse to the open stable doors.

Cue Stephen Laurence on a horse, clinging to its mane for dear life with one hand and with his other wrapped around a semi-strapped saddle; bursting forth from farmer Brain's stable and knocking the stable boy clean out as he jumped from the path of danger. He didn't have time to go and check on the kid, and he had no idea how to stop the horse even if he wanted to. Instead he bound onwards towards the forest trail. As promised Abigail met him on the path and, in an astounding feat of foresight, with a solitary sugar cube held in the flat of her palm. That solitary sugar cube was enough to slow the galloping horse and allow him to escape with his life.

Abigail fastened the saddle whilst the twins played tag in the trees. Stephen glanced from the two boys back to her and shook his head.

'They're just children-' he began

'They're Illion Marks' children. I'm sure they are more than capable of killing any big bad gribblies in the forest. Besides, they're eleven. It's time they learned.' she claimed confidently.

'Abigail.' he reproached.

'Stephen.' she said with equal measure.'Trust me. This is a cart horse: it won't stray from the path.'

They held each others eyes for a moment before Stephen nodded.

'I'm going to regret this.' he realised.

'Not until you've been rowing for at least an hour.' she replied. 'Right boys, time for an adventure!' She called with excitement in her voice. 'Who wants to go off down the trail and find daddy, eh?' she spoke, leaning over the snot-nosed twins. They grinned and cheered at her feet. The smile she gave them could cut glass.

Another ten minutes later and the two of them were walking along the tiny wooden pier and choosing from the best of three boats. One was halfway underwater already; another looked like it wasn't far behind...perhaps 'choosing' was not the correct word, after all. They climbed into the third boat and broke out the oars.

'I have to admit-' started Stephen, then paused to grunt as he pushed the rowing boat away from its mooring, 'it's not a bad plan.' he finished. Abigail beamed, then opened up her bag to see what there was for eating. She exclaimed in happiness when she found the copy of *'Flowers and Folklore'* stashed in beside her clothes and a few rations.

'Elena thought you'd want that.' he told her sheepishly.

'Elena...' she said, and looked back across the water to the white-washed house standing not a hundred yards from the beach. For the first time that day Stephen watched the happiness fade from behind her eyes as she remembered the people that they were leaving behind.

'One day I'll come back.' she said coolly. She was looking back at the book on her lap, and she opened it slowly, and ran her hand over the fresh, clean paper. 'And I'll put Catherine in the cellar to live.' she added. Stephen said nothing...time would heal her wounds. In the meantime, his days work had only just begun...and it was going to be a very, very long afternoon.

In the quiet of a late autumn afternoon the sound of a longhorn rung out across the still farms of Beeton. People came from their homes, half eaten lunches still in their hands, to see what all of the fuss was about. Out in the forest the hunters stopped, put down their tools and headed home through damp undergrowth at high speed. The longhorn meant they were under attack – but Freisch was a peaceful nation full of peaceable people, and there was no war here. Under the eves of the trees a large, shabby grey wolf pinned back its ears and sent out a call to its mate...Beeton was in trouble, and the hunters were being recalled to their masters side.

Chapter 3

Siara Teel swept loose hair off her forehead and cursed against the wind that had risen constantly since they had left. She could handle the rain; but the wind was dangerous...it shifted direction every other moment and gave away the party's scent to all and sundry.

'We need to huddle down out of this weather.' she complained to Illion. The tall elf made a fluid motion that might have been a shrug. 'You're not expecting to be attacked, are you? He's just a butler.' he cooed in a voice that might move mountains. Siara sighed, and allowed her mount to keep pace with the others. There was a rustling in the bushes some thirty yards ahead and beside her both Pat and Aitken drew weapons. Illion made a dismissive sound and drew his pale stallion to a halt.

'George. What news?' he hailed. Sure enough George Dickson's naked body emerged from the trees. Whilst the men grinned Siara blushed and averted her eyes. There was no shame in the Wanderer's movements, no embarrassment. They were a strange species indeed. A second glance told her two things; one, that his body was a lot...furrier...than a normal man's, and two, that George Dickson had very little to be ashamed of. She blushed again and tried to ignore the fact that Pat was laughing at her discomfort. She hoped he hadn't seen her take that second glance...George Dickson was a married man, after all. She really hoped Greer didn't emerge from the bushes naked as well, the boys couldn't take much more before they broke out into catcalls and someone's jaw got broken.

'Nothing so far. I can smell them though. They haven't left the path. Greer and I are going to head out farther.' informed the Wanderer. 'Not tonight George. Tomorrow. We need to get out of this wind.' answered Illion coolly. George Dickson looked at the elf, considered the sky, and then stared back at the elf again.

'Very well.' he agreed. It was the longest exchange Siara could remember them ever having. Nobody spoke to the Wanderer couple; the people back home bought their meat and furs but they didn't dwell on them. They were different, and odd, and entirely too reserved to get to know. The people left them alone, except for Siara of course. She was curious, and friendly, and she liked Greer's wild spirit and free thinking. Illion said she was a bad influence...he was probably right.

They turned off the trail and struck camp for the night. Illion started a fire whilst Greer and George (now dressed) hung back from the flames and ate their meat raw. The other four shared a hog and Siara stripped the carcass down for everything that could be sold, eaten or used. It was a process they had gone through together a thousand times. Siara used salt to preserve the leftovers and carefully hung the pack of meat outside of camp and from the highest branch she could reach...you never knew what the smell of blood attracted in the darkness of the night...what might come to tare your camp apart in the hunt for it. She also volunteered for first watch, because it would buy her the next two nights off and she still felt full of energy in spite of the drizzle. As the others were bedding down the Wanderer couple argued, voices coarse and harsh in their own, guttural, mother tongue. They squared towards each other, heat in their body language and fret in their tone. Siara watched, fascinated, as George's fangs slid out from behind his lips in what seemed a lot like a growl. Greer responded by raising clawed hands to strike away his touch. It was a strange sight; disturbing, to see two humans behave like two animals instead...she wondered how hard it would be to be stuck forever in between, like they both were. George had raised his hand, and looked like he might strike his wife. Siara was on her feet and with her hand on her sword hilt before she even realised what she was doing..Memories bit at her; of a drunken father who liked his fists too much. George snarled at her, whilst Greer looked confused. The scenario finished with George taking his wife roughly by the arm and leading her off into the trees, fangs still perched menacingly between his lips. Siara relaxed, and noticed Illion had his hand on her shoulder. She followed the hand up to his face.

'Don't get involved.' said the elf discreetly. 'I will take this watch. Get some rest.' He told her in a voice that could not be argued with. Siara yawned, and wondered why she was suddenly so sleepy. 'Wake me for the next one then.' she told him, and stumbled off to find a place to rest her suddenly weary head.

In the morning Siara wakened the others with a fresh, meaty breakfast and welcomed them to the fire. Greer came first, looking for something bloody for she and her husband. Siara stared at the bruise around her eye and handed over the meat mutely. She couldn't help herself. Before the other woman had taken two steps she stopped her.

'Why don't you leave him?' she asked in a whisper. Greer tilted her head, like a lost puppy who was trying to understand.

'He is pack.' she said simply. It was quite obvious. Humans were strange. Siara frowned at her response and swept hair from her eyes.

'There are other packs.' she replied. It was Greer's turn to frown.

'You know...my father used to- my father was like George. I got out.' she tried; but George was waking and he wanted fed, so Greer spun on her heel with an air of panic and went back to him, like she always did. Siara shook her head and handed Illion his breakfast. He took it from her with a cold glance of warning. He didn't say 'I told you so...' but the look he gave spoke volumes.

They had been moving for no more than an hour when they encountered the horse and its two dreaming riders. I don't know, stranger, how best to describe the hunters reaction...except perhaps to say that they weren't very happy. Siara was the only one to have to conceal her smile when she realised who the assailants they had been tracking all day and night had turned out to be. Illion was perplexed – which in itself was hilarious. She had never seen him in such disarray before. Illion Marks was a man of control; and in that moment, on that dusty forest path, she witnessed him roar a curse so loudly that he woke his own children – who were delighted to see him. The adventure had been long, and precarious, but they had survived! Better; they had found father, and succeeded in their quest. Lady Abigail would so happy with them! Even if, for some reason, daddy didn't seem to be very happy at all.

Chapter 4

In the very early hours of the morning an exhausted Abigail pulled the oars a final time and grabbed at an overhanging branch to pull them to a stop. She stabbed an oar vertically into the grass embankment. She looped the rope around the makeshift pole and threw both bags onto dry land. The sudden lack of movement woke Stephen, who twitched under his jacket and jerked awake, realising he didn't quite know where he was. He stared at her on the bank a moment and ran a hand through his short brown hair.
'What time is it?' he croaked. Abigail shrugged. She handed him a water skin and watched him drink.
'Ronton's just around the outlet there. I don't fancy rowing into the harbour, we'll get squashed in this little boat.' she said with a croak. Her voice betrayed how weary she was.
'We should camp. The hunters won't be moving at this time.' he told her, concerned, and handed back the skin. She shook her head.
'We're a half mile out. We can sleep when we are on a boat.' she answered, the same tiredness causing her to sigh as she picked up her pack. 'Ooo-' she added, and darted off into the trees.
'Abby!' he shouted, and clambered clumsily out of the swaying boat and scrambled up the bank and after her. She hadn't gone far, and was digging in the dirt at the base of a tree. He gave his own sigh, and rubbed another hand over his tired face. He knew this routine well – too well. She got it from her father.

Right as he was about to speak out she produced what she was looking for; some kind of gooey, sticky, brown root. She held it up like a prize with a wicked smile on her face. When she saw his expression she fumbled it away into her pack.
'It might come in handy.' she told him. The marin root was an awfully good replacement for smelling salts if it was dried and dusty.
'Ooo!' she exclaimed, and darted off again. Stephen sighed, and looked towards the ever-lightening sky. It was going to be a far longer journey than he had expected...wherever it was that they ended up.

It was after nine when they finally made the gates of Ronton Bay. Ronton was the biggest town on Freisch; it was also the only port town; and at nine in the morning the gates were busy and the streets had already been bustling for over an hour. The pair slipped in with the steady stream of farmers, traders and tourists that came through the open gate. Stephen wished he had a hood to hide behind; but Abigail strode through like she owned the place, and even threw a cheerful wave to the solitary (and exceedingly bored) guard. Stephen's smile froze to his face until they were out of earshot. 'Try for a low profile, eh?' he reproached her. Abigail threw him a tired smile and shifted her over-full pack to her other shoulder. Without any further communication they walked the length of the waking town to the harbour. The streets were cobbled and clean; the alleyways were not. Abigail held her nose as they passed one and wondered why people lived in big towns. There was no place for the rubbish and judging by the smell most of the houses didn't have a privy. The scent of fresh baked bread overlaid the smell of excrement and filth; and the pair had to keep dodging into the road to avoid the chamber pots being emptied from the stories above.

'I don't like this place.' she said quietly to Stephen as they pushed their way onto the crowded promenade. A dirty young man with one missing leg thrust a cup into her face and pleaded for her gold. Stephen was between them at once, and guiding her to the less-crowded jetty. She gripped onto his arm, her nails digging in...the laughter gone from her eyes.

'You OK?' he worried once they emerged. She shook her head.

'Feel funny.' she breathed. He looked around for a place to let her sit down and spied a nearby building with an open door. That would do. He all but dragged her through it and into a chair in what appeared to be a waiting room. He sat her in one of the seats just in time for her to swoon.

'Hoi! Stay with me.' he told her. Across the room an unsubtle cough drew his attention. He turned to see a middle-aged, balding and short man who adjusted thick glasses and peered at him over the top of them.

'May I help you?' asked Mister Greene.

'Do you have any water?' asked Stephen. The clerk disappeared through a door whilst Stephen fought to keep his charge upright. He came back momentarily with the water and between the two of them cajoled her into taking a few sips.

'I just need a minute.' she said breathlessly when the faint had passed. She just needed to sleep...and maybe something else...something to do with the boy with one leg and how he hadn't been able to afford a healer. She shook her head in an effort to clear her twisted thoughts. They needed a boat, they needed to leave. Illion would be furious and rushing here on the wings of the Gods to rage at her. Illion Marks was almost as terrifying as Catherine; with the added bonus of being able to hypnotise you with his...elf...ness. 'Would you like me to call you a carraige? I can send the boy-' started Ollie Greene. Stephen interjected before he could go any farther.

'My lady has had no breakfast yet. I did try to warn her...' he half-lied.

'Father is just across the way. I'm quite sure I'll manage the walk.' lied Abigail, although she wasn't sure she hadn't slurred. Ollie looked at her tired smile, contemplated Stephen's five 'o' clock shadow, glanced back at the lady in the chair and pursed his lips. He hadn't failed to notice the tare in her dress, or the mud on her butler's shoes. They both looked tired; and whatever they were running from they appeared to need the help.

'There's an inn a few buildings down the promenade. Just back out the door and to your left. It's run by a man named Oran Grimes. He's a good man, but his clientèle is questionable. Mister Grimes is the tight-lipped type. Probably doesn't like to ask questions. Can't account for the food though.' he said thoughtfully, then he added 'If your father is looking for a place to stay whilst he's here, of course.'

'Of course.' agreed Stephen, gratefully. He turned back to the lady. 'Think your strong enough to go back out there?' he pressed her. She gave a single nod.

'Can we just avoid that beggar with the cup?' she responded. He frowned, but nodded anyway. Whenever he thought of the Jones family – any single one of them – the first word that came to mind was 'eccentric'. He was too long in the tooth to start questioning them now. He thanked Greene for both of them and took her to the inn, fed her, and put her to bed. It was much later, after he had rested himself, that he realised he had never thought to ask the helpful stranger his name.

About six at night an exhausted group of hunters finally reached the steadfast gates of Ronton Bay. They split off into groups and headed straight for the extensive harbour. It did not take long for them to stumble upon Ollie Greene; who wrote down their message with a steady hand and waved a cheerful goodbye to Siara Teel as he closed up for the night. He left the office, walked the length of the promenade and turned up the hill. At the top of the long, cobbled, street he strode up a path and towards the houses in the 'nicer' end of town. He picked his house, approached, knocked the door three times, and waited for his boss to answer. The man who came to the door was impressively broad, had little-to-no neck and met him with amusement in his eye. The quartermaster nodded.

'Join us for one?' insisted his Captain.

'Sir...We have a problem.' he said instead, and watched the man before him go from merry to straight-laced in the same amount of time it took him to buckle on his boots.

'My entire life savings are in that tin.' explained Stephen as Abigail turned it out onto the bed. She fingered through the meagre coins and looked up at him. She was trying not to judge. He shrugged. 'I guess it's too late to ask for a raise?' he offered. She stuck her tongue out at him and sat back from the table. She glowered from the window at the view out and across the harbour. 'We've got enough for the inn. Maybe for one ticket. I could go down and sell some of the ingredients we found-'

'Absolutely not. Not one foot outside this door until it's time to leave. They're out there. Let's just hope Grimes is as tight-lipped as that guy said he was.' mused Stephen. He closed the shutters and sat back down on the bed. Abigail bit her lip in thought.

'Maybe we can find a Captain willing to trade?' she suggested.

'Trade what, exactly?' he questioned, then shuddered at the thought. 'No.' He scratched at his itching beard and realised he needed to go out there and get money somehow. For that he would need a disguise...

A sharp rap on the door had them both on their feet and facing it. Stephen repressed the urge to swear in front of the lady. 'Fresh water!' called a woman's voice from beyond the wood. He relaxed with a deep breath and unlocked the door.

'We don't need-' he started...and then Greer Dickson wrapped her clawed fingers around his throat and pushed him backwards into the room.

He recovered quickly – quickly enough to stay on his feet, anyway. She came at him again, her attempt at a punch thwarted as the man behind her tried to push past her. George Dickson's face was fanged, his lips pulled back in a snarl, his forehead and sideburns hairier than they should be. He stalked into the room with a purpose, pushing his long suffering wife so that she fell in to Stephen's grip. He grabbed her by the neck and raised his fist. Then he caught sight of the bruise on her eye, muttered a curse and pushed her away behind him to fight with her partner instead. Greer landed on the floor and waited...she would jump back in if there was an opening. In the meantime George sprung at Stephen, knocking him again to the ground where they struggled. It was less of a fight and more of a beating as George laid punch after punch on Stephen's face, his arms pinned under the hunters legs. Abigail leaped for Stephen's sword, and lined up a shot with the flat side of the blade, she hit him hard over the head. Hard enough, she had thought, to knock him out...but their physiology was different from a humans...they had harder skulls. The hunter growled and turned to snap at her. She held the length of the blade between them as he sprung to his feet. She had changed his focus at least, and she backed away until the hunter had her in the corner by the door, the sword forgotten at her feet. He tilted his head at her, grinning a row of pointed canines that reminded her of fangs she had seen once, long, long ago. She froze, aware that she was in trouble. He moved in one fluid motion, knocking the sword away with his left whilst he let fly at her face with his right. Abigail went out like a light, and fell to the floor for the second time in a week. Stephen, unable to reach her in time in his half-concussed state, peeled himself from the floor to leap on George and grab him from behind in a choke-hold. He raged when his eyes fell on Abigail, and let out a growl of his own. George was not choking out easily, and he punched him a few times whilst he had the advantage. The hunter clawed at the arm around his neck and thrashed, then he switched tactic and brought an elbow up to take Stephen in the eye. Whilst he reeled George jumped him again, bearing him to the floor and attempting to land more punches around his face and eyes. By this time it had occurred to Stephen Laurence, as yet another blow cracked into his jaw, that he was not going to win this fight. His head snapped towards the opposite end of the room with one punch, and he blearily took in Greer in the corner. He briefly wondered why she looked so scared, and then the thought was cut short as another punch he failed to block with his flailing hands snapped his head back the other direction. He blinked at the fire, trying to clear the blood from his eyes...and then he remembered something about Wanderers...something about Wanderers and fire, and how to scare off a wolf in the night.

His hand sizzled on the log and he choked on the instinctive cry that rose in his throat but held on anyway. He brought it up to thump into the side of George's super-thick skull. It had no impact, not until the hunter turned his head to see what had hit him, and then there was pure panic in his eyes. He crossed the room to his wife in a hurry, springing on his hands and feet like a dog that had been startled and patting at his hair and arms where the sparks had landed. Both of them watched the flame as Stephen rose, somewhat unsteadily, to his feet. He leaned against the fireplace and caught his breath, the log brandished ahead of him as a weapon. He checked his wounds while the two wolf-folk panted and stared. He risked a glance to Abigail, still in a heap on the floor...Gods but she hadn't moved a muscle.

'You. Check she's alive.' he ordered, pointing the slowly burning log at Greer. The woman shot a look to her husband, but the man was focused on the flames. When Stephen took a step towards her she scrabbled around the room and, surprisingly tenderly, checked Abigail still breathed. 'If she's dead I'm going to burn you. You understand?' he told George while he was waiting. The hunter kept his eyes locked on the flame and seemingly ignored his threat. Stephen narrowed his eyes, he had the sudden urge to burn the son-of-a-bitch anyway and took another step towards him.

'She lives.' said Greer to his right. He stopped, still heedful of George, his hand burning hotter and hotter as the flames devoured the wood he held.

'Bring her over to the bed.' he told her.

'She needs a compress.' said the wolf-woman. Stephen grunted. He had a wild idea how to get out of this...but it meant he didn't need to kill anyone. Probably.

'You know medicine?' he asked her. She bobbed her head.

'Field medicine.' she explained. She ripped a strip of material from the girls dirt-sodden, silly, daytime dress and folded it up into a square, which she rinsed in the jug by the bed and pressed against Abigail's swollen skull.

'You.' Stephen said finally, pointed the flaming log at George. 'Get the hell out of my room. I'm keeping hold of your wife for now. You come after us again and I'll burn her at the fucking stake, you hear me? Now get the fuck out of here.' he commanded. The Wanderer pulled his lips back in another snarl but Stephen simply took an idle step towards him and then stopped to watch him bolt for the door. He sagged against the fireplace, desperate to drop his flaming weapon.

'I'm not going to have any trouble from you, am I?' he asked the huntress.

'Not if you put away the fire.' she answered, pulling a blanket over the girl. He gave a relieved grunt and tossed the log back where it belonged, then he crossed the room and stuck his hand in the water jug. There was a sizzling sound that he might have imagined, and then a sweet, high-pitched tinkling sound that it took him a long time to realise was Greer's laughter. He turned his head to her slowly. She calmed herself when she saw his expression, and reduced her laughter to a tittering.

'You need to let me look at your face.' she giggled. He wondered what kind of figure he cut, battered and swollen and bleeding and without a mirror in the room and in the presence of a lady no less. After a few beats he started laughing too...because he was just a butler; yet armed with nought but a stick he had still managed to fend off the big, bad, wolf.

Chapter 5

Abigail awakened with a start. There was a strange man leaning over her, young and blond and terrified by the fact that she had his wrist in an iron grip.

'What are you doing?' she queried in a quiet, troubled, voice.

'T-trying to heal you...' he answered with a stutter. She sat up, pushing him away from her in the process.

'I'm fine, thank you. Where am I?' she challenged him. She looked past him, to the iron door with the bars on the tiny, too-high, window.

'You're in Ronton Bay-' he started

'In the cells? Am I in a prison cell? Let me out of here. Now.' she commanded, there was the familiar cold feeling creeping up from her toes. She swung her legs around and off the itchy straw mattress. She crossed to the door and tried the handle. Locked, obviously, she was locked in a cell. She quelled the sharp stab of panic that sunk in her stomach and was quickly imbibed by the rising cold.

'Guard?' tried the healer. She crossed the two steps of the room and knelt beside his open bag. 'Hey!' he started, and then stopped as she produced a black dagger that he had never seen before. 'How did you-' he spoke, right up until she yanked his arm around so that she could hold the knife against his right temple.

'Well...shout for him again.' she told him, an inch from his left ear. He gulped, he was hired help, he didn't come to work to get assaulted.

'Guard!' he shouted, a little more urgency in his voice. The lock clicked and the door swung inwards...and there was Greer Dickson. She stared at Abigail, and Abigail stared at her...and then she growled at the healer who ran from the room in such a panic that he left his bag behind. Greer followed the length of Abigail's arm and then raised an eyebrow at the knife, which promptly fell to the floor. The huntress sniffed the air and then turned, gesturing with her head for Abigail to follow. She didn't argue. Being free from the cell was all the proof she needed of trust. On the floor in the empty cell the black dagger *dissolved*.

'We have a group of hunters in town.' started Captain Charles Echan. He removed his tricorn hat and threw it onto the desk in the middle of the room. 'I believe they are looking for you, Mister Laurence...well; you and your young companion, anyway.' he finished. He sat in his leather chair and pointed to the wooden one opposite. His two men brought Stephen around and one of them pushed him down into it. Stephen sat without resistance. He looked a little pale, perhaps a little more dishevelled than he was evidently used to...but he didn't look or act like a criminal. In fact the man looked from guard to guard and leaned forward conspiratorially. 'Am I allowed to talk?' he asked politely. The Captain nodded once. And waited.

'I...I'm not a kidnapper. I mean I am – but I'm not. That wasn't my intention at least, when we left.'

'You stole a child Mister Laurence; regardless of your reasoning you are, by definition, a kidnapper. We'll keep you whilst we find your hunters, and they can take you back to your Mistress.' finished the Captain. He nodded to the clerk, who made to leave, and turned to the pile of paperwork on his desk.

'Wait please, please- lady Catherine is...Well she's not right. I mean there's something wrong with her.' Stephen protested. The Captain raised his eyes and held a hand up to stop the questioning glance of Ollie Greene. The clerk, the Captain and the guards all waited...but Stephen said nothing else.

'You better start from the beginning Mister Laurence. If you're going to be hanged the least I can do is hear your excuses.' admitted Echan. He leaned back in the chair, arms folded across his chest, and listened.

'Abigail Jones is Samuel Jones' daughter. 'The mad alchemist'; the doctor that went missing during the riots – you remember him? He was my employer before Catherine came. I'd have left but I made a promise to the kid when her folks died. I promised I'd keep her safe. That's why I had to get her out of there...' Stephen began, and outside the early evening rolled on to a damp dusk.

Abigail picked nuts from the bowl on the table and chatted happily with the Captain whilst Greer sat at the desk, stone-faced. Abigail was a smart nugget from a long line of smart cookies, but right now she was destroying his centrepiece. They were sitting in the big chairs by the fire in the far corner of his office – and he didn't have the heart to tell her that the nuts were ancient and for decoration rather than snacking on.

'I know you're lying about who put Catherine in the cupboard. Your butler already admitted the act. He will have to be charged...' said Echan. Abigail watched him warily from the chair.

'He's lying to protect me.' she shrugged. The Captain hid his grin with his coffee cup.

'Is he now?' he purred. Abigail narrowed her eyes. He knew she was lying, and she knew that he knew she was lying; the question was: what he was going to do about it?

'You wouldn't take the word of a mere servant over a Lady...would you?' she asked innocently. She took a sip of her own coffee and was instantly transported to heaven. The flavour of sunshine on green leaves danced across her tongue and warmed her throat. 'Oh that is *divine.*' she sang eagerly, and drank more. The Captain leaned back in his chair. The girl had her feet curled up under her so that the horrific day dress she wore crinkled all over. She cut a strange figure; like a little doll that should be perfect but who'd just fallen in the river, been found by the dog and dragged back home through a hedgerow.

'I would, but the establishment wouldn't. If you stuck to that story you could save your man's life...but your aunt would know the truth, irrespective of what I do or say.' he answered. She tilted her head.

'What does that mean?' she pestered. He sighed.

'It means that your aunt sounds like a woman who won't be crossed.' he told her, but she shook her head and her little red-brown curls bobbed.

'No. Irrespective. What does irrespective mean? It's in my book.' she explained. She frowned. 'Never mind. My book is in my bag, and my bag is gone. Besides. I don't think I have a pencil.' she finished. The Captain watched her with his mouth slightly open.

'I said your aunt might kill your friend. Don't you care?' he questioned her in his disbelief. She stopped eating the centrepiece and stared at him.

'It won't matter to me, I'll be dead by then. I can't be sad if I'm dead, silly.' she said seriously. Echan felt a chill run the length of his spine.

'And why would you be dead?' he asked, though he wasn't sure he
wanted to know the answer. She sipped, and set the empty little cup
back on the table.
'Because aunt Catherine wants me dead. With me taken care of she
has her life back and she gets my father's inheritance. Now that
Stephen has been caught kidnapping me, all she has to do is murder
me in my sleep and point the finger of blame at the resident criminal.
Put simply Captain; if you send me back there I will die before
Stephen does. I'm not saying that I wouldn't defend myself of
course; but she has a lot of weight and strength that I don't, and I'm
not like her Captain...Regardless of what she has done to me she is
still my only real family, and I could never hurt her. Not really.' said
the girl. She broke the intense eye contact they'd had and cracked
another walnut in the crocodile shaped nut cracker. She put the nut
between its teeth and slammed down on its tail so that the nut
smashed to pieces between them. The Captain picked his hat from
the table and spun it thoughtfully on his finger.
'Now can you please tell me what irrespective is? I'll remember it,
and write it down later.' she said, suddenly a child again. The
Captain stopped spinning his hat and leaned forward to pinch the
bridge of his nose.
'What in all the hells am I going to do with you three?' he asked
rhetorically. Abigail chomped down on pieces of ancient walnut, and
shrugged.
        Siara pushed the door open and behind her George gave a
low growl as the bell above tinkled unexpectedly. The Wanderer
pushed past her and stalked into the room, nostrils flaring. He
crossed to a seat and pointed to it, then toured the rest of the space.
'Can I help you?' asked Ollie Greene. He pretended not to notice that
one of them was furry.
'I was here last night remember? We got their scent at an inn nearby.
We followed it to here. Where are they?' explained Siara. She kept
the man's gaze and one hand on her sword. The clerk licked his lips
and adjusted his spectacles.
'I don't know what you're talking ab-' began Ollie, but stopped,
because the Wanderer was close enough for him to count the hairs
on his eyelashes. He gulped.
'Please, there's no need to threaten Ollie...He might not be the best
looking chap but he keeps good logs.' wafted the Captains voice

from through the open door behind the desk. Echan beckoned the hunters into his office and gestured for them to sit whilst he, himself, sat on the edge of his desk. Siara came first, followed closely by a fanged George, who decided to sniff out the room instead of sit. He came to a stop at an empty bowl of nuts on a table. He picked it up and raised his eyebrows at the Captain., who nodded.

'You're absolutely right of course. We caught your two fugitives. We have them in custody.' confided Echan. Siara looked from he to George.

'Great, where are they?' she entreated, all business. The Captain gave a half a grin.

'They are in my custody.' he answered.

'You said that already.' Siara retorted. The Captain responded with a deep sigh and walked around his desk to his chair.

'I have no intention of releasing either of them. You may tell the Lady Jones that her beloved niece was caught stealing gold from one of my very own officers. The other is a kidnapper, a thief by nature. Both will remain in my cells until I can transfer them to a suitable jail. If the Lady would like to say goodbye to her niece she is welcome to do so; provided she arrives here before I can relocate them, that is.' he answered with the tone of a man who had partaken of this very conversation many times over the years. Siara frowned.

'Do you have the authority to do that?' she questioned the Captain, who smiled disarmingly.

'Forgive me, I should have introduced myself...I am Captain Charles Echan; Commander of the home guard in Ronton Bay. And when it all comes right down to it...I can do *whatever* I like.' smiled the Captain. Siara gave a measured outward breath to steady her temper. George, thankfully, hadn't been following the conversation.

'She won't be happy.' she told the Captain. The man placed his tricorn hat over his crew-cut brown hair and stood. He had not failed to see the fear in her eyes when she'd spoken last. He gave her a nod, and a solemn pat on the shoulder on the way out.

'Give her my name. Let her blame me and not you. I cannot, in good conscience, send that child back to live with a psychopath. I trust in my situation you might do the same.' he said as he passed her. He patted her shoulder once more and then left the pair of them to show themselves out. In the waiting room Ollie kept the desk between himself and the Wanderer, and didn't let out the breath he had been holding until both of them were swallowed up by the night.

Back at the inn it was she who had the pleasant job of passing on the message to Illion Marks. The elf laughed, to her surprise, and then demanded to be shown where this 'Captain' was. George and he left, presumably so he could turn his temper on the poor office clerk...but the pair returned fruitless not one hour later. After a dry supper of toasted bread and ship biscuits she retired to her room, sharpened her sword, and tried not to think about what would happen if they ever caught up with her old friend.

Stephen flinched, watched the tray slide under the door and closed his eyes again. There wasn't much to do in the cells but sleep. After a while he sat up, and immediately groaned at the tightness across his shoulders...that's what he got for a day at the oars. He tried fruitlessly to crack his neck and picked up the tray. He was in the middle of breakfast when the door swung open and Greer Dickson stalked in. He froze, spoon halfway to his mouth, and watched the strange Wanderer woman sniff out his cell. There wasn't much to sniff, and it wasn't long before she was leaning over him and inhaling. Vaguely disgruntled, Stephen was about to protest at the weird intimacy when he noticed the bruises up and down her neck. He grabbed her arm and she hissed. He pulled her sleeve up to see the bruises continue. George Godsdamned Dickson. He made no effort to disguise his anger. He met her wary eyes.

'I'll kill him.' he warned her soberly. Greer Dickson was the type of woman (furry or not) that deserved to be worshipped; not beaten around like an old, useless mule. The rage he felt made his hands shake. She tilted her head and made a noise that might have been a whine. He rolled her sleeve back down and patted her arm gently, as if it were made of wet paper and might tare.

'Don't go back.' he said in his best no-arguments voice. She watched him another moment or two and then gave him the sweetest smile. Then she did the strangest thing Stephen Laurence had ever seen in all of his young twenty-five years...she went wolf.

There was an inward rushing of air, a noise that sounded like a high wind was tumbling past his ears and then the woman blurred as if she were moving faster than light. The bedsheets flapped around him and the breakfast tray overturned, spilling now-cold oats all over the hay mattress. He jumped to his feet in his fright, not knowing whether to run or help – not knowing what was happening *at all*...and then when the blurring, rushing and tumbling stopped there was a large, pale-yellow wolf where the woman had been. The wolf sat down on the wet floor and watched him. He wondered if it was safe to move. Slowly, oh so slowly, he sank back down. The wolf tilted its head in *exactly* the same way that the woman just had, not thirty seconds ago. It stood, its defined muscles moving languidly as it flowed the two steps to the bed. It turned once, twice...five times on the spot and then lay down, curled in a ball. After a long while, Stephen reached out a hand and patted it on the head. The wolf growled slightly, and he didn't do it again. It was another hour before the Captain came to see why his visitor hadn't left...and then another before they realised that she wasn't planning to.

And so it came to be that Stephen, Greer and Abigail boarded Captain Echan's ship that very night. They were bound for the Gold Port to transfer a handful of prisoners. As *'the Relentless'* pulled away from the Jetty and worked her steady way towards the harbours mouth: The hunters watched in stolid silence. As far as they were concerned Abigail and Stephen were bound for the harsh punishments found in the mainland's many prisons, never to be seen again – and it was a long way back to Beeton empty handed. They could only watch from the promenade in silence, glowering after the ship until it was a mere speck on the horizon, distant and remote, and then they turned and headed for home. Only Siara Teel, much later and only once she was alone, allowed herself a satisfied smile. Stephen Laurence had gotten away...and now she didn't have to worry about how to stop them from hanging him.

Chapter 6

'Irrespective: ADJ. Without respecting any other circumstances, particularly a specific event. (Think irrelevant)' she scribbled in handwriting that was never neat enough as it was...irrespective (!) of being on a boat and with the paper being wet. She squinted at her book and hoped it would still be legible when it dried. The stub of pencil she was using needed sharpened, so she moved from the chained prisoners on the oar benches upstairs in the hope of finding someone with a knife.

Up top Stephen sharpened her pencil whilst talking idly to the first mate. Talphibious was a tall man when compared to other men; but beside Abigail he seemed monstrous. He was a good natured man though, so where he should be scary he tended to be jolly instead. He had taught her all about climbing the rigging; the benefit of oranges at sea and the many reasons that sailors liked rum so much. She had helped scrub the deck, briefly held the rudder and even caught a fish. Stephen had spent the long days at sea in the Captain's company, for the most part...and poor Greer had spent the entire time puking over the side with her hair standing almost on end. It would seem that wolves were not water lovers...and this wolf had to endure five days on a boat...and they had only been at sea for two.

The third morning even Abigail was getting sick of the endless blue scenery. Sea met sky and sky met sea, over and over. Greer was beneath deck, groaning and clutching an empty and painful stomach, and Stephen had been closeted away since breakfast, apparently playing poker in the cabin with Mister Talphibious, the Captain and the Quartermaster. Left to her own devices she thumbed through 'Flowers and Folklore' for the third time and put it away. She 'hrumphed', and then noticed she was unsupervised. With a wicked grin she realised that there was one thing she had been absolutely desperate to try ever since she had set eyes on it – but Stephen wouldn't let her. In fact he had expressly forbidden it...making it all the more tempting.

Five minutes later she was hiding round the back of the cabin and had marked an 'x' on the wooden wall with her pencil stub. She hefted the short-bow, surprised once more by the weight it held.

Now Abigail was a lady; and ladies weren't allowed to play with weapons...but she'd seen the hunters fire them all the time back home...so it couldn't be that difficult for her to work out. She took an arrow from the quiver by her feet and placed it against the string. She fumbled a little trying to work out the balance, then she had a go at pulling the string taught. She let the arrow fly and it all but fell from the bow, prompting a bedraggled dance to remove her toes from death-by-arrow . The offending wood clattered to a halt. She looked at it thoughtfully, picked it up and strung it again. She pulled the string back further...this time the arrow flew four yards and clashed uselessly into the floor. She pursed her lips, retrieved the arrow and tried a third time. This time she managed to hit the wall, and right on the cross too – but there wasn't enough strength in her arm. She picked the arrow up and narrowed her eyes at it, as if the arrow were somehow to blame, then she strung it back into the bow with the absolute and certain knowledge that she would not be beaten by wood and flint.

     'I'm really, so, so sorry...' Stephen half-whispered in shock. The Captain, Mister Talphibious and himself had rounded the corner and come to a halt. They had spent a few moments in silence, broken by Abigail, who lowered the bow and accidentally discharged an arrow into the deck. Her borrowed shirt was soaked with sweat and bloodied around the cuffs – worse – the back of the cabin looked like a porcupine.

'Um.' stammered the lady. Captain Echan had turned a vibrant red. Mister Talphibious eventually composed himself enough to step in and save the day.

'We're stopping in at Calle to trade. We're less than an hour out. You should make yourself ready, we'll need all hands on shore.' he explained in a meticulously careful voice. Abigail gave him a slow nod.

'Sure...I'll just...clean this up.' she replied tightly. She looked from the bow in her hand to the wall and back to Stephen. She didn't remember firing so many arrows...what kind of quiver was this anyway? She picked up the empty quiver and looked inside of it. In one nearly invisible motion the Captain reached a hand out and took it from her. He said nothing, but the look in his eyes was one she recognised...anger, annoyance, disappointment. She mumbled an apology and scuttled off to find her gear, knowing she had upset the

Captain. It was a queer feeling, and a new one. Not to have disappointed someone (she had so often disappointed Catherine) but that she actually cared about the person whom she had hurt. Downstairs she frowned at the blood on her cuffs. She didn't seem to be bleeding. After awhile she gave up trying to figure it out and took off the shirt to scrub the damn thing with salt. She packed up her bag, gave her face a wash and tried to think of ways that she might make up for her mistake.

They rolled into Calle late in the afternoon, the Captain wanted to pick up a shipment of wine to take on to the Gold Port...specifically he wanted Estoran wine; and there was only one place in the whole world that you could buy Estoran wine outside of Estora; and that was The Golden Fox in Calle. It would cost a hefty purse, but would fetch a heftier one – and was therefore one of Charles Echan's favourite trade routes.

'Prisoners and wine on the same ship? Sure about this?' teased Stephen. Talphibious grinned and shaded the sun from his eyes as the men dropped anchor. Greer pranced from foot to foot, eager to be on dry land. The harbour around them was magnificent – Stephen had always thought of the Bay as a busy place- but this was immense.

'Relax, we do this all the time. Besides...free labour.' grinned the Captain. He ushered the five of them towards the gangplank whilst they wondered if he was serious or not. They crossed the water into the busy port and all talk was forgotten for a while. Other ships docked and departed all along four separate jetty's, the promenade ran a mile in each direction and the high, white-washed walls towered above all as far as could be seen. Abigail had never seen – or felt anything like it. She gripped onto Stephen's sleeve and didn't let go.

'Follow me!' said the newly jaunty Captain. He turned quickly and began pushing a path through the crowd. From Abigail's perspective faces swan past everywhere, high and low, ugly and beautiful, rich and poor. Some were toothless, some wore chains, some were branded. There were merchants and sailors, uniformed guards and their prisoners, peasants and beggars and rich men come for the sight. There were inns and taverns and shops all along the promenade and they passed them on bleached cobble streets – who had more people cleaning them. After a while she shut her eyes and trusted her steps to Stephen. It was a funny thing about people; but every time she passed a stranger it felt like it took a little out of her...and in this sea of people she could easily drown.

They turned off the promenade and up a main street...There must have been other main streets though because the city was just too large; but it was bigger than any of the island streets Abigail or Stephen had ever laid eyes on. The press of people eased somewhat. Here there was less milling around, less crowding. On the street people were going or coming, not simply waiting and loading or unloading. The air here was freer, less full. Abigail opened her eyes when her feet turned sharply and she heard a bell ring ahead. They ducked into a tavern and away from the bleached, sterile streets of Calle.

The Golden Fox was a special place run by a fierce manager named Gribbles and stocked to the hilt with home mixed Estoran produce. Rumour had it that an actual, *real* Estoran owned the place – a novelty these days, and a tourist attraction. Since the riots a few years before all trade with the island had stopped, with the single exception of the desperate folks who lived in Salston, the most northern point on the Isle of Porta. They traded because if they didn't they would starve, and the legend said that many of them already had. The Fox was a different breed altogether, offering the finest of unattainable wines, spices, luxuries and other culturally specific produce. The origins were a secret, though many (the Captain included) believed that the goods were smuggled from the island itself. Another theory was that the Estoran owner made it all himself; but if there was a secretive owner he never once showed himself – not even to Gribbles; who was known for his ability to be a little loose tongued in his cups.

Gribbles leaned two overtly muscular and tattooed forearms on his bar and watched the newcomers with a welcoming smile plastered onto his face. It was his default expression...that or fury. When you came into his bar you hoped it was this face that you got. 'Aye aye Cp'n!' he greeted Echan warmly, and raised his two massive arms to clutch his hand warmly. 'The usual, is it?' he asked in earnest. The Captain grinned in response and slapped the man on the bulging shoulder.

'Straight to business, I like that Gribbles, that's why I keep coming back!' he answered warmly. 'But add two this time.' he added. The barman grinned and waved him off.

'Oi Kid!' the barman shouted, and a broad shouldered young man with dark features came through the doorway from the back. He stopped a moment, looked at the customers and froze.

'Serve these gentlefolk whilst'n I sort out their order.' Gribbles said gruffly. The young man scrambled over and nervously asked the counter what it wanted. The Captain ordered for everyone and they picked a table.

Greer refused to sit, shaking her head and pointing to the door. Stephen frowned.

'You can go outside if you wa-' he began, but she interrupted him.

'No. Your back is to the door.' she quietly warned him. Her voice was silky (when she wasn't growling) fluid and well formed like the wolf was. Stephen realised she was right and moved, and then she sat down.

'Everyone comfortable?' asked the Captain sardonically, once they were all seated. Greer flicked a wolves eyes at him, and he grinned in response because he greatly approved. On his own the butler was dead meat, but with her around they might stand a chance. 'Good.' he announced finally. 'Because you three are staying right here.'

'What?' exclaimed Stephen in surprise. He sat forward and thanked the young man, who was setting the drinks on the table. Abigail was hopeful, then looked at her orange juice in dismay. The young man shrugged an apology and disappeared. She had caught a glimpse though, under all of that messy, nearly black hair, of the clearest blue eyes she'd ever seen. She watched him polish the spotless bar whilst she sipped.

'Catherine will come looking for you and I am going to tell her that I took you to the Gold Port. I'll keep this stop out of the logs. You, Mister Laurence, are going to take your entourage here, and disappear into the city.' the Captain explained.

'Perfect place to get lost, is Calle...' added Talphibious. He smiled innocently and sipped at his wine. 'You could get a ship from here to anywhere in the world.'

'Very nearly.' agreed the Captain. Stephen closed his mouth and looked from one to the other. The Gold Port was farther, and in his mind it was therefore safer, but they were quite right in their speculation...a man could lose himself in a city this size...besides which, Abigail had caused a reasonable amount of damage to the Captains favourite ship, and he strongly suspected he didn't have much of a choice. Abigail was dejected. She had adapted quickly to life on board a ship and had concocted romanticisms about the three of them becoming sailors. She liked the Captain, and she liked the friendly Talphibious...and she wanted more time to repay what she had done with the bow. She bit down on a response and watched the young man at the bar smash a tumbler. He disappeared, presumably to find a broom, and when she rejoined the conversation the men had already moved on to something else. That was it then. The decision was made and her heart sank...because if there was one thing Abigail Jones hated it was a crowd; and in Calle, there was nothing but.

It took about an hour for Gribbles to return and during that time Greer and the men had become more than a little inebriated. Abigail sipped a fresh OJ and tried not to roll her eyes at the revelry. Stephen was approaching the stage where he might either burst into song or have to be put to his bed, whichever happened first. Greer was very still and quiet, but she was making gruff noises in her throat when she breathed. Abigail suspected she was sleeping, but her eyes were still open...she sounded quite a lot like she was snoring. Gribbles didn't approach them, more he cuffed the boy on the back of the head and he scurried off out back again, and then the grizzly manager threw a nod to the Captain, saw Abigail watching him and treated her to a wink. She turned away, vaguely disgusted by the gesture, just as the Captain and Mister Talphibious rose to leave.

'Well ladies, it has been a pleasure...' drawled Talphibious. He mimicked tipping an imaginary hat on his flowing locks and discreetly hid a hiccup.

'It has indeed. And don't take this the wrong way: but I hope we never cross paths again, for your sake, Lady Abigail.' added the Captain. Abigail stood but Greer didn't even blink. She frowned.

'I think she's sleeping. But- I wanted to make it up to you...what I did with the arrows. I didn't mean it. I get a little...obsessed. I wanted to do something to make it better but there isn't any time now-' she tried, fretting and with her eyes on the table. To her surprise the Captain slapped her shoulder light heartedly.

'I can assure you mi'lady, *'The Relentless'* has seen worse foes than you. You can repay me by getting lost, so to speak, and never letting me see that pretty face of yours again.' he said. Once she was blushing a suitable pink he grinned and thumped Stephen. 'The girls will be alright here for the moment. You can walk us to *'the Relentless'* Mister Laurence.' he added, and it was so much like an order that Stephen didn't even think to argue.

On the street the Captain sent his first mate ahead whilst he and Stephen enjoyed a leisurely stroll. He bit the end off a cigar, lit it, and handed it to Stephen (who didn't and had never smoked) who took it and almost lost a lung in a fit of coughing. The Captain slapped him hard on the back until it passed and then lit another for himself...despite Stephen's attempts to give his back.

'I've left some coin with Gribbles, I've traded with him many years and he is trustworthy...but I don't recommend you stay here long. You have a room at the Fox for the next three days; but after that you are on your own. I won't be back in the Bay for another week...in short Mister Laurence, this is all I can do for you. If your hunters come looking for you it would be wise for you to be gone.' advised the Captain. He took a long drag on his cigar and breathed it out happily. Stephen was taken aback, and trying not to drunkenly reflect on what would have been had the Captain turned him over to the authorities.

'Thank you.' he said through a tight throat. 'But why? Why go to all of this trouble for strangers? We appreciate it don't get me wrong, but...why?' he asked. The Captain gave a heavy sigh and was quiet for a long time as they walked. He took another long drag on the cigar and, in a faraway voice, spoke.

'I had a daughter once. I had a wife that- well. She didn't travel well.' he stopped to clear his throat and offer a smile. 'Both lost now of course...in the riots. You know, it's the silliest thing. Her hair was the same colour as your Abigail. It's a unique colour. You don't see it often...native to the islands, don't you know?' he finished, with his eyes on the horizon. As if somehow he might search it until he found his family again.

'I'm so sorry.' was all Stephen could say. The Captain waved a hand bravely.

'Don't be, it's not your fault. But I know what it feels like to fail, Stephen. I failed to keep my daughter safe. Do not be like me. Don't fail.' he explained uncharacteristically gently. Stephen swallowed, and offered a nod. After a few more steps the Captain turned to him once more.

'Aha! You are not getting away quite so easily, butler. Tell me about the girl...You know you won't be able to take her to the Guilds if you are both outlaws?' he asked. Stephen shook his head, suddenly defensive.

'Why would I take her to the Guilds anyway? There's nothing wrong with her. They'd test her, and push her, and she's not...she's not strong.' he replied, shoulders tense. The Captain watched him carefully.

'There are ten arrows per quiver on my boat, Stephen. She had one quiver and more than a hundred arrows. You tell me...There isn't anything wrong with her per say; but that is magic. Like it or not...and it's a magic that I've never seen before. She will need a teacher.'

'She's fine.'

'She will need a teacher before she hurts the people around her.' the Captain persisted. Stephen set his jaw.

'You don't understand. She doesn't know.' he told him. The Captain gave a heavy sigh and stopped walking. Stephen was surprised to find that they had made it back to the docks. In the quay '*The Relentless*' waited, the final boxes of scrumptious wine sitting on the jetty whilst the crew loaded her.

'Well someone is going to have to tell her. Sooner rather than later Stephen. There would be no point saving her if she managed to accidentally kill you both in the process.' he said finally. He held out a hand and Stephen shook it.

'I'll tell her.' he assured, and wondered if he would. The Captain nodded, but doubted it. Above them and along the pier '*The Relentless*' still had arrows in her stern.

'Till the shadows take us.' he parted jovially. He turned on his heel and strode towards the boat. Before he crossed the gangplank he turned, and gave one final tip of his tricorn hat, and then was gone, lost amidst the crew and the crowd and the glorious winter sun. Stephen smiled, and would have stayed to wave them off had it not suddenly occurred to him that he was hopelessly and irrevocably lost. He fought panic, and left to go off in search of the tavern.

Chapter 7

Siara Teel closed the door behind her and breathed a sigh of relief. Catherine had been quite calm, actually. She had listened to their account and become alabaster at the mention of the Captain; and at the mention of Greer's strange disappearing act and George's subsequent blood-hunt had turned a mild shade of red. Only the four of them had returned to Beeton to spread the good word; and of them all had now been dismissed with the solitary exception of Illion Marks, who was in the room behind her and was now (by the sounds of it) being exposed to the full wrath of the lady Catherine Jones. Siara breathed a deep sigh of relief and followed Pat and Aitken down the hallway and towards the stables.

'Whatcha think she'll do now?' asked Pat, his massive shoulders tensed almost up to his ears. Aitken shook his head.

'She'll need to appeal to the Mayor...I guess.' contributed Siara. The three of them went straight to the stables, where four tired mounts needed tending and two stable boys needed overseeing. The cook brought out some food after they had been waiting a while, but Siara had a strong suspicion that she did so of her own volition...a pleasant gesture like that would never have come from Catherine Jones.

'Thought you could use the snack.' Elena Whitbrack greeted them with a tray of bowls and stew. They helped themselves greedily, and talked freely, and by the end of the meal Elena Whitbrack left them with a smile on her face...and they never even suspected her smile had nothing to do with their safe return- but everything to do with their failure.

By the time Illion Marks emerged from the building the dusk had turned to night and both Pat and Aitken had gone home to their families. Siara didn't have a family, not any more, so she stayed and waited; and passed most of the time chopping up firewood because she didn't have anything better to do. She looked up as the back door closed behind him and lowered the axe to the ground slowly. Illion's eyes were reddened, his face pale and drawn in the poor light cast from the house in the background. She stuck the axe back in the chopping block and crossed the yard towards him, wiping dirty hands on her leathers.

'What's the news boss?' she greeted him. He waved a hand and took a long breath out.

'We are escorting Lady Catherine to Ronton Bay in the morning. Only us...it's too late in the year for the town to be without hunters, so the other two can stay here.' he stopped, even his elven lull had sounded world weary.

'You OK?' asked Siara, sweeping her hair out of her face. Illion gave a weary grin, and raised her hand to his lips to give a gentle kiss.

'Go and rest, Siara Teel. Tomorrow we have even more work to do.' he said in a tone that might have been considered warm, had it not been for its source. Siara was halfway back to her own, run-down little shack when she realised he had charmed her into tiredness with his words. She gave a stubborn half-laugh...a night in a warm bed between clean sheets was all of the convincing she would have needed.

The next morning the horses were saddled and waiting and the horn sounded with the sunrise. Siara Teel mounted up and looked around her town. Something, deep down in her stomach, felt wrong. She didn't know the child but she did know Stephen Laurence and she knew Illion Marks perhaps a little too well...She hoped her childhood friend had the good sense to take himself far, far away.

And in the Gold Port George Dickson dangled his legs over the promenade and watched '*The Relentless*' make its slow arrival, negotiating its way around the grand harbour entrance and sailing into sight. He jumped to his feet in one swift movement, and tossed the remains of the chicken leg he'd been eating into the sea below. He watched a long time...waiting...waiting. The gangplank descended for a man in a tricorn hat, and behind him a man who was six foot if he was a day and was equally as broad. George tilted his head at the third man – shorter, balding, bespectacled – bulls-eye. He waited until the men had passed him with the intention of following the third man until he was alone; but as they passed he picked up an unmistakeable scent...the lingering remnants of Estoran wine. George Dickson grinned, then turned back to the boat as the crew busied themselves with unloading their cargo...two dozen prisoners, and twenty-two boxes of Estoran wine. Now George Dickson was not an educated man, but he was a man who savoured his alcohol...and he also happened to know that there was only one place in the world where a man could buy such a speciality without venturing to the island itself.

George Dickson bought himself a one way ticket to Calle and went off to find his traitorous bitch of a wife.

The traitorous bitch in question was out in the cobbled streets of Calle, following her nose downstairs to breakfast. She followed it all the way to the kitchen, where Gribbles wife politely told her to go 'pull up a pew.' She was redirected to the bar in frustration and worse, made to wait with a grumbling stomach. When the food came it was porridge, and she looked at the meagre fair as if it were vomit...which it might well become if she ate it.

'Meat.' she all but growled. The woman looked at her with a kindly smile and then noticed her fangs. She followed the overly hairy length of Greer's arm all the way down to the hand that gripped her sleeve. The woman nodded profusely and promised to return with pork. Greer waited a full thirty seconds before following her to the kitchen and eating the bacon near raw from the stove.

'More.' she said with a mouth full of uncooked pig. Her hostess gulped, and wondered if she would get the chance to cook it this time.

And that is how she got Stephen his breakfast.

At the top of the stairs she knocked and entered. The other two were still sleeping so she set the tray down and opened the window. The city hung about them like a fog, everywhere you looked and without specific detail. Everywhere there were houses, shops, people, smells...too many smells. She closed the window again and the noise of the slam was enough to wake the others. It was their third morning in Calle, and if they wanted to stay any longer they had better sort it out before the landlord tufted them out on the street. Stephen barely had time to sit up and clear his throat before she was speaking.

'I don't like this place. We should go somewhere else. Somewhere with forest.' she told him in her fluid, silky voice. Stephen coughed, realised he was shirtless and pulled the sheet up around himself.

'Well, we don't have to stay here...' he started, but stopped when his charge groaned her agreement from across the room.

'No more cities...but can we go see the Alchemists before we go?' she asked hopefully. Stephen rubbed sleep from his eyes and thought fast.

'I know how much you want to Abby, and believe me I'd love to as well...but you can't go in there and announce yourself, not now...' he coaxed gently. The Alchemist's Guild had a headquarters and school here...he should have realised she would want to see it sooner.

'But some of them might have known my dad.' she pined honestly. Stephen sighed.

'I'm sorry Abigail. I'll take you once you're eighteen I promise. Your aunt won't be able to do anything once you're an adult. It's just too dangerous now.' he said, hating himself for the sadness in her eyes. Abigail understood. In the logical part of her brain she knew he was right...but her emotions raged inside of her, urging her to make a run for it. She rose and dressed and tried to quiet her brain. She might be emotional, but she was not stupid...and Stephen's word was law...especially after the boat situation.

'As for getting out of the city...I think that's a great idea. Any preference as to where to?'

'Porta.' suggested Greer in a firm tone. Abigail and Stephen both looked at her like she had gone mad. Porta was just south of Estora and, if the rumours were to be believed, was still mostly uninhabited...except for the ghosts and the zombies, that was.

'Why on earth would you want to go to Porta?' asked Abigail. A shiver passed down her spine as she realised she had been to Porta before...at the request of one Laird Partridge.

'It is my home.' answered Greer. Stephen stopped making his bed and turned to her. He hadn't known Greer very long, but now that he thought about it, she and George had turned up not long after the riots, when Catherine had placed an advert for hunters in the Bay. It made sense that she came from Porta...on the other hand, so did Partridge. Going by what Abigail had since told him about their last encounter he doubted the man would be of help to them.

'You sure that's a good idea? I don't think it will be the same as you remember.' he said. Greer shrugged.

'I have been back already. There is much difference. There are whole towns in the north that are deserted. They would not think to look for us there-' she answered

'Ooo we could have a farm, Stephen...I could grow herbs and we could get a cow and a horse and-'

'Hold on Abby, just hold on. Porta...is a little close to home for my liking. We could find a farm if we went inland.' Stephen pointed out.

Greer's wicked grin spread to his own face as she answered them both with a raised brow.

'Not one that we could *defend*.' she said, and flashed a wicked row of fangs at them... it really didn't take much more persuasion than that.

The docks were busy as usual; and particularly smelly today. The wind was high and at this time in the morning the catch of the day had been out long enough to turn. The rotted fish would be shipped inland and away from the city, where it would be ground to bones and blood and spread out over the fields as fertilizer in early spring. Nothing was wasted here; everything served a purpose. Everything except Abigail, who leaned on the wooden banister and watched the fish fight over the crumbs of stale bread she was feeding them. Funny...in other places you fed ducks. Not Calle. In Calle you fed the fishes.

'He's coming back.' said Greer from behind her. The Wanderer had been watching the fish too, but with a hungrier expression than Abigail. She had picked Stephen's scent out of the crowd, indicating that he had come back outside.

'Three thirty from the fourth pier. Ships called: '*Ebenezer*'...weird name.' Stephen's voice cut through the crowd towards them. 'We should walk over there and get the last of our supplies.' he added when he had found them. He shot a careful glance over Abigail, who seemed a little worn, and resolved to leave them in an inn somewhere and find what they needed himself. They set off towards pier 4, every passing person setting Greer's already packed senses tingling.

George Dickson arrived in Calle at three in the afternoon. He was already too late: but not late enough. As the three outlaws boarded the '*Ebenezer*' a curious twist of fate saw George look up, and pick his wife's face out of the crowd. The passenger ship had already lifted anchor and he was too far away; but the scent of Greer Dickson hung heavily on the wind, accompanied by the smells of 'kidnapped' and 'traitor'. He pushed his way through the crowds until he could make out the name painted on the hull, and once more felt the agonizing rage of letting his wife get away. On the pier, in the middle of the afternoon, George Dickson threw back his head and howled.

Out on the waves Greer's ears pricked up. She stood on the deck and waited for the wind to change. She didn't need to; she could pick out her estranged former Alpha even from a hundred yards out. She pursed her lips, watched him get smaller, and then succumbed to the inevitable first wave of seasickness. Porta was two days south...and she wasn't sure how much more of this 'boat' business she could take.

Chapter 8

Catherine Jones reclined on a chaise longue and waited for
her host to pour the tea. Robert Decotte was an illustrious hotel
owner, of old money and good stock, and was also a very close
friend of Catherine's late father.
'Milk?' he asked sweetly. Catherine nodded, then thanked him after
he passed her the cup with an old and slightly trembling hand.
'Terrible business...absolutely terrible.' murmured the elder into his
cup.
'Yes Robert, quite. She is in terrible danger of course...Jail! Can you
imagine? She's just a girl! Anyway, the Mayor will be able to
change this...Captain's mind.'
'I do hope so child...but perhaps not. The system is fickle you know.
There are 'other' methods, however. Now...let me think.' said
Decotte. He rose and crossed the room to a dresser. He unlocked it to
reveal a filing cabinet of sorts. He fumbled in a drawer in painfully
slow motion before holding his monocle up to his one good eye to
get a closer look at the card he was holding. He exclaimed,
victorious at last, and returned clutching his prize. He passed her the
paper, and then spent a further minute resettling himself into his
chair. Catherine looked at the card. On it was an address and nothing
else.
'A new butler?' she asked hopefully. Her friend chuckled and patted
her hand gently.
'A useful man, my dear, but not a butler, no. This is the address of a
man your father and I used to resort to when we had no other options
left. He would be able to make your Mister Laurence disappear
without too much trouble...for a small fee of course.' he explained
surreptitiously, and tapped his nose. Catherine looked at the card
again.
'There is no name on this card.' she noticed. Robert grinned
wickedly.
'He is not a man who needs a name, sweet heart. Send for him, and
you will see. In the meantime you're welcome to stay here as long as
you like. Cherize and myself are tragically in need of a bit of young
blood about here.' he answered. Catherine fanned herself idly with

the card before placing it carefully into her purse. After all, one never knew when such a thing might come in handy.

The following morning Catherine took herself to the Council Offices. She made an appointment to meet the Mayor in the afternoon, and then took herself to the Job Market to try and find a new butler. A good man was hard to find, and on the notice board she found she had the choice of three. Ever a woman to get business done with she selected a man based on experience alone. Hugh Clarence had eight years serving a good family in Skart, and three years prior to that with another family name she recognised from Porta – before the war. She took the card from the wall and noted the address of the inn she might find him at. After that she had Decotte's carraige take her to another address. She knocked three times and was furious to be kept waiting in the street. The man with no name did not answer the door of his run-down little hovel in the cheap end of town. Catherine neatly dodged a puddle of filth on delicate feet and managed to make it back to the carraige unscathed. The driver took her to the hotel, where she had a bath drawn before she met with the Mayor.

Late in the afternoon Robert accompanied her, in her best, over-starched, black lace dress back to the Council Offices to meet with Mayor Marquez. The man was fat, there was no other way to put it...certainly not to one as likely to judge as Catherine Jones. He was also red faced and stank of Gin. She would have lost her temper had it not been for her in-bred sense of composure and the presence of Mr Decotte, who had forever seen her as a beloved niece. The Mayor took down her requests in a scribble of handwriting that she very much doubted he would be able to read once he was sober enough to do anything about it. Decotte didn't have the heart to tell her that she was wasting her time. The popular Commander Echan was the real authority in this town, and he seemed to be the man that she had a grudge against. Politically speaking, the Mayor was a figurehead and no more, at the beck and call of the Navy in regards to trade, protection and reputation. Politically speaking, there was no future for Catherine in an overt move against the Commander...but as I have already said stranger; he did not have the heart to tell her. And so he went with her to make her complaint and kept quiet, and the two returned disgruntled to try and ready themselves for the evening meal.

In the evening she sent for Illion Marks. The hunter was a man she approved of; stubborn, resourceful, strong. Illion was not a man who was used to failure, and she played on the fact as if it were second nature. She met him in the quiet dining room after she had finished a pleasing meal of roast pheasant and sweet potatoes. She sipped golden Apple Wine from a luxurious glass tumbler and watched the man approach, stalking towards her like he was wary of attack. He carried himself exactly like that: a hunter on the prowl. She grinned in a satisfied manner...If a man with no name could not kill Stephen Laurence for her then, in his absence, Illion would have to do...she just wondered what his price was.

'You sent for me, my lady?' he purred. Catherine firmed her jaw. Despite his many good qualities he was still an elf, a second class citizen as far as she was concerned. Filthy creatures who could charm with their words. She was immediately wary.

'Sit down.' she told him. He looked uncertain, and then glanced rather longingly at the door...and then he sat down.

'Is there somethi-' he started, but Catherine held up a finger and silenced him.

'Tell me, Illion: what is it that you want?' she asked him instead. He frowned, a single crease along his otherwise unblemished brow.

'What do I want?' he repeated dumbly, the eleven lull of his voice fraught with uncertainty.

'Yes. What do you want?' asked Catherine. Then let out a deep breath as his confusion failed to dissipate. 'What do you want out of life? What is it that you strive for? What is your dream, Illion Marks?' she clarified for him. He sat back in the seat with his arms folded across his chest and met her gaze fearlessly.

'Why lady? Do you intend to get it for me?' he asked, very carefully keeping the sarcasm from his voice. Catherine raised a solitary eyebrow.

'Perhaps...but there are certain factors to take into account-' she began, but it was Illion's turn to interrupt.

'If, for example, I were to do something for you...Something you can ask of me and no other...something you would be willing to reward with my greatest wish- hah. Ask me lady, and I will tell you my terms.' he grinned, figuring out the mystery as he went. The question was: could he? Even for the thing he most wanted in all the world...could he? And what did he want? What could he ask for that was worth a man's life?

'Well. You seem to be a clever man. You know what I want. The question remains the same. What do you want?' she asked. Her finger traced the rim of the glass. Illion watched it rather than meet her eyes.

'I want a boat. I want land. I want to lead your guard. I want a lifetime of comfort, as many wives as I please and...ten percent of the town's annual tax. Give me that, and I'll take care of Stephen Laurence.' he said. When he finally met her gaze she was smiling softly, and in the low light she looked almost human.

'Done.' she agreed simply.

'Done?' he asked in disbelief. She gave a sigh and nibbled her lower lip.

'I need a strong man beside me...and who is stronger? We could do great things, you and I. You will have your terms...but I want that man dead. The humiliation he has brought the house cannot be suffered. Kill him and come home.' she said softly, her cheeks flushed with wine. He stared at her rudely for a long moment, and then stood.

'I will leave in the morning.' he said. He put out his hand and she shook it, and then he walked away. The hunters were staying with the rest of the servants at a cheap inn on the poor side. Catherine watched him go with a smile and tapped her lips thoughtfully. She was the sister of a famed alchemist after all...she hadn't gotten this far in life without getting to know a thing or two about poison herself.

Catherine opened her eyes and tried to scream, the unmistakeable cold press of steel lay across her throat. A hand covered her mouth and stopped her reaction. A faceless voice whispered by her ear.

'You came to see me. Why?' asked the male whisperer. The hand moved from her mouth once she had calmed enough to process the softly spoken question.

'Are you- him?' she asked the darkness. There was a soft, throaty laugh.

'Who else? Why did you come to my house? Did someone send you?' the voice repeated. Catherine tried not to swoon as the blade bit into her skin and she cried out a little.

'I want to hire you. A man has wronged me. I want to pay you-' she explained. The blade left her flesh, her skin breaking out in goose-pimples in its wake.

'Then that is a different matter.' spoke the mysterious voice from somewhere nearby- yet still in a whisper. Catherine shivered as she slowly sat up. She pulled the sheets up to her chin against the stranger and the cold. 'Who is my target?' he asked. Catherine was wide awake by this point, and had no trouble remembering her cause.

'Stephen Laurence, my former butler...and perhaps others, depending on your price.' she answered. She could almost hear the man crack a smile in the darkness.

'I know that name lady, and I know you. Quite a scandal...and I would guess that you have bigger problems than one simple butler. Yes. I will work with you. And you will meet my price. The desperate always do.' said the still-faceless voice, and the coldness of it was enough to send a chill down even Catherine's spine.

In the morning, after the deal had been made, Catherine wakened feeling better than she had in days. Her strength had returned with the exorcism of her will. She would have her way, as she always did, and no little brat with an ego problem was ever going to shake that. If there was one thing in the world that Catherine Jones could depend on it was the strength of Catherine Jones; and that morning it had returned to her in droves. She had to look on the bright side of things. There may have been a scandal, but now the town (such as it was,) the house and the farms all belonged to herself, and with no protests from her damned niece. If Abigail didn't return then Catherine was heiress to it all. Wouldn't it be such a pity if some terrible fate happened to her whilst she was in prison? Catherine would continue to wear black, she would continue to mourn...and all the while she would be laughing all the way to the bank.

After breakfast a maid announced the arrival of one Mister Hugh Clarence. Catherine met with him in the dining room for lack of a private study. It was a triviality to her and nothing else. She told the new butler that if she liked him by the end of her stay in Ronton Bay then he would have the job. Until then his position was provisional and no more. The man was tall, slender and very well presented. His cuffs and collar were starched to perfection and his shoes shone...exactly as Catherine had known that they would. She liked him instantly. He was the model of decorum. She went about the rest of the morning making plans to leave the very next day, now that she had concluded all of her business in Ronton. A letter in the afternoon changed all of that however; when Mister Decotte himself chapped excitedly on her door and waved a fine parchment in her face so that the Royal Seal was clearly visible.

A Royal Prince was coming to Ronton Bay...and Catherine Jones had every intention of being there for his visit. She had the money, she had the breeding – she even had an invitation to the hastily arranged ball that was to be thrown in his honour. All that Catherine Jones needed, in fact, was a dress that wasn't black.

Chapter 9

Abigail screamed and ran off along the road, laughing her head off. In the end Greer caught her in one easy bound and she fell about herself giggling raucously.

'If you keep running away you are never going to learn. Stand your ground.' barked the huntress through her clenched teeth. Abigail's amusement was not to her liking. If she didn't take her training seriously it might get her killed or worse...taken back to her aunt.

'I'm sorry Greer, really I am...it's just when you have fangs and claws and stuff you are really scary-' the young woman answered, breathless.

'Then why are you laughing at me?' demanded the Wanderer, whose knowledge of human interaction was still a little minimalistic.

'I don't know. Laugh and run... it's my natural reaction...aren't the good guys supposed to laugh in the face of danger?'

'We're the good guys?' asked a tired Stephen. They had been walking all morning...life on the run consisted mainly of walking, or so it seemed to him.

'Yes laugh...but without running away.' added Greer sceptically. Abigail frowned.

'We are the good guys...aren't we Stephen?' she asked with too much uncertainty to her tone. Stephen scoffed and shook his head.

'Of course!' he said brightly, then, under his breath, added 'I just don't know what that means for the rest of the world...'

A few miles later and a town crept into view on the horizon. Greer stopped them sharply, because the smell of other humans came to her on the breeze.

'Why are we stopping?' asked Stephen from the back. Abigail squinted for a better look at the town ahead, and recognised it at once.

'A town.' explained Greer.

'Specifically Rapton.' warned Abigail. She shot a look to Stephen, who shot a look to Greer.

'We go round.' he decided. Greer looked into the forest, the briefest, fleeting look of worry in her eyes. The forest around them was unlike any other – except for perhaps the forests of Estora. The trees were dead or dying, the forest floor brown, putrid mush where nothing remained. There were no plants, no animals, no sounds. She knew every twist and turn of it – every nook and cranny...but the forest of her childhood had been thriving and beautiful, and she did not want to step into it. They had come to Porta to find a town where they could be forgotten, not to roam in the dead forest. She appealed to Stephen with her eyes, and he gave a tight grin and patted her arm in reassurance.

'We have to go around. They know us here.' he explained. Greer gave an almighty sigh and readied herself. Before too much longer she gave a firm nod and stepped foot into the trees, fighting with the wolf every step...the wolf that wanted to do nothing more than laugh...and then run away.

And so it came to be, stranger, that the wandering trio wandered around the outskirts of Rapton. What they were not expecting was that the whole town would be encircled by a great wall, perhaps six feet in height and made entirely of rough-cut sandstone. Worse still; the wall ran out of town on the other side, and continued seemingly endlessly north. By the time they reached the far side of town the sun was already low in the sky. After another two, much slower miles spent off-track it became clear that they were spending the night amidst the trees – whether they wanted to or not. They skirted the solid wall until they found a gap in the trees that one might optimistically refer to as 'a clearing', and spent a half hour building the biggest fire that they could. There might not be any wildlife out there...but there was something causing the hair on the back of Greer's neck to stand upright...and that was all the warning of danger the other two needed.

When Abigail wakened in the night it was to a tearing sound like claws scratching stone. Subconsciously she slowly realised something was wrong. Something huge and heavy fell on the fire a half-inch from her face and she sprang to her feet without further pressing. There was a growl from behind her, and she turned to see the pale wolf springboard off the wall and leap at a hunched figure. The fire was low, and the...thing...writhed on it and let out a fast-paced, guttural clicking noise.

'Huh?' she asked the air. She gawked down at the humanesque form struggling in the fire. Something about the noise it made had frozen her feet to the spot. Something about the clicking, about a voice that was trying to speak but couldn't. The wolf was a mass of claws and teeth. It got hold of something and shook it ragged. Abigail broke from the sight of Greer tearing at darkened flesh with her teeth – what was that smell?

'Stephen?' she called through the night. Amidst the trees; a silver set of eyes turned to her. 'Stephen!?' she shouted, then giggled. She took the three steps to where he had been sleeping and her foot hit something solid...something cold. She went to her knees at once and was relieved to find his pack- just his pack – but that meant his gear was here somewhere! She fumbled for the small crossbow in the darkness, going by touch alone. Stretching her hands around and searching until she grasped string, and pulled both crossbow and bolts towards her. Greer gave another violent shake of the thing she worried at. Whatever it was it was almost certainly a corpse by now. She hadn't figured on it being a corpse to begin with until she caught sight of Stephen being pinned against a nearby tree by one of its companions. From this point of view she could see torn, faded and ancient clothing draped loosely on what was left of the rotted man beneath. The creature had patches of white, dirty hair clinging to a skinless skull...she walked closer, suddenly oblivious to the danger as her scientific capacity took hold.

'It's not possible...' she whispered to the night. The flashing firelight burst into brilliant flame as the creature rolling in it finally caught fire and what was left of its clothing and flesh burnt in a bright, blue-tinged flame. Abigail watched the creature before her; its white-fingered hands tighten on Stephen's throat. She was close enough now to see that Stephen was being suspended above the ground, his face red and his legs flailing uselessly beneath him. He was not a tall man, but this creature might stand a full foot above even the tallest...like some kind of ragged, un-dead giant. Stephen wrapped his fingers around the creatures bony hands in an effort to free himself. Around Abigail the world faded to slow motion. With perfect clarity she hefted the already loaded bow, instinctively took aim and fired at the creature that held Stephen. The shot hit it where its heart should be. The creature did not even react, but got on with the task at hand. It leaned forward, opened its bone white maw and sunk its pointed teeth into Stephen's shoulder. He cried out and kicked but to no effect. Abigail heard a thud behind her, and turned to see the wolf slide down the wall. Un-dead...right. How did you kill something that wouldn't die? Well...you could burn it...but her bolts were metal, and metal didn't burn. She tried to think critically, her mind racing as to the possibilities. If she wanted to alchemically bring someone back to life...how would she do it? Not the heart therefore-

The bolt hit the creature square in the back of the head and it tumbled forward, releasing Stephen in the process only to bear him to the ground with its weight. Abigail turned, reloaded – wait...how did she load it for that second shot? She fired at the creature closing on Greer. She looked suspiciously at the loaded crossbow, shrugged, and put a bolt between the pair of silver eyes watching her from the tree line, just for good measure. There was a 'whooshing' noise behind her and she turned with crossbow at the ready to face a human and very naked Greer.

'Help him.' was all she said. The pair turned as one to their fallen friend, his body still crushed under the weight of the beast that assaulted him, a single arm protruding from the mess of blood and rotted flesh that had felled him. The fingers weren't moving. The fingers weren't moving and Abigail blinked. There was an arm in the dirt. Stephen's arm. Something in her soul turned cold.

Chapter 10

Greer and Abigail grabbed the fallen Stephen and dragged him free of the mass of rotted flesh and bone that had him pinned. Between them they propped him against the same tree the monster just had and looked frantically for signs of life...there were none. Abigail pulled up one of his eyelids, but his pupils didn't change. That was bad, she'd read it somewhere but where wasn't important, not right now. She took off her cloak, and then the sailors shirt she'd been wearing since '*the Relentless*', and pressed it against the open tare in his shoulder to try and stem the bleeding. He was soaked in blood all down the front. She slapped his face gently, and then not so gently, and then remembered the marin root she had picked up back on Freisch. She ran to her pack and threw things out of it until she found the marin. She brought it back and snapped the now-dry twig open under his nose. The yellow, odorous powder that emerged from it floated in with his faint breath, and sent a jolt of adrenaline straight to his brain. He opened both eyes, babbled something incoherent, spasmed with his whole body and then fell back to unconsciousness. Greer and Abigail looked at each other.
'I don't know what to do...' said Greer, the fear in her voice palpable. Abigail turned to her, white faced and serious.
'Neither do I.' she confessed. She had no moss here to treat the wound and stop infection, no antiseptics or salves or even a clean bandage. Out here there were no books to tell her what to do; and Stephen was *dying*. There were flashes through the trees, and when she glanced up silver streaks still laced the air, unable to fade quickly in the darkness. Beside her Greer let out an involuntary growl from low in her chest.
'Can you carry him?' Abigail asked, breathless, nauseous, terrified. Greer looked from the silver in the trees to the fast-fading Stephen, and scooped him up in a fireman's lift with apparently no effort at all. She didn't know where they were moving too; but even if she could get them through the wall they were still miles from civilization – and the nearest town was Rapton...would she risk exposure to save Stephen? In Abigail's crowded, buzzing mind there wasn't even a question. Stephen was the only person who had ever cared about her, and she wasn't about to lose him to save herself.

'We have to get through the wall and back to Rapton, there will be a healer there...every town has a healer.' she repeated the mantra, knowing even as she said it that it was a lie. Healers didn't like people, it came with the gift, and Beeton had been exceptional in this instance...probably the only time Beeton was exceptional for anything – other than beets of course...

Abigail shook her head to clear it. She needed focus. She didn't have time to be thinking about beets right now. The wall...rope...or vines- damn this dead forest.

Greer, Abigail and the prone Stephen tore along the wrong side of the wall back towards town. They knew there were no gaps, no loose stones that might be freed or climbed. They had already tried that on the way here, and in the daylight. There was no escape, just a steadily encroaching tightness in Abigail's chest brought on by whatever was chasing them. She stopped for the third time and let off two, consecutive shots. The two closest sets of eyes went down in a tumble. She didn't stop to wonder where the bolts had come from this time, just fired blindly and was surprised that the eyes blinked out, leaving a silvery traced outline of where they had been. They were saved – quite a while after 'in the nick of time' - by a flare from deep in the forest. The flare was a fantastic, brilliant, luminous green...and it lit up the night sky for miles before it faded, just as quickly as it had come. The three stumbled to a stop in stunned silence. Abigail pointed to the sky, tracing the faded green streak with her index finger. She followed the after-effect of the flare across the sky and down, down, down, into the trees. The flares source had come from further north, up the hill and through the trees. Once again Abigail and Greer exchanged a mutual look, and without further discussion they changed direction, left the wall, and headed towards the unknown, deeper into the dead forest.

After an uphill struggle in the dark, grunting and struggling, slipping and sliding on the muck that made up the forest floor- stopping intermittently to shoot a magically replenishing crossbow at creatures that shouldn't exist...after all of that; the three tumbled from the dense trees and into a clearing that could not possibly be there. A house stood in the clearing, a little chimney puffed smoke. A tiny waterfall cascaded down one side of it and formed a stream that cut a path downhill to their left and the whole place, the whole place was illuminated by a soft green glow. The two stood, Greer with Stephen balanced precariously on a shoulder, and tried to understand what lay in front of them.

'What?' asked Abigail of the air. The neatly trimmed grass ahead of her was purest green; the stream was lined with flowers and plants, there was a vegetable patch on the other side of it, and a little wooden bridge across...there was a herb garden and, ringing it all and beneath their feet, was a yard-thick and continuous border of edelweiss. Abigail took a step forward so that she was no longer crushing the poor, silvery plant. Edelweiss was a tough one, it would take more than Abigail's sturdy black boots to break it. Beside her Greer remembered they were being chased and spun; Abigail took a look over her shoulder and then turned too, to marvel at the silver eyed creatures, who hung back a few yards and seemed unable to come any closer. She let the tension go out of her shoulders and relaxed a little.

'Magic.' she said, nodding decisively. Even as she spoke she could feel the thrum of it in the air about her...the gentle warmth that felt much like lying in a warm ocean and letting the gentle waves wash over you. It was a heady feeling, and could lull one into a false sense of security. She checked on Stephen, whose breathing was weak but constant. She lifted the makeshift shirt-bandage and saw that the bleeding had finally stopped. She let out a deep sigh and would have slid to her knees had it not been for the elf.

The figure was six foot five at least, and built like an ox. His shoulders were almost a full meter across, his head bald, his attire at first glance seemingly composed of colourful rags...Abigail's mouth fell open, not at his appearance, but at his entrance. The large, bald, elf stepped *out of* the rock wall beside the waterfall, muttering a string of words in what Abigail deduced to be elven, and carrying all the gear they had left behind in their panic. Greer tensed, but she couldn't fight with Stephen on her back, so she made a move to lay him down but Abigail stopped her. She was watching the elf, who was watching her, and who was coming closer. When he stepped into the green glow she gasped; because he was covered head to toe (or the bits she could see were, anyway) in tattoos. She approached him against Greer's better judgement, to get a better look. She had never seen a tattoo before...and the magic in the air was affecting her focus.

'What is that?' she asked him, when she was no more than a foot from him. She squinted up at the massive elf, and wondered if he spoke any common. The towering figure bent to her level and peered in her eyes.

'Tatt-oo. For White Wolf. Mmmmm. Me.' he tried. His voice was gentle as a giant, his manner more contradictory to his appearance than anyone she had ever met before.

'You're White Wolf?' she asked him, pointing to the tattoo of a great wolf howling under the moon on his forearm to help the understanding. He hummed again, as if trying to figure out what she asked. Then grinned and nodded.

'Asa. Asa Lupine. You Abigail Jones. I waiting...for Abigail.' he said with evident pleasure. Abigail's smile froze on her face. He looked past her, towards Stephen and Greer, and frowned.

'Why you no heal?' he asked her, but she couldn't answer, because she hadn't gotten over the last shock yet. The elf took her by the arm and dragged her back to Greer and Stephen. She let him do it, since he had just walked out of a wall. He took the man from Greer's unresisting grip and laid him out flat on the grass. He hummed and 'ahh'ed' a little, and then signaled for Abigail to come and crouch beside him.

'You heal.' he said confidently. Abigail laughed a bitter laugh.

'I'm not a healer Asa Lupine. I hit things with the crossbow.' she answered. 'But you have herbs?' she asked him, knowing that's what she had seen when they had stumbled across his home. The elf shook his head, and the jumble of beads and feathers around his neck danced. He smelled of earth after the rain.

'Mmmm death...rot...mmm needs healer. He catch.' the elf tried. Abigail had gone pale as a ghost. She was getting desperately close to loosing Stephen, who was even paler than she was and whose eyes moved fitfully under his closed lids.

'I can't heal...' she appealed once more. The elf turned to her, and peered at her as he had before.

'Heal like mother.' he persisted, and nodded.

'You knew my mother?' she asked. Asa Lupine pointed to Stephen on the floor.

'HEAL.' he all but shouted, drawing out every syllable for its importance. 'He DIE.' he told her. The girl looked from him to Stephen, from Stephen to Greer and then back to the elf. It couldn't be that hard, could it? After all...Abigail Jones was just desperate enough to try.

She leaned over her fallen friend and again raised his eyelid. The eye beneath was no longer brown, but brown swirled with silver strands, etching their way through his system.

'Nonononono.' she mumbled, and wondered what the hell she should do. How did you heal a person anyway? What? Did you take some of yourself and just...sort of insert it here...so that their energy has a bridge and you can be the conductor-

She blinked and the whole world around her changed. She was in an empty plain, the grass beneath her feet marshy and squelching. Her shoes filled with water. Endlessly, in any direction, there was masses of muddy grass and what seemed a lot like dusk...after the sun has gone but with its light still bright enough on the horizon to keep the darkness at bay. She felt heavy, like when she tried to chase the blue fairy in her dreams. There was a choking noise coming from somewhere, and the only thing she could do that made any logical sense was to search for its source...ahead of her there was a movement, what might have been fingers raised in the twilight. She headed for it slowly, her movements being dragged down like she was trying to walk through Elena's lentil soup. It took her an impossibly long time to reach the flicker of movement that she had seen, and when she got there all she could see was a hand about to disappear beneath the surface. She fell to her knee's, grabbed the hand and tugged hard- and then the scenery changed.

She was in a room – it was Stephen's house, she recognised it from memory although she hadn't spent much time there. There were bodies on the floor, there was an old, tired chair, there was Stephen before it, his eyes locked on an object in his hands. She walked around him until she could see what it was; a crossbow...the one she liked to borrow. There was nothing else in the room although there should be; there should be an old man, she realised, sitting in the chair and muttering curses at the world and how much times have changed. But there was no father...just a curious, lingering, emptiness. In the memory Stephen raised handsome, hurt, brown eyes and looked at her, and what she beheld in the man was no longer a butler or friend, but a hero. She felt a tear on her cheek preceding the world fading to darkness.

They were in the dining room. Catherine scraping cutlery across her plate made the solitary sound in the room. Abigail pushed at the food on the porcelain and looked up in confusion when her aunt spoke.

'I know you've taken it. A night to think about it perhaps...' she was hinting. A cold chill ran down Abigail's spine...the closet...hours in the chilled darkness awaiting release. Across the room and ready by the door Stephen cleared his throat.

'Lady Catherine, I believe the Lairds seal was in the bottom of the box we donated to goodwill. I almost certainly remember catching a glimpse of it-' he tried.

'Then why didn't you say anything you imbecile?' the matron snapped. Stephen gave a calm and very polite smile.

'You ordered me not to ask any more questions ma'am, after I questioned your judgement about the portrait.' he responded readily. Catherine gave a deep, angry, breath but said no more. Abigail was spared the closet that night, and Stephen was (as always) the one who had saved her. The world sank to black and she cried because she was alone again, and because she was terrified that when the time had come for her to repay her friend she had been unable to. What was she but a burden to him? What was she but a child whose dreams had been far outweighed by the consequences of real life. She had been nothing but trouble to him...and it had led to this...to Stephen dying in the dirt and she as useless as ever, at the mercy and kindness of strangers. Exhaustion finally ebbed its eager way across her soul, still glowing green amongst the darkness, the only light in a place where her feet still squelching and the twilight was now gone. At some point she closed her eyes and fell asleep on her feet.

When she awoke she was in a real bed, with real, feather-stuffed pillows and soft, warm sheets around her. She tried to sit up but two large hands pushed her gently back down.

'Did it work?' she asked the elf. The man above her gave a comforting smile and raised a clay bowl of water to her lips.

'All fine. Rest.' he cooed, and the charm in his elf infused words sent her softly back to the world of *real* dreams.

Chapter 11

In the Gold Port Siara wakened slowly. Something was tickling her spine. She rolled over onto her back and discerned the feeling to be caused by Illion's fingers, as they started tracing the tip of her breast. She groaned softly, and removed his hand.
'We have work to do.' she told him. In the night his words could charm her, in the day he was just another boy. Their relationship was a functional one and no more, constructed in each others loneliness and occasionally taking solace in each other. She sat on the edge of the bed and pulled her shirt back on. She could feel his predatory grin on the back of her neck.
'Yes...work. Retrieve the girl, kill the butler.' he purred at her. He came closer to caress her shoulder.
'I'm not killing anybody, thank very much.' she snipped. 'Help me with this.' she added, and stood so that he could lace her bodice back up for her. He rose with her, and kissed the back of her neck whilst he went. She rolled her eyes.
'I'll do it then.' he said without thinking. She stopped, took the ties from him and finished it herself.
'We're not killing him. We'll bring them both back.' she told him, her voice bristling. Illion laughed at her, and finally went to dress himself.
'That's not what she wants. She wants him to die.' he said in his mirth. 'You are very naïve Siara Teel. It's sweet.' Siara bit into her bottom lip, then tried to do something about her hair. Illion Marks had no reason to lie, and so Catherine wanted him to hunt down and kill Stephen Laurence. In his arrogance, Illion had thought to invite her along for the ride...he hadn't told her the full plan. She quelled a rising fury in her stomach and pulled on her boots.
'Where are you going?' he asked dumbly, and with an extra helping of charm. For the moment, in her anger, she was immune to him.
'I'll meet you downstairs.' she snapped, and left him there wearing nothing but his shirt.

In the bar downstairs Siara fought to keep down runny eggs over porridge and silently cursed whoever cooked such a foul concoction. After a few more mouthfuls she pushed the plate aside and let her forehead hit the table. For all she was a good hunter she could be really, blindingly stupid. She was on a manhunt, after all...what did she expect? That they catch their targets and skip off merrily into the sunset? She turned at approaching steps but it was not Illion, just a stranger who did not meet her eye, but rather skirted around her and out the front door. She sighed again, wondered why she stuck around with the elf, and thought about her options. They came down to two things really; stay or go. Neither was particularly appealing. If she left she lost her job and probably all of the respect she had spent years earning in Beeton...if she stayed she would have to watch an old friend die...but still, an old friend who had broken the law...

After an hour had passed she went to see what was keeping him.

'I'm sure you look lovel-' she started, as she unlocked the door and went inside. She closed it behind her and stopped talking immediately. Illion Marks, in just his shirt, was sprawled on the bed and not moving.

'Illion?' she asked gently, and took a few timid steps towards him. The elf did not move, did not blink, did not snore...she got a little closer still and learned that he no longer breathed, either. His head rolled at an odd angle...his neck broken...his last thoughts probably annoyance, and aimed at her. There was no blood in the room. There were no signs of a struggle...just a body on the bed that grew colder by the second. Siara stood over him a full minute in contemplation before the reality sank in. The hunter had been taken entirely by surprise. His un-touched weapon sat a dozen paces away...whoever killed him had done it just after she left the room. She walked to the sword in its ornately decorated silver scabbard and dully picked it up, feeling its weight like a solitary comfort in a room gone to madness. She peered again at the pale, sprawled figure on the bed, and brought the sword to him. She lay the sword beside him, and wrapped his cold fingers around the hilt. Illion Marks ought to have died with a sword in his hand. He would have been furious, in fact, to learn that he did not. She sat on the bed and looked at him. After while she wrestled him into his trousers...it wouldn't do to be discovered like that. After a further while she snapped out of her trance and looked about herself in horror. Illion had been murdered. What did that mean? It certainly wasn't Stephen Laurence who did the deed...no. To get past Illion Marks a man would have to be smart, quick, and most of all- professional. This was a hit...and though the danger was long since passed she should not be here a second longer. Siara Teel grabbed her gear and left the body of her former lover to be discovered by the inn's staff. She left the building in a hurry, and didn't stop until she got all the way out of town and onto the prison road. There was only one person in Siara's reasonably small world who could afford to pay a professional killer – and that was Catherine Jones. If that was the case then she had to find Stephen before the assassin did...if that *was* the case then there weren't many choices left in Siara's rapidly shrinking world. Her mind clambered to a halt somewhere in the forest north of Calle...about the same time as she realised that there would be no going back now. The notion of returning to the life she had built for herself fled from her like a bird from a cage. She was a witness now, and very likely the next name on Catherine's list. Her hope lay in Stephen Laurence...if only she could reach him before her own hunter did.

Chapter 12

Catherine Jones twisted in the dress to get a better look at herself in the mirror. She liked what she saw – although not quite enough. There had been a time when her beauty was rivalled by no other; when her long, greying hair had shone black under the lamplight, and when young men queued around the ballroom to ask her to dance. She snatched the proffered fan from the shop's girl and fluttered it a few times provocatively, wondering if she could use it to hide the slight sag she had noticed recently around her chin. She was pleased with the result, but when she moved the fan away the rigours of time were still there, still plain to see on her body. Her bosom had shrunk somewhat, her bottom had become misshapen...her legs and arms moved by themselves if she walked too fast...no, time was not being kind. The dress seemed garish, balanced on her frame like it was made for someone younger. She shook her head at the black and blue lace number and moved the serving girl by the shoulder until she had a full view of the monstrosity .

'Take it in here, up at the bottom, in at the hip by at least two sizes...bring the straps off the shoulder so that I can show off my décolletage...it's the sole part of me that is still pleasing to the eye. And for goodness sake get rid of the slit, I'm not twenty, you know.' she ordered. The girl gave a half curtsy and then began to scribble notes on a clay tablet. 'Now help me change.' she commanded. The girl curtsied again and led her into the changing room, where she busied herself untying knots and undoing laces.

A few moments later Catherine emerged in her regular black and spoke with the tailor himself, just in case the girl was unreliable. She was pleased to hear that the alterations would be complete in time for the celebrations the following evening; but she was even more pleased to hear that Robert Decotte had insisted on fitting the bill for the dress. He might be an old man now; but Robert Decotte was the best fake uncle a girl ever had.

On the street a sudden murmur of energy had arisen. She stopped in the doorway and glanced at Clarence, who held the door open for her.

'Mi'lady,' he greeted her formally. 'It would seem that the Prince's ship has arrived in the port...might I suggest an early lunch to avoid the rabble?' he asked primly. Catherine was at once grateful for the suggestion. They were a reasonable distance from the hotel and she was in a good mood; she didn't want to risk it in having her temper tried by the assembling peasantry.

'A splendid idea.' she admitted.

'Very good ma'am.' said the butler. She left the rest to him, and let him guide her to a nearby inn of suitable reputation.

Inside Clarence ordered for her; the duck and some wine to match. The wine was white, from the Golden Hills and absolutely terrible – the duck though, the duck was slow roasted and dripping fat, and was absolutely exquisite. For a few moments she lost herself in a food heaven, the meat dissolving on her palate like it was made of spun sugar. Before she remembered her manners she had scraped the plate clean – and a commotion at the door was announcing the arrival of a very, very important guest.

Prince Marius of the human Royal family stopped in the doorway and eyed his surroundings. He wore a ruffled shirt and tight, fawn-coloured leggings of finest brushed suede. His hair flowed like a silver mane from his head to rest loosely on his shoulders. Prince Marius was the King's brother, and he had come on a tour of the islands to inspect lands that had been damaged since before the war. His eyes fell on the people in the bar, and he watched with amusement as, one by one, they noticed his presence and fell about themselves to bow.

'My Lord, the Quincy has rooms prepared for us-'

'I like this one.' announced the Prince, and watched the barmaid flush pink. This one would do just fine. 'Show me to my rooms, Miller.' he told his entourage. The man who had just spoken waved frantic hands at runners and guards, and within moments the inn was declared safe and the Prince was striding towards the staircase. On the way past Catherine Jones he noticed something unusual; a scraped plate before a refined lady. He smirked, and turned to her bowed head.

'What did you eat, lady?' he addressed her. Catherine straightened herself from her curtsy and smiled demurely.

'The duck, your Majesty.' she answered, and then dabbed at her face with a napkin. This prompted the good natured Prince to laugh raucously.

'I see it was delicious?' he pressed. Catherine used his amusement to hide her embarrassment.

'It was divine, sire. Had I known you were coming I would have saved you a bite.' she answered properly. The Prince laughed until his face turned red, and then he touched her shoulder with his royal hand.

'I dare not ask about the wine!' he told her warmly, and then turned and was off out of her life for the time being. On the way up the stairs she heard him call to Miller to 'bring me the duck!' She sat down until she could compose herself once more. Suddenly all was forgotten but one important detail. A Royal Prince had come to Ronton Bay...and forever more he would remember her as 'that duck woman'.

Commander Charles Echan tossed back his third drink and ignored Mister Talphibious, who was frantically clearing his throat beside him. They stood five paces behind the Prince's Guard...and not nearly close enough as far as he was concerned. He passed his fancy glass to a nearby servant and quietly ordered another.

'Captain...Go easy.' warned his first mate. He growled a quiet response.

'It's bad enough that I have to be here, don't make me do it sober, Jake.'

The Prince and entourage finished this particular introduction and the entire party moved one pace forward. Another person was brought to be formally introduced, and they hadn't even made it into the ballroom itself yet, they were still in the entrance hall. Rumour had it there was a buffet in there, but Charles wasn't drunk enough yet to believe in fables. They took another step forward, and watched as yet another trembling old man brought forth a bride twenty years younger than himself.

'Decotte! Is that you! My goodness me but I didn't know you were still going.' the Prince's voice floated back to them. 'And this must be your lovely wife- ah but we have already met!' The elderly gentleman muttered something in response and the Prince's booming laughter cut through all other noise in the room.

'Lady Jones is it? Forgive me my dear, let me show my humblest apologies by offering you the first dance.' he announced. Mister Talphibious stood pointedly on Echan's foot.
Jones...Jones...Oh...*that* Jones. Aha.

Ahead of them the Prince waved off any other introductions and led the Lady Jones towards the dance-floor in the adjoining room, and his entourage fought to keep pace. The dancing began, the Captain tried not to drink any more and the night wore on.

At the end of the evening they stepped out into the fresh air and were thankful for the coolness after the stuffy ballroom. The buffet had been awful, the wine had not been rum and the music had not included drums. To the Captain and his first mate it had been a roaring disappointment, particularly given that their duties, it seemed, were not to end here. The Prince decided to walk home, to enjoy the 'fine sea air', and completely ignored the solid gold carraige the Mayor had dug out of storage and polished specifically. The entourage walked in the street, the guards the only ones that were alert, and Echan's men fanning out before and after them to guard against the dangers of side streets and alleyways. It took a full half hour to get the fool back to his inn, and then another half an hour to get the whole party safely inside the building...and then, just when he hoped it was over, the Royal Prince, brother to the King, pulled him aside for a 'personal chat'. The command was plain; return the girl to her aunt. Without missing a beat Echan repeated the story he had been concocting since the moment he saw the Prince talking with the lady Jones.
'They escaped, your majesty, when we made a brief stop in Calle to pick up a shipment. We never brought them as far as the jail...I had hoped the mistake would be forgotten amidst the paperwork...' he mock-confessed. The Prince eyed him, weighed him, and found him as honest a man as they came...if a little less than sober.
'Then do your best to find her...her family are frantic.' the Prince decided, and left the Commander and his men standing in the street.

In the quiet peace of his own chambers Prince Marius of the human Royal family kicked off his boots and donned his soft, lambswool slippers. He blew out all but one lamp, and that he carried to the balcony. He set it on the table and went back inside for wine. When he returned he set two glasses on the table and poured both, then took his own glass with him so that he could gaze over the near-city that bathed in the sporadic lamplight below. Far across town and to the north the gates were solidly closed, steadfast against the dangers of the night. He took a deep, cleansing breath of sea air and counted the watchmen wandering the streets below, easily recognised by the torches they carried. He could see twenty-four. He was reasonably sure there wouldn't be that many on an ordinary night. A shift in the air around him told him that his guest had arrived, and he smiled so that his white teeth shone in the deepening darkness.

'How on earth did you get here? The gate's not even open. I didn't think you would make it.' he said dryly. The air on the opposite side of the balcony chuckled, and a rough and grizzled hand appeared from the shadows and snatched up the second wine glass.

'It takes more than walls to keep out Estora...Though for some reason you humans build them, regardless.' replied his companion. The Prince waved the response away, and sat on one of the balconies wire chairs.

'How much longer?' he moaned, more to himself than to the man present. The shadow tilted his head, and took a slurping drink of the wine. It was good wine, it almost tasted of home...almost.

'We await the final location. There are one or two small matters-' he started.

'Did they agree our terms?' the Prince interrupted. The shadow-man let out a deep sigh, his hulking shoulders loosing any tension he'd been holding there as he did so.

'Contact has been made. We will have an answer soon. Do you have the location?' asked the man, who leaned forward so that his teeth shone in the meagre lamplight. A heavy beard covered a dark and scarred face, a face worn that had fought in every battle that the Prince was old enough to remember- and more.

'I have the location. I need time. A few weeks should suffice, General.' the Prince answered calmly. The Sage Lord Mo'ash turned his toothy glare into a toothy smile, and the two sat in silence a few moments longer.

'This is the last time I will contact you.' said the Prince, after a time. The old Estoran nodded, and looked out across the horizon.

'Do not get too used to the view, my Prince.' he began cautiously. 'It will soon be changing.' he finished, and carefully set the glass back on the table.

'I won't.' answered the Prince, but even as he spoke he already knew that he was, once more, alone.

Chapter 13

'Remember me?' asked Siara Teel. The clerk almost jumped out of his spectacles when he saw her. She knew immediately that she'd been had the last time she was here. The expression on the snivelling Mister Greene's face told her all she needed to know. 'Where are they?' she asked him. She strode past him and pushed open the door to the back office, but the Commander was nowhere to be seen.

'He's guarding the Prince-'

'He ought to be guarding you.' she retorted, then drew her sword. To her surprise the clerk watched her, but made no move to run or fight. He gulped as she lay the sword against his throat.

'Where are they? I went to the Gold Port and the prison officer at Blakely never checked them in – he hadn't even heard of them. So where did he take them?' she asked. The man remained silent, so she pressed the tip of the sword home a little and was rewarded with a satisfying squeal. Still he held his tongue, even though his whole body shook from head to toe and a trickle of blood dripped onto his white collar.

'I don't know-' he started. She moved the sword and punched him, then forced him to straighten with the tip of her blade.

'You're going to tell me or you're going to die. Stephen's in trouble. Catherine Jones has sent a professional assassin after him – and frankly, I would rather kill you than him, so- last time now: where are they?' she tried. The clerk pushed the blade away from his chest and met her eye. He pushed his glasses back up his nose with a shaking hand and produced a handkerchief, which he used to dab neatly at the wound on his neck.

'We let them off at Calle. When you find him, tell him to go off-road. The Prince has ordered warrants for his arrest on every noticeboard from here to the Capital.' he said in a steady stream. Siara could hardly believe her ears. Calle. She had passed it twice in the last week and a half. She sheathed her blade and turned to leave. The clerk stopped her at the door with a call.

'Perhaps people would be more cooperative with you if they knew which side you were on, Miss Teel.' he said, with hardly a trace of malice in his voice. It was enough to make her stop and turn on her heel to stare hard at him for a few heartbeats before she left. The insult she'd had ready dead on her tongue. The man was right, after all...it *was* time to pick a side.

In Porta town George Dickson slid down the bar stool and then pulled himself back up. He ordered another from the wench with the big- from the wench behind the bar, and tried not to ogle. He was drunk, he'd been drunk for days. His wife had come to this island; and he could track her as far as Rapton; but after that the scent disappeared completely. Nothing, nada...just a cold hole in his heart where there used to be a woman that took care of him. It would have been the perfect relationship in fact, had she just loved him. He wouldn't have to hit her if she had loved him. He slid off the stool again and wondered if she loved Stephen Laurence, and if that was the reason their two smells mixed together on the breeze. Maybe that was why she left? Maybe she had been screwing him the whole time? His poisonous thoughts were interjected with the appointment of a fresh ale. He brightened immediately at the prospect of one more drink and sipped the froth from the top. His chin smacked the table top as he did so.

'You OK, friend?' asked an unfamiliar, cheerful voice. A hand reached out and steadied him before he slipped from the stool again. 'My wife left me for the butler.' he tried to say, but even to himself it sounded slurred and difficult. He dug his claws into the bar to stop himself slipping any more, and then took a long pull of the beer. It was his last one, he promised himself. Tomorrow he would stop feeling sorry for himself and start getting back to business. He would search the whole island piece by piece, tree stump by bloody tree stump...but he was going to find his wife...and then the bitch would pay.

'Your wife left you for the butter?' the stranger repeated. George laughed out loud and thumped the bar.

'Yip.' he giggled, let out a burp and then he slid finally from the stool and scooped up his jacket.

'Where you going?' asked the helpful man.

'Bed.' said George Dickson. He stumbled towards the door and fell over a stool. The patrons laughed and cheered him on, and a solitary, friendly hand reached down to help him up.

'Come on, I'll take you, just point the way.' said the man.

Outside George stumbled sideways and felt the wall of the building catch him. He pointed down a side street and let the stranger lead him. They turned the corner and had gone a few yards when a thought worked its way to attention in George's addled brain. 'S'awful kind of you...but I don't have any money if you're planning to rob me.' he warned the stranger. The man chuckled and held on to his arm as George connected again with the wall. He straightened the hunter as he spoke.

'Oh no, George, I have no intention of robbing you.' the man with no name replied. George squinted at him in the night. Something was setting off alarm bells but he was too drunk to pin down the thought that nagged him.

'What's your name, friend?' he slurred. There was a flash of white teeth in the darkness and a sudden, piercing, gut wrenching pain in his chest. He looked down to see a sword through his heart, and followed the length of the blade to the strangers eyes. There was no time to react, no time for vengeance, no time even to utter a curse. George Dickson fell helplessly to his knees as his once strong body failed him, for the first and last time ever.

'Don't have one.' answered the kindly stranger dully, just before he twisted and ripped the sword free and walked away, leaving George Dickson to bleed out a lonely, meaningless death all over the cobblestones of a dank alleyway in Porta town.

Chapter 14

Abigail finished taking the dead heads from the lavender and listened to the conversation behind her. It was the last item on her list of chores...a list that apparently grew every day. Greer had gone out early...hunting. The forest around them was stone dead; but above their little clearing there was a rock pool and a river; and around the river life blossomed.
'How can that be? When everything else is dead? Is it magic too?' she had asked the bald elf. Asa Lupine had nodded, beamed (as he often did, when her curiosity forced her to blurt out questions,) and stopped to dip his hands in the river. He mimicked washing his hands.
'Wash...see? Wash, wash, wash...All the time wash. Is clean.' he finished, shaking his hands and then drying them on his furs, he pointed up and down the shore and winked at her. 'Clean.' he said, and grinned so she could see the whiteness of his teeth.
Abigail loved Asa instantly. She had never met anyone like him before; eccentric and brilliant and all locked away from the world in his little patch of sunshine. The first day she'd been here he had wakened her with a cinnamon infused tea; and she'd known from then on that they were going to get on just fine. They had been with him for nearly a week, and after two days she had begged Stephen to stay there. They didn't need a town; not when they had a magically protected plot of land and their own healer and Shaman. If they could stock enough food for the rest of the winter they would be all sorted...hence today's little trip.
She wiped her hands on her apron as she straightened. Behind her the same argument that had been going on for three days raged on. Stephen had given in to her demands to stay with the elf for two reasons. One was, like she, he had been wakened whole in a comfortable bed and with a breakfast that included bacon. He trusted the Shaman immediately, perhaps for no other reason than that he had saved all three of their lives the night before. Secondly – and most importantly – Asa had asked them to stay...and he was a magic user. He was a magic user who had known Isabel and Samuel through the Alchemist's Guild, and who was familiar with the tragedy. Who had heard tales of Abigail Jones, and who was willing

to teach her...even if she didn't know that was what was happening at the time. For now she learned about herbs and healing...they could address the summoning of ammunition some other time.

'We need weapons...would you just buy the weapons, please?' he pleaded with Asa. The elf sucked in his lips and shook his head.

'No need. Is safe.' he repeated for the hundredth time. Stephen rubbed a hand over his eyes. They were gathered around the endlessly burning fire that strangely never took any wood, outside the cabin. Asa was whittling down a bowl with a file and mallet whilst Stephen paced and raved.

'If we get attacked here all we have are four bolts and two swords. We need weapons.' he tried a final time.

'That's not true. I have a dagger...and Greer doesn't need any weapons.' asserted Abigail, joining them from the herb garden. She dumped the dead lavender out onto the table and spread it out to dry.

'Cover it.' said Asa, so she found an old sheet to spread over the flower heads.

'There are people hunting us. If you don't get us weapons we need to move on.' Stephen half-threatened. Asa stopped whittling, and stood to his full height. He looked serious, which was unusual in itself, but he said nothing. After a few seconds of disapproving silence even Stephen gave in.

'Just please...The people chasing us are...Well they're professional hunters. And we – Abigail and I – are not.'

Asa grunted, and walked to the cabin. He reached inside and produced the simple wooden staff he liked to carry. It was dark oak and almost as tall as he was. He brought it over to the fire and beckoned to Abigail, who took off her apron and came to his call.

'You no need we-pins. You need magic.' he corrected, still more serious than Abigail had ever seen him. Asa thumped the end of the staff on the ground at his feet and there was a cracking noise, accompanied by a dozen flame red sparks which shot up from the impact and fizzled out on the perfect grass. Asa raised his chin and nodded to Stephen.

'Is safe.' he said. After a while Stephen closed his mouth...and Asa began his usual, cheery humming.

Fifteen minutes later Abigail and Asa had loaded up a little push cart with furs and beads and other...Asa-ish stuff...and were on their way to Porta town for market...which was apparently happening

today...even though it was gone ten and they hadn't left yet. Stephen watched from the fire, curious, whilst she panicked. The Shaman led her to the stone cliff in the clearing and had temporarily let her go so that he could dig a knife into his hand. Before she could look at the wound he had dragged his open palm down the rocks surface, and in front of her eyes it rippled like water. She touched it, and it sucked her whole finger in before she could free herself. Asa watched, nodding and humming and grinning. She was awe-struck.
'We go.' he said, and took hold of her arm.
'But how do you breathe?' she asked...just before the rock face swallowed her whole.

She stumbled out onto her hands and knees and within a stones throw from Porta town...She could see the wall. She filled her lungs with air and sat on her ass, trying to get her bearings. There was a sort of a giant-waterdrop noise behind her which was closely followed by a low pitched hum and a few clicks. Asa stopped beside her, brushed some brick dust off his shoulder and then produced his pipe. He filled it from one of his many pouches whilst he waited. She got unsteadily to her feet and tried to convince herself the land beneath her was steady.
'That. Was. Awesome.' she breathed. She tried to straighten, and laughed nervously. 'The world goes back to normal soon, right?' she hoped. The elf shook out his match and took a deep breath of smoke before he answered.
'Practice.' he said, and led the way to town.

They set up a stall along with the other handful of traders using the push cart as a table. They didn't have much to sell; they were there mainly to buy grain. Asa left Abigail to manage the stall and went about the business of purchasing. He didn't buy any weapons...but he did pick up a new set of whittling tools. There was no reason the girl shouldn't have a staff of her own; and any true staff was crafted by a loving owner, not soullessly selected from a blacksmith's shelf. In an hour he had the supplies they needed, inclusive of enough oats to feed a small army, and was back to see what Abigail had managed to sell. He tilted her chin up to look at her and noted the tiredness in her eyes. He frowned. The girl could not block out others energy yet...huh. Until she did, every interaction that she ever had would cost her a part of herself. He couldn't allow that to continue. In the middle of the marketplace in Porta Town, Abigail Jones got her first 'official' lesson.

They packed up the cart and Asa sent her for water to refill the skins. She was nervous, or excited, definitely one of the two. When she came back with the water he took the bucket from her and dumped it, unceremoniously and without warning, over her head. It was freezing cold and the shock of it froze her to the spot...thankfully, because her instinctive reaction would have been to punch him in the face otherwise.

'Wash, wash, wash!' the large elf sang whilst she fumed and trembled from the cold.

'What...the hell?' she asked, her voice shaking...possibly with anger.

'Wash...mmm...urgh!' he exclaimed, finally as frustrated as everyone else was by his inability to speak properly. He resolved to work on his common, but in the meantime...He let out a long breath and muttered a few ancient words. It was no big effort for a Shaman to see the magical threads that connected the world together...it was a bigger trick however, to make someone else see it. Abigail was a healer, and therefore her power came from the earth, and therefore...

He placed a hand squarely on her shoulder and to Abigail Jones the world swept into life in a way she could never even have imagined before that moment. Everything was normal and as it had been before – except for one difference – everything that was alive had hundreds, thousands even, of thin green threads flowing outwards and connecting them to everything else that was alive and that they had interacted with. Two farmers wives talking in the street connected around their heads, their green threads reaching out to join, weave and caress each other. Abigail took a few steps towards them but felt Asa's hand on her arm. She looked at him; and he was the only person in the whole square whose face she could see properly. Everyone else was obscured by the threads at least a little. Outside the inn a stray dog wandered, hunting for scraps. A bar wench shooed the beast with a broom, and the green threads on the animal retreated and bounced away from the broom...a green jolt shot along the hair and wood and back into the threads of the bar wench; whose colour was a little darker than those around her. She scanned the crowd for another who was slightly darker than the rest, and found a merchant, two stalls down. The man sold trophies;

animal heads mainly. She couldn't see anything different about him other than that.

'What does it mean when they are darker than the rest?' she asked Asa, who was watching her carefully and absent-mindedly producing his pipe. He gave a small grunt.

'Ai. Karaca. Mmm...bad join.' he tried to explain. He put his pipe between his lips and knotted his fingers together. She tried to think in Asa speak. She found a third, darker one, and watched the lady emerge from the carraige and turn her nose up at the beggars that bothered her driver. She had money didn't she? A coin to them meant a meal...to her it probably meant absolutely nothing- and she understood. The man selling animals heads; smiling as he handed over a stag's head...no purpose to the kill...just decoration. The wench chasing the dog away – they weren't bad people they just...weren't helping.

'I see.' she said, and she looked at her own hands; covered in a green layer so thick she couldn't see herself. 'Wash.' she voiced, and looked at Asa's clean face. The elf beamed a smile at her, and then nodded at her hands again, eagerly. She looked again at her hands, and this time they were clean...come to think of it, she felt much better...lighter.

'Remember.' reaffirmed the Shaman, and held up the empty bucket. She laughed – and then stopped, because someone across the square was fading out; like a green light that was puttering out in the night. She knew what it meant without thinking about it, and was across the way and running before Asa could stop her.

Chapter 15

The beggar was leaning over one of the many horse trough's scattered throughout the town. His chest rattled as he leaned over to drink, his hands shaking with the strain. He slaked his thirst and leaned his back against the cool metal. There was something in his lungs...some steadily growing mass that choked him in the night and made him have to fight for every, single, breath. He rested a hand on his aching chest, and was surprised to find another hand laid over his. Jack Mason was just that, a stone mason...or he was once...before the Estorans took everything from him that he held dear. He was in the memory suddenly; his wife dead in the back yard of their beautiful, Salston home. She was grizzled, bloodied, and with a look in her eye he had never seen before. The evil glint of silver leaked out of her as she slashed down on whatever it was she straddled. Again and again she slashed, over and over. A streak of blood flew upwards into the night from that clawed hand- a streak of blood that told him where little Oscar had gone...

And then peace.

A cool hand on his forehead, soothing words in his ear, crisp, clean, fresh water on his cracked lips.

'Mummy...' from his mouth...but somehow he had become a little girl and lay in a room he didn't recognise...a concerned looking butler mopped his brow with a soft, white cloth.

And then peace. And beautiful green life everywhere...and the ache in his lungs floated up from him like a very literal weight off his chest. When he opened his eyes the little girl was a woman, and she smiled at him, swooned a little, and was scooped up by a huge, towering, ox of an elf that was dressed in a druid's clothing and was tattooed just the same. Jack grasped the woman's hand and thanked her – she had done more than heal him, she had brought peace to his troubled memories...she had soothed his loss.

'I have nothing to pay you with.' he uttered with tears in his eyes. The woman shook her head and giggled, even as she struggled to stand on her own.

'Why would you pay me?' she asked him, and he was still struggling to understand when the large elf spoke.

'Come. People.' he said, and indicated the crowd they were drawing. As he started to lead the woman away another grabbed her shoulder, a middle aged woman with two teeth in her skull and a shock of greying-blonde hair.

'Come and look at our Helen for me? Please Miss?' the woman pleaded. Another grasped at her and asked for help with gout, another wanted her to fix an aching spine – Asa led her from the crowd, muttering, and when they wouldn't stop he slammed his staff into the ground and stared from his six and a half feet; and the crowd blinked at him, turned back to Abigail and started grasping again. Asa sighed, took her by the arm and frog-marched her out of there, a stream of people following them all the way to the gates.

They walked in silence the whole way back to the rock, and then they walked farther because there were still people following them, and Asa didn't like to reveal his tricks to people...at his height and with his appearance humans found him terrifying enough without watching him disappear into a rock wall. He was annoyed; she could feel it through the threads! But he was annoyed...worse, he wasn't saying anything about it...which meant he was letting her figure a conclusion for herself. It didn't take much figuring.

'He was going to die.' she tried. The elf kept his eyes on the road, but nodded. 'The others weren't...they were just...'

'This why healers mmm...no heal.' he stated gruffly. She let her chin fall to her chest. How were you supposed to help the world if you couldn't do what you were made to do? How could you help people if every time turned out like...like that? Maybe...maybe you did it in private...maybe you charged exorbitant fees so that the majority would leave you alone...maybe you lived in a hut in the woods because all the connections all the time would wear you out. Perhaps. She took a deep breath and let it go slowly, thinking about all of the mistakes she had just made. 'Oh.' she mumbled, after a while. Asa grunted, and nodded again, and pointed to a nearby rock. They drew the cart to a stop in front of it.

'I won't do it again...not like that.' she said to her shoes. Asa gave what might have been a grunt, or what might have been a chuckle, and drew his knife down his palm. He clicked to the rock a few times and muttered the spell, then watched, satisfied, as (at least) the rock did as it was told.

The pair stepped back into the clearing with much less effort and fear than it took for them to leave in the first place. When all was said and done stranger, they had achieved the days mission, which was to secure enough basic grain to see them through the worst months of the winter that lay before them. Abigail's lessons had begun, and from then on ranged from the thought provoking to the mad, from the roots of plants and up into the very sky itself. Yes, Abigail Jones loved Asa Lupine very much...and I hate to think what would have happened to us all, had it not been for that strange, tattooed man who welcomed them into his home and ever-after swore that the earth had told him they were coming. I hate to think.

Chapter 16

In the great city of Calle lady Mariana DeBossa adjusted her
sun hat and snapped out her fan. She fanned herself delicately,
especially delicately, carefully so. Under her pale complexion and
demure appearance she longed to fan the flimsy material as fast as it
would go; yearned for the cool air it promised, but could not provide.
It was winter, and it was a coastal city, but the sun shone at its zenith
and the presence alone of the huge, burning beast in the sky was
enough to set her to sweating and perching on the edge of her seat,
ready to flee.

Mariana DeBossa was drinking herbal tea with lemon. It was
absolutely disgusting, and tasted like watered down piss – but it was
what ladies drank...so she sipped it and smiled, and beneath the table
she kicked off her sandals and revelled in the cool, fresh air that
immediately soothed her poor sweating toes. She let out a small sigh,
grateful for that singular pleasure in this hub of...of...humans.

A young couple passed, and the sailor tipped his hat to her
whilst his partner, noticing the act, hit him on the arm with her purse.
Mariana felt the smile freeze to her face and hoped the young man
tripped and broke himself. Mariana DeBossa hated humans, but she
particularly hated human men and their roving hands and eyes.
'Go inside, this is too open.' said a voice by her ear. There was
nobody there, of course, and so far all was exactly as she had
expected...if somewhat...disconcerting.

Mariana DeBossa scooped up her purse and slid her sandals
back on. She did as she was told and went inside. She ordered a
'glass of something cool' and was rewarded with a mug of nearly-
cold milk. She smiled, so as not to look disappointed, and then
picked a table that would offer a good view of the door and any
guards that might somehow be on to her. She was barely in her seat
before the disembodied male voice rang again in her ear, deep and
steely.
'Very good. Book a room here. I will return.' the voice informed her.
She checked herself before she replied. She was alone in the room
but for the innkeeper, who wiped his mugs with a dirty cloth and
smiled a gap-toothed grin at her. She held in a sigh and fixed the
smile to her face. She wanted to know when? When she could expect

her midnight caller?..but if she broke his cover her neck would not be the only one on the line. She had been specifically told not to ask questions, not until the meeting was properly arranged and certainly not in public...one did not tend to 'blend in' if one was caught talking to oneself. She steeled herself with her best smile and approached the keeper. She needed a room for the night, and that meant being as absolutely normal as any human lady would be.

Mariana ate a light salad and then ordered a bath drawn. The salad had been terrible but the bath, at least, was worth the effort of waiting an hour for the inn's solitary serving girl to fill it with hot water. She climbed in with a relieved sigh and closed her eyes to dip her head under the water. When she emerged the growing-familiar shadow was with her...although how she knew that he was there she could not tell. She did not address the invisible presence, rather she washed out her hair and bathed herself as she normally would, but with extra, careful control. Mariana was a political Goddess, and if there was one thing a Goddess knew, it was that her greatest weapon was her femininity. She spent a full ten minutes in the bath, conscious of being watched and hiding her anger beneath a mask of neutrality. She did not speak, not until she was out of the tub and had a bathrobe wrapped around her, and the previously disembodied voice popped into existence across the room.

The creature fondled through the collection of clothes she had brought with her with hands she could barely see. The shadows cast by her candles dipped and wove around the man, making it difficult to place his features.
'What is so important that we must meet in this place?' asked the voice. The face behind it turned to regard her, and she straightened and held her chin high. The figure was cloaked, and shaded, and difficult to make out- but it was probably the most any other species had ever seen of a Reaver.
'The Masters send their greetings, and we request your services.' she told it. The man let out a droll laugh and came a little closer, his head tilted, his movements reserved and stinted...like an iguana on the hunt. Beneath the cloak she caught a glimpse of scale; green and purple and reflecting the light back at her to make her think she hadn't really seen anything at all. She held in a gasp, turning it into a gulp and giving a delicate little cough to cover her indiscretion. The creature didn't seem to notice.

'Our path's have not crossed in a thousand years, dark blood. Why now?' it all but hissed. The thing was mere yards from her now, and coming closer by the second. She could feel the coldness in the air, hear the thoughts of a thousand different humans all around her in the packed city – see glimmers of blue and green out in the streets from the open window- but she could feel and hear and sense nothing from the creature before her. She was as blind as a mole, stumbling around in the dark and relying optimistically on her other senses...like...like a *human.*

'There will be war.' she told it, trying desperately to calm her nerves. The creature stopped in its advance, its head tilted to one side, she caught a glimpse of yellow, pointed teeth – or maybe fangs – through the mists of its face. A chill touched her spine and she folded her arms across her chest protectively.

'A war? That is a grand thing to say. And what would your 'Masters' ask of us in this 'war' of theirs?'

Mariana finally smiled. She couldn't help herself...from now on he was in the palm of her hand...terrifying or not. The question of price was all that remained. What did Reavers want? They wanted to stay hidden. They were a species hunted to near extinction; a species who had long since turned on their human counterparts, and therefore lived their lives in the shadows, and by the sword.

'We require you to do nothing...and once it is all over, you won't need to walk in the shadows any longer.' she expressed simply, and went to find the carafe of wine she'd had with her salad. She poured the creature a glass and crossed back on tiptoe (and with lots of hip) to give it to him.

'Nothing?' he repeated.

'Nothing at all.' she answered, with her sweetest smile. The creature drank the glass in one. Evidently they were not creatures prone to manners.

'That will be costly...' he intimated thoughtfully.

'Cost is not an issue. Our races have similar interests...we want to ensure your...resources...do not fall into the wrong hands when the time comes. We will have a handful of contracts, of course,-'

'But you want to know we are on your side.' finished the creature for her. The Reaver spun on its heel and crossed the room in a swirl of black tendrils. It poured itself another glass from the carafe and drank it, once more, in a single gulp.

'You will have your answer tomorrow. I cannot speak for all my people without consulting some 'Masters' of my own. You will stay here and wait for my word,' the creature commanded, it turned its head as if listening, and then grinned its pointed fangs at her one last time. 'Mariana DeBossa, fourth generation of the family...first of your name.' it finished. Mariana watched it walk to the window, her perfect smile twitching, her composure temporarily forgotten with the knowledge that the creature had managed to do its homework. Nobody knew her, nobody here anyway...only on the island, only at home, did they know her name...only on Estora.

Chapter 17

Abigail picked up the basket slowly, carefully, and most of all with her right hand. Her left was shaking uncontrollably, and she dared not move it from its grasp on Asa's huge fur cloak, which she had draped around her shoulders. There were crabs in the basket...there was a man in the trees. She was sure he was watching – no – observing – her...but she could feel the threads that leaked from him across the rock pool and they were *not* good threads. They reached and groped and flashed across the space towards her like feelers or tubers, the green in them so dark it was almost black. The crabs in the basket clambered sideways and into each other, struggling to escape from their trap...and Abigail found herself doing the same. The water was between she and the top of Asa's clearing. She was dripping wet and unarmed...so what could she do? Heal him to death? Make him feel really, really invigorated as he killed her? She let out a shaking breath and counted the crabs out loud.
'You're too small, little buddy.' she said to the littlest crab. She scooped it up in between her hands. 'Let's put you back in the water.' she finished, and dropped the cloak...hoping those weren't her last words. She turned and, in only her shirt and pants, put a toe back into the water. If she could get to the other side of the pool she could get to the clearing the hard way...via waterfall...A click behind her froze her in place.
'Abigail Jones?' a soft, unbelievably gentle (considering its source) voice drifted to her across the shifting water.
'You have me mistaken with someone else.' she answered without turning. She bit into her lip.
'Your aunt sent me.' the voice purred, closer than before and filled with nothing but menace, in spite of its dulcet tone.
'To take me back.' she said flatly. She could feel the metal in his hands if she concentrated hard enough, feel the rushing of blood inside his ears and the relentless pounding of his heart. It was a crossbow, probably...maybe two swords...but he definitely had metal in both hands. She looked down at her own hands, and watched the frightened crab disappear inside of its little peach shell. Abigail wished that she had a shell.

'You think she wants you to come back?' murmured the man with no name. Abigail swallowed, it did nothing to help her suddenly parched throat.

'Mind if I let him go?' she gestured with the crab, her own voice distant. There was no need for the innocent crab to get hurt. His buddies were still in the basket, still fighting to escape. She hoped the others found them when they found her body. She didn't want their little lives to be taken in vain. The man laughed as she set the little crab down. She watched it scuttle away and plop itself gratefully back into the water.

'If you do it here the blood will get in the water. They'll see.' she said. If she could get him into the trees she had the advantage. She knew the land here and he did not. She knew of one particular spot not too far north where the river cut a dangerous path through some potentially deadly rocks...she turned to him, to see a very plain looking man. He was dressed in greens and browns; the colours of the forest around him. He was armed beyond reason with swords and daggers and a bow *and* crossbow. Abigail shook her head. Save for the weapon overkill there was nothing memorable about him...brown hair, brown eyes, medium height, medium weight...no defining features. His nose was normal, his lips thin, his face expressionless...the man before her was a walking exercise in anonymity. She felt a giggle begin in her throat...helplessly, she laughed at him. He looked from the water back to her, and then jerked with the crossbow towards the trees.

'Move.' he ordered her, anger in his voice for the first time. She followed the end of his bow and took two steps towards the trees, the crabs and cloak forgotten by the water. He moved so that he was behind her – and then somebody- some sweet wonderful soul- saved her life.

The shot came from above, from the canopy of the trees, and sported a beautiful light-wood, white feathered arrow, which struck right between the strangers eyes. She couldn't see or feel the person who fired it, and she spun in a circle and tried to process events. The assassin lay in a heap behind her, the tree line was empty and she could sense no one, even with the new skills Asa was teaching her. She jumped in fright when an elf dropped onto the path ten yards in front of her. She stared at him, and he stared at her. He was as tall as Asa, but much less broad (and much less bald.) He looked young, his face and hands strangely elongated from a humans, his long frame dressed in a green tunic that looked like there might once have been more of it, and his long, light brown hair was tied back in a simple but colourful green thread. His arms were wrapped in tattoos...just like Asa's.

'You're a druid.' she breathed in awe.

'Supres ino uman.' the druid said with a grin. She nodded.

'Thank you.' she bowed, and pointed to the dead assassin. The druid's grin got wider, and he offered a bow with his hands clasped before him, as if at prayer. She didn't know what he had said, but his voice had struck her like it was liquid gold.

'Liandor.' said the druid. He placed a hand palm-flat on his chest.

'Abigail.' she responded in kind. Liandor grinned broadly, and nodded.

'Asa.' he answered. She turned from him to the body, and then back again.

'Yes. We should probably fetch an adult.' she agreed, shaking with adrenaline and trying not to relive her near death experience. She remembered the crabs at the last second. She somehow didn't have the stomach for crab any longer, so she turned them free – much to the druids pleasure – and then the two of them went off in search of someone who might be able to make sense of all this.

In the safety of the unending firelight the strange druid spoke fluently with Asa whilst Abigail dried her hair and Stephen and Greer fussed. Once they were finally assured of her safety and Stephen had calmed down enough to think straight; they all had a long chat about the nature of druids, their role in making the forest live again and their presence in Asa's clearing.

'Why didn't you tell me?' Stephen whined to Asa, who merely grinned and tapped the side of the his nose.

'I did. Is safe.' he reported almost smugly...and Abigail hid a laugh behind her hand. The poor druid didn't seem to know what was going on. Her merriment and Stephen's annoyance were interrupted by a rustling across the clearing, and all of them were on their feet at once. Another two druids shuffled into view: Finan and Vernon specifically, although she didn't know it at the time.

'Geez, how many of them are there?' Stephen asked of Asa, who shrugged.

'Many.'

The new arrivals were similarly dressed to Liandor, in plain robes. Both were tattooed and muscular, both with the same light brown hair and green eyes. They were dragging something behind them on a rope. The older looking one – Vernon – came forward and spoke to Asa and Liandor in a steady stream. He saw the lost looks on the others faces and stopped to give them a wide grin.

'We found this one. She is yours?' he asked. He dragged the bundle behind him through the edelweiss until a tangle of soft brown hair came into view.

'Good Gods, is that...Siara Teel?' gasped Stephen...and so it was.

The morning rose on the little hut...where it was slowly dawning on Asa Lupine that there wasn't enough space. He left the others whilst they were still sleeping and went out into his little clearing. At the rock wall he stopped, and slit open his palm. He needed a favour...he needed some home improvements...and what better way than to merge the little hut into the rock itself...By the time the others showed up for breakfast he was wiping sweat from his brow and brewing tea, and the little shack in the forest had become a little cave system in the forest. Imagine Greer's surprise when she woke up in her own bedroom, with her own space, and her own bed. Imagine Stephen's happiness to find he no longer had to share with the snoring druid, and Siara's surprise that she wakened in a room, unharmed, and not in a prison cell. She wasn't dead, and she wasn't even tied up. When she came out to the fire the others were waiting for her, and Siara Teel sat down to tell her story.

An hour later Greer straightened from her seat and turned her longing gaze to the forest.

'You are sure he is dead?' she asked coldly. Siara had expected more than that – she had expected hysterics, she had expected tears. Instead the huntress looked distant and uncaring. Siara nodded slowly.

'I'm so sorry, when they said it was a Wanderer that was murdered I just knew. I buried him in the cemetery outside the north Temple...I did what I could. If you ever want to visit him-' she said softly. Greer laughed bitterly.

'I left him for a reason...you saw. It was the best decision I ever made. But this, at least, tells me what has happened to him. Thank you.' she said carefully. Then she strode purposefully away from the fire and off into the morning.

'Greer don't-' started Stephen, but she had already gone; nothing but a bundle of clothes on the edge of the clearing. Stephen looked at the trees and wondered if he should go after her. Behind him Asa chuckled lowly, he was eating a bowl of oats and dribbled it everywhere as he laughed. He gestured towards the fire with his spoon.

'Wolf will be fine. You...mmm...not so much.' he mused, still chuckling. Abigail tilted her head and shot him a look that told him she agreed. He brought Greer's things back, carefully trying not to touch any of it, and dropped the gear on Abigail's lap. He stopped by the fire and towered over Siara for a moment, then he brought her a bowl.

'So what now? I don't think we can let her leave...' he said idly to Asa. The large elf shrugged, and peered at Siara the same way he had once peered at Abigail. He leaned over and sniffed her neck. Abigail laughed outright whilst Stephen scowled.

'Don't scare her Asa, if she goes to the guards we're done for...I'm not in the habit of killing old friends...' he let the thought trail off. He shot a look to Abigail, who looked up from her bowl long enough to shrug.

'But I was hunting you?! Why aren't you...angry?' Siara Teel's voice rang out in her confusion. The last few days had been hard, made harder still by two druids dragging her the last two miles face down in the dirt. She realised she didn't hurt with some surprise, and shot a hand to her face...she should be scratched, bruised, there should have been blood...Instead there was nothing. She had been healed whilst she slept. She wondered which one of them it had been.

'I kidnapped a kid. Asa is aiding and abetting, Abigail has obstructed the course of justice and I think...I think that plant by the fire there induces paralysis. Welcome to the party. The first rule is try not to get killed...the second is don't get caught.' said Stephen. He fetched his own bowl and began to eat. Siara watched him a while, and then eventually picked up her own spoon. She wasn't quite sure what she had stumbled into here; but it was a whole lot better than the situation that she had stumbled out of. She enjoyed her first breakfast in the camp, whilst Stephen worried about Greer and Asa worried about druids and Abigail...Abigail worried about the assassin...whose body had not been there when she had gone out in the grey dawn to look for it, and whose presence was potentially the first of many. Catherine hated her, and she hated Catherine, and ultimately she had known this day would come. Why, then, did it hurt so much? There were two Beeton Jones' left in the world...it was a sad thing to realise that sooner or later there would remain only one.

Chapter 18

Across the sea and many miles to the north an old, old man entered the cold and abandoned house of his youth. He opened the creaking door before him and pushed it inwards; the hinges screeching protest all the way. He stepped over the threshold and filled his aged lungs with the musk of more than forty years. He had kept a family in this house; a wife and a child...and he had left them here whilst he worked...work, work, work...sometimes it felt like he had wasted his whole life with his work. What did it matter to him now? What did a life of work mean once one had received the calling? It was his time to exit, his time to leave. His work could live on through his son and heir, and he could go on to join his beloved wife in the Otherdark.

The God had appeared to him in a dream. In the dream he had been young again. He had been in this very same house; he had been sitting right here in this chair, right beside the dinner table. He had been on his own fathers knee, and the impossibly old man had looked down at him, his face creased and wrinkled with age, his kindly, sea-blue eyes shining in the lamplight.

'It is time.' his elder had told him with the voice of Shade. He had kissed his wife, hugged he and his brother and ushered them all upstairs. In real life he hadn't seen his father's body again until it had been laid out in the catacomb under the Temple; the Convocation gathering with the family to say their final farewells. In the dream however, his younger self sneaked back downstairs and watched...The ancient man at the table in the present echoed the movements of the ancient man in his dreams. He removed his scarf; his badge of office...a thin strip of silk worn around the neck of his heavy, black, velvet robes. He folded the silver cloth for the last time and set it on the table. Next he removed his rings, one at a time and with great effort. These rings had not left his crooked and bony fingers in a hundred years at least...in truth it had been so long that he could not remember. He set the heavy gold rings on top of the cloth, ready for his successor and heir. Lastly, he produced scroll, ink and quill from the deep folds on his robe and set them on the table. He began his letter with the words 'Dear Aaron,' and ended it with leaving all of the love his weathered body had left in it to his only boy.

In the endless dark of an Estoran evening, the Shadow Lord Wreather dug a dagger into his own wrist and strangled a cry at the pain it caused. He switched hands before numbness set in and sliced into his other wrist with the silver ritual dagger. He dropped the dagger on the table and sat back, careful in his dying moments to make sure the blood didn't drip on the parchment. In his final moments the Shadow Lord Wreather reached out into the night towards his long lost love...and left the shattered remnants of his once-strong body behind him.

Across the island, the dense, all-consuming noise of the Temple bells ringing drowned out all other sound. The bells signalled one thing alone: the death of a Shadow Lord...the weakening of the Convocation...and across Estora peasants downed tools in the fields, initiates fell silent, tutors closed books – and the Lords gathered. In his own study the Shadow Lord Mo'ash felt the loss like a link had been broken in his head, like he had completed a jigsaw but for a single piece, and that piece was lost and never to be found again. The Convocation must have twelve...and given that the God Shade occupied one of the seats that put their number down to ten. There would be a mourning period, and that mourning period would set their plans back by weeks. That coward Wreather had known it...that's why he had killed himself. It was not a calling from his God, but a flight in fear to escape the coming war. The Wreather's hid behind their science, used their alchemy as a shield to protect them from the retribution of their elders. With the old man gone the son had no such protection...not that he needed it. Aaron Wreather was a torment all unto himself...however, Adrian Wreather, the old man's brother, was compliant, helpful, reliable...and more importantly: he had no interest in science.

The Shadow Lord Mo'ash smiled to himself in the soft blue light of the many strategically placed crystals that lit the shelves he sat amidst. Adrian would suit his purposes just fine, and the fiery younger man could wait another few years...hopefully until Mo'ash was in his own tomb, and not in a position to grudgingly accept another ten years of 'research' warnings, and obsessive cataloguing. Now all that remained would be to convince the others of his choice. He connected his fingers together, the act symbolic and part of his subconscious. As a young man he had learned the symbol; an outward action prescribed by his tutor to help him connect his mind with those around him, a technique that came naturally to most of his kind, but that had never come naturally to him. He silently conveyed his reasoning and his decision to the others. He felt agreement from most, lack of interest from some and resistance from the Lord Underridge alone. The Lord insisting that the chair should be offered to the progeny before the sibling. The chair belonged to the Wreather family, on that, at least, they were all agreed.

The Convocation gathered at the long table in the big hall, the largest room in the Temple and probably the single room capable of holding both they and the minor Lords at one time. The bells rang until every last one of them was tracked down and brought back, or in a few cases were otherwise accounted for. The bells rang for a long, long time. And only after they had fallen silent did the gathering begin.

'My father, the Shadow Lord Wreather, has passed to the Otherdark.' announced the young Wreather. Mo'ash nodded approvingly at the lack of emotion in the young man's mind. He watched him re-take his seat in the front benches and cleared his own throat.

'The mourning period has been set for twelve days. After which the replacement shall be selected.' he announced, his booming voice echoing around the huge hall. He noted the young Wreather flick cerulean blue eyes at him from under his mess of black hair. If his eyes weren't so old he might have seen the young Estorans grip on his armrest tighten till his knuckles turned white- but they were not. And instead, he continued on with his speech, oblivious. In his chair Aaron Wreather fumed, stranger...because that seat belonged to him...and now he was going to have to fight for it.

In the dark recesses of his laboratory Aaron Wreather touched his blood to the round, blue-tinged crystal and watched it ripple out in response to his essence. The crystal lit up exactly like the lights in the room, and glowed a swirl of reflections in its surface. In those reflections shadows danced; and faces swam in and out of focus. He watched a long time, obsessively, some might say. He watched a Wanderer pleat a young woman's red-brown hair, and he waited. He barely noticed that the door had opened and a breeze blew through the room, rustling the papers on the desk.

'They want us to call them.' said the Lord Marcus Lester from behind him. He opened his mouth to reply but found himself lost in his thoughts instead. After a few moments spent inside his own head he turned to his friend with purpose.

'They can't move! They are ten.' he answered, his voice soft and with a slight accent that he hated and tried fruitlessly to hide. Marcus patted his shoulder companionably.

'About that. They opened to suggestion because Mo'ash wants Adrian. This war is happening Aaron. We have to call them.' he tried as gently as he could. In a flurry of movement the young Lord Wreather picked up the blue crystal and hurled it into the wall. It lodged there, undamaged, whilst stone dust pattered to the ground around it.

'They are not ready.' he rasped once he had caught his breath. The two of them peered at the wall as the crystal slid out and hit the earth with a heavy 'thunk'. Marcus offered a smile.

'None of us are.' he told his friend. 'But if we spend our whole lives waiting until we are ready, we will never get anything done...and look on the bright side...if we're right, this will change *everything*.' he finished...and his wicked amusement was just as contagious as his grin.

'And that, stranger...friend, was that, so to speak. Or that's all my voice can handle for one day. All the players are on the board- almost- and the story proper can begin. It has been a long afternoon, and the setting sun is bothering my old eyes and making me weep. Perhaps tomorrow I will tell you some more, and perhaps tomorrow we will go up to the high meadows to gather lavender. It's nothing magical – not any more – but it makes a fine pot-pourri I can sell...The plants, at least, are one thing that the Cataclysm did not take away from me.'

Part 2

Chapter 19

Abigail stalked through the trees, the half-finished staff raised protectively across her body, the afternoon sunlight playing through the branches of the old oak trees that surrounded and supported the druids encampment. Beneath the canopy there were dark clusters of shadow everywhere, and any one of those shadowy nook's might hold her enemy. There was a rustling a few yards ahead of her and she smirked; because even if she wasn't getting any better with the staff at least she was learning his tricks. She spun on her heel and struck out lengthways as if the staff were a sword. Liandor laughed and parried easily. When she brought the staff back to cover her body he simply pushed against it and shook his head. 'I told you...already.' the druid grunted as he worked. His common was getting better faster than she was able to learn. Abigail gave ground, taking step back after step back. She knew the score. Asa's voice rang in her head 'You too skinny. No weight. Use head.' he repeated. She would have sighed if she'd had any breath left. She dropped suddenly into a leg swipe – her favourite move – and was rewarded with the druid's maniacal laughter. Apparently she was not the only one getting used to the others tricks. The druid laid his whole weight on his staff and pushed against her own. He careered over her head in a cartwheel and landed behind her. She turned just in time to see the base of his staff was two inches from her eyeball. She dropped her staff and put her hands in the air.
'You dead.' said Liandor.
'You are dead.' she corrected. He nodded, determination knotting his green eyes together.
'You aarrrr dead.' he repeated, and then grinned.
'I still beat you with the bow.' she teased mock-bitterly. She picked up her staff and pointed to the sky.
'Asa?' she asked. Liandor shaded his eyes and examined the position of the sun. He gave a decisive nod.
'Asa.' he agreed.

They found him in the camp – oh but the camp! What a place it was. Druids lived in trees you see, specifically their number mainly consisted of wood elves, and wood elves lived in trees. They found the oldest, wisest and strongest trees in the forest and they moulded them into homes. Up amidst the branches of the old oaks on Porta you could find enclaves made of woven leaves, homes the size of individual tents; you could find platforms, and ladders, and softly glowing green plants enchanted to provide light. You would find coloured threads woven amongst the leaves, beads and feathers and colourful birds. All of the animals that had fled from the blight on the rest of the forest had taken shelter here...the druids prayed, they chanted, they had rituals morning, noon and night. They kept the darkness at bay and slowly, oh so slowly, they were taking back the forests once cursed by the Estorans and their dark God. Liandor led Abigail up the spiral staircase that wound around the base of a pale tree and up into the upper platforms. With a little walking and a few ladders they were in a sort of communal area, an open space between where they ate and where the Chief's hut lay. Asa's box of supplies, reagents, bandages, alcohol – everything an alchemist might need, lay open in the doorway and in disarray. Abigail sighed when she saw it, and went to clear away his mess before he gave her 'the look'.

'Wait.' said Liandor, and pointed to the floor. She nodded and got on with the packing. He ran to the end of the platform and climbed over the edge and out of sight. Before he could return the enclave's ragged but bright purple curtains opened and Asa came out, closely followed by both Uthar and Celeste, the tribe's leaders. The spoke in swift Druidic and walked out onto the platform. On the way past, Celeste put a gentle hand on Abigail's head. She froze, and then quickly dropped into a bow, her hands in front of her as if in prayer. The high Priestess beamed, and patted her gently. She put her hand on Abigail's upper arm and urged her to her feet. She regarded her a moment, taking in her pleated hair and dirty knees. Then she smiled like she knew something Abigail didn't and took a small pot from somewhere amidst her voluptuous curves. She opened it, put her thumb in it and wiped a streak of it under Abigail's left eye. She blinked in shock, her eyes straying to Asa (who, in spite of her best efforts, was giving her 'that look') and then she remembered herself and smiled and bowed her thanks. She felt Asa's anger fading, felt the Priestess' approval, felt the Chief behind her knowledge her existence rather than his usual solid and cool tolerance. She even felt Liandor bounce back up the stairs towards her. Wow...what was this stuff on her face? All the green threads glowed in importance and connection. The sky flowed into the trees, the trees flowed into the ground, the ground flowed into herself, and everything else that lived on it...and in turn everything alive bled excess life into the air and it all went back into the sky to start the cycle again. It was beautiful, and intricate, and could merit years of study. She turned to the canopy of trees and gazed out over them to the ocean and not too-distant waves. In the distance thunder rumbled, miles and miles away and out over the sea where dark clouds gathered ominously about the horizon to the north and east.

'There's a storm...' she mumbled to herself.

'See Celeste, now you have distracted my apprentice.' said Asa in Druidic. The Priestess gave a wonderfully gentle laugh.

'She has a curious mind, distraction comes naturally to her, I think.' answered the Priestess.

'Samhain falls in a few days. Will we see you this year?' questioned Uthar. Asa gave a firm nod.

'Of course. Someone needs to bring the cider. You won't see me until nightfall. What about them?' he asked, and jerked a thumb towards Abigail.

'The humans?' started Uthar, but he stopped at his wife's gentle touch.

'Bring them to the celebration. It will be good for them...but the prayers...' she hinted. Asa nodded his understanding.

'The prayers are not for humans.' he agreed idly. He laughed at Abigail's face. Liandor had handed her an orange stone and she had turned it in her hands a few times and then jumped a half-mile into the air because he was trying to untie the necklace she kept hidden under her shirt. On the necklace was a ring, a very important ring, so important that she never let anyone know of its existence...and yet everyone knew it was there...an unspoken agreement...the last possession of her fathers. Stolen from her aunt Catherine and kept like the treasure it was, close to her heart. The druid looked hurt, then he took the stone he had given her and pointed to the hole in the centre of it. She watched him, wary, then decided she didn't want to hurt his feelings. She took the necklace off carefully, and let his happy face drop the rock onto the leather. She tied it back on and dropped the ring and stone back beneath her vest. Then she thanked him with a bow whilst he beamed. Asa watched with approval...the ring had been a signet ring, the family seal, if he had to guess. A silly thing, to hold on to possessions in such a way, like they could provide a link to the person that was gone already. The only real link was in memory...but perhaps that was the difference between an elf and a human. Without much more arrangement the two packed up the travel bag and headed back to their clearing, their jobs done for the day. Besides anything else the night was coming, and the last thing you wanted to do on Porta was to be stuck out in the forest in the dark.

In the clearing the two settled into what was fast becoming a regular routine. By the fire Stephen had left her nightly chore- a batch of hooked fish he had spent the day on. There were rabbits, three of them, that needed skinned. They would treat the skins into furs and use it or sell it; and with three meat eaters in camp none of the animal was ever wasted. Abigail could no longer stomach to eat animal flesh, it came with the green threads and the connections. She could treat the fish though, salt it or hang it by the fire for smoking. She put Asa's tools of the trade away inside the cabin and went to the coolness of the caves to splash some water on her face. Liandor had beaten her a fair few times that day, and a dirty face at dinner earned the dreaded 'look.' When she finally emerged Siara was on cook duty and dishing out something fish and rice based. They ate together, sharing information, the days stories, chatting about nothing...it wasn't too bad a life...Especially not when night time meant they were all trapped in the clearing, and once her chores were finished she and Asa would spend the time they had left before bed sitting studiously in the shack, Asa's trunk of herbs and potions unfolded into a sort of self contained desk, and Abigail would sit on the floor whilst he talked her through basic potion making or herbology. She had a reasonable knowledge already, taken from her father's study: but there was always more to learn. She was a willing student, eager to get the work of the day done so she could spend her nights wrapped in beakers and powders, roots and plaster-pastes and cream bases. She had most of the theory already, but the practical experience blew her mind. For two weeks Asa tried to keep up with her desire to learn and after that he left her in the spare room to play whilst he slept. She was expressly forbidden access the poisons and explosives, those he kept separate and to himself, hidden from her over-eager fingers and need for knowledge. Abigail had the air of the dangerous, the slight hint of obsession that had driven her father to great things – but also driven him to the edge of madness. There was a fine line in science between doing something because it *could* be done and doing something because it *should* be done...and Abigail was still a little young to properly consider the results of her actions. For that reason alone he kept the hemlock safely out of her reach, and considered how much he could actually teach her before she needed the guidance and safe practice found only in the Guild...Then there were the herbs...the ones she had been using constantly for two weeks now...the ones that should have long since needed replenished, but that were still full every time he opened the individual little drawers that shelved them. It was just like the arrows Stephen had warned him about, and it was unlike any magic he had come across before. A summoner could summon; but not a healer. Perhaps she was a hybrid of the two? Unlikely as it seemed, it was not unheard of. There had been a mage who could heal once, legend had it he could smash your face in with rocks and then fix it afterwards – but they were of the same element, both earth. Summoners were of the air, and Abigail was not, and none of it made sense. So he let her work and taught her what he could and when she was done he hunted her to bed and cleaned away the mess and wondered, wondered, wondered where all of those damned herbs kept coming from.

The first snow came in the morning, but it didn't lie. It never lay in the islands, just floated down and dissolved in the salt-laced air – but it had come, and all through the forest a sort of quiet peace had descended. Abigail came out the cave entrance without passing through the hut, it was literally first thing, and waking Asa after she had kept him up so late would be to sign her own death warrant. She tended the little herb garden and some of the water herbs, and then thought about breakfast. They'd had bread and cheese for three days in a row, and the cheese was running low, so this morning it would be oats. She took the bucket to the waterfall and held it under the stream...where she saw something more than passing strange. As she was filling the bucket the world around her pulsed; and she assumed it to be her own heartbeat blurring her vision as sometimes happens. When it happened a second time she timed her heartbeat, and found it to be out of sync with the blurring. Her sleeves got wet as the bucket overfilled and she turned her attention to it – but the water was red...all of the water was red...the stream ran bloody as if in a nightmare, splashes became globules, the gentle lap on the banks became a sloshing, another woman would have screamed. Abigail let out a soft giggle and then collapsed at a sudden and sharp pain in her head. She might have muttered a swear word or two as she went down, taken unawares and uncertain what had just happened. She screwed her eyes shut tight and covered them with her palms in an effort to block out the light that suddenly burned her.

'Stephen!' she choked through the pain. The pain in her head stopped, and moved through her body just like the waterfall until it became a stabbing pain in the soles of her feet instead.

'What the-' she asked the air – and then stopped. She had opened her eyes again, and Abigail Jones was no longer in the clearing.

Chapter 20

Stephen looked from the oats in the bowl to the place the bucket should be and frowned.

'I might kill her.' he told Siara. The huntress swept a few loose hairs away and tried to hide her worry for his sake. She wasn't in the forest...and that left two places that she might be. Asa was with the druids as they spoke and Greer had gone into town on the premise that Rapton didn't know her, and that if Abigail had been caught and taken there she would be able to catch her scent. Siara had a very strong suspicion that she had not run away...given that the only thing she appeared to have taken with her was the groups solitary steel bucket. Abigail wouldn't go anywhere unarmed...not unless she had been taken.

'Stephen...I don't think-' she began, then stopped abruptly.

'What is it?' he asked, too hopefully.

'Greer's coming back. Stephen...she's alone.' she told him, echoing what her senses told her. The wolf was running fast towards them, but without any threat of danger, instead she had the urgency of a woman who had lost her charge.

'Then she must be with Liandor, they're damned near inseparable nowadays.' he said thoughtfully. He tapped his chin a few times. There was a growing pit of concern in his stomach that wasn't going away. Why would she be with the druids without so much as her jacket? It was snowing, after all. He watched the snowflakes fall fruitlessly onto the endless fire to sizzle and spit away to nothing. Besides Greer's assurance that her smell had not left the camp and that no strangers had visited in the night; he was dubious. Abigail wouldn't leave him, not without at least a goodbye. The more time passed the more sure he became...this felt wrong...it felt bad. It felt like she had been stolen...kidnapped for real this time. When Asa returned with a string of druids in tow and no Abigail, his heart finally sank. Abigail was gone, vanished in the night...and all he could think of were the Captain's words...'Don't fail.' Charles had warned, but something deep down inside was terrified that he already had.

Celeste tasted the water in the stream...magic. A different magic to Asa's which she could easily distinguish given how long the two had known each other. This magic was unusual, it tasted of over-salted shellfish, with a weird underlying taste of something like nettle, and then a whole lot more salt. It was bitter magic, and bitter tasting magic meant it was dark. The metallic twinge the nettle taste gave to her palate told her all she needed to know.

'Blood magic.' she said aloud, in common, and with her words cut with fear. Stephen let out the breath he'd been holding and screwed up his eyes. He cuffed at a stray, frustrated tear before the others noticed, and clenched his jaw.

'Where is she?' he whispered. Celeste and Asa exchanged a look.

'No way to tell.' said Asa.

'But I find out.' Celeste assured them with a decisive (if fearful) nod.

'How?' he asked. He should have known better, for the high Priestess merely offered a coy smile, and muttered something in Druidic that had her entourage scurrying off after her in the direction of their camp.

'Hair.' she told Asa on the way past. He nodded, ducked into the house and then came out again. When he also walked away into the forest there was very little anyone could do to stop Stephen and the others from following too.

Greer didn't like it in the trees, she fought to stop the wolf from trembling as she climbed down yet another ladder. It wasn't the actual climbing, nor the trees themselves, but rather a combination of both height and...well...the *wrongness* of it. The wolf complained that birds lived in trees, and wolves (very pointedly) did not. She tried to relax her shoulders down from her ears a little, and was actually quite glad when the whole group came to a stop on a wide platform. That way she could lean her back against a tree and know she wasn't about to fall off anything. There was a little wall of woven branches to one end, but she didn't realise it was a house until Celeste emerged with a scroll in one hand and a red potion bottle in the other.

'Hair.' she demanded again of Asa, who produced a lock of red-brown hair. The hair had been cut from Abigail's head, Greer could smell her on it. Siara jumped and intercepted the lock of hair.

'Hey. Where'd you get this?' she asked suspiciously. The big elf shrugged and took it back from her. Siara sulked. 'It was you that cut my fringe wasn't it? And you let me blame Abby...' she scolded, then let the thought trail off sadly. Abigail and Siara got on ninety percent of the time...but the other ten percent? Arguments like 'Did you cut my hair while I was sleeping?' had occurred more than once in the last few weeks. Even so the pair had grown close, close enough to take Siara by surprise at how worried she was. She watched Asa give the hair to Celeste, who dropped it in the potion bottle where it fizzed.

'It should be blood.' worried Asa in Druidic. Celeste gave a slow nod, her concentration elsewhere.

'I assumed you wouldn't have any.' she answered. She stopped to place a gentle hand on the elf's arm. 'This will work.' she assured him. She had known Asa Lupine a long time, long enough to notice that he hadn't hummed to his spirits all morning. Long enough to know when he needed that extra little bit of reassurance that a touch could give. She refocused and took the red ribbon from her scroll. The druids were not a race given to paperwork; but there are some items that everyone owns, and this was one. A map of all the known world. It was drawn in fabulous colours, from the tip of the mainland in the far north to the point in the south that connected with their little islands, tiny and obscure at the bottom of a sprawling land of mountains and rivers, pasture-land and forest, and there, in the centre, the focal point of it all: Capital City and the Ring of Ten Sisters that protected her. The cities were picked out with white crosses and elegant script. The islands were nothing but dots...but she suspected she would find her amongst the Guilds. There were not a whole lot of people in the world who knew how to use blood magic, and of those very, very few were permitted to study it. If a blood magician 'went rogue' they were put out of their misery on the spot. The Mages had a zero tolerance policy. The probability that they had summoned her was the safest conclusion.

Celeste stirred the potion to make sure that the hair was properly dissolved. It wasn't necessary to the spell, it was just that the thought of drinking hair turned her stomach. She downed the little bottle in one go and put it aside, then removed one of her many necklaces. The chain was of leather, the beads of white bone, and a solitary, clear, quartz crystal hung on the end. She hung the necklace over the map and held it steady. She started with Capital City and worked her way outwards in slow, wide circles, carefully keeping her hand steady so that the crystal hung straight down on its pendulum. She frowned as she passed over the first of the Ten

Sisters and nothing happened...Sterling City was where the Mages Guild resided in its gleaming white castle...Abigail was not there. She passed each of the other nine cities in turn, nothing. She swung the search wider, Stephen looking increasingly more like he was about to interrupt with every passing second. She held up her other finger to silence him. She knew their history well enough. She moved the search from the cities to the coast, down, down, down to the islands to hover over Freisch. The crystal fell solidly, Stephen held his head in his hands and Asa narrowed his eyes...for he could see what she could see. The opposite end of the thin crystal lay on Estora. The map was too small.

'Do we have a map of the islands?' she asked her Priestess-in-training Melody. The girl ducked back into the hut to search.

'It said Freisch didn't it? Catherine's got her-!' Stephen started, frustrated at his helplessness. Celeste quieted him with a hand.

'Map too small.' she tried to explain. Asa grunted his agreement and they all waited a few moments. When Melody popped her blonde head through the door and shook it so that a spattering of flowers came loose from her hair Stephen's heart sank yet again. Asa restored his faith by shrugging. From somewhere amongst his many pouched, many-furred person he produced a stub of chalk. He began drawing a map on the floor – a very crude one – but a map none the less. Celeste watched her friend with a smile on her face and her head tilted to one side. There was a five minute silence broken intermittently by the scratching of chalk on wood. After he was finished she once again held the crystal steady, but before she could even begin the necklace whipped out of her hand and fell straight down. They all looked at the crystal, which had landed square in the middle of Estora.

'What the hell?' muttered Stephen under his breath. 'How could she possibly?' he wondered aloud, hoping someone could tell him. His brain rushed to keep up. 'Wait...why? What could the Estorans possibly want with her?' he asked...but nobody was answering him...instead they were staring at the map on the floor and deep in thought. After a while Asa raised his head, turned red eyes to Stephen and asked:

'What is th-u plan?'

Stephen met his gaze steadily, grimacing at information that didn't make sense to him.

'I don't know.' he answered honestly. 'But we better think of something soon because I'm not- I'm not willing to lose her just yet.' he finished with a shrug. 'Especially not to the same people I lost her parents to.' he added in his head alone...because some thoughts were too painful to ever be repeated out loud.

Chapter 21

Abigail popped back into existence in an old stone building. She waited until her stomach caught up with the rest of her before she opened her eyes. The room didn't stop swaying so she turned her head to the side and narrowly avoided vomiting on herself. She stayed on the floor for a bit, just to be safe. The room span; sandstone and iron bars, a straw mattress, the bucket she had brought with her upturned and blood all over the floor. In a daze she reached out a finger, for some reason expecting the blood to be warm. It was not, and Abigail Jones remained on the floor.

When she wakened everything hurt, indeed, it had been the pain that had woken her. She dragged herself, sticky with blood and still in her night clothes, to the makeshift straw bed, where she fell face forward and rolled onto her back. There was no relief. She groaned and fought the urge to be sick again as the room continued to rock around her. The pain moved with her actions, from shooting and cutting down her front to slicing and aching at her back. Her brain rushed the information to her as she was jolted near upright by another wave:

'*Get off the ground.*' her own voice told her. She opened an eye and heard herself whimpering. The bucket. It was solid steel. She forced herself onto her knees and used the wall to right herself. The coolness of the stone was almost comforting by comparison to the weirdness of everything else. She stumbled the few steps across the small space and flipped the bucket upside down with her foot. It took all of the energy she had left to get on top of the damned thing – but once she was standing on the bucket with a solid layer of steel between herself and the ground the room around her slowed down to walking pace. The pain subsided and, most important of all, she could breathe again. From the top of the upturned bucket Abigail caught her breath, looked at the iron bars of her cage, and swore like a sailor.

After a few minutes on the bucket things made even less sense. She was in a jail cell. The rest of the room was probably where the guards were supposed to be, but for some reason whomever had brought her here wasn't bothering to guard her...probably because of whatever spell they had cast with the bitter tasting magic that had made the room spin. Whatever the spell was, it was coming from the ground and seeping into the air and everything else like a rot. It stank of sulphur and decay, but the taste in her mouth was of blood. She wondered where 'here' was. Then she figured it was probably Catherine's fault and tried to work up the courage to make her way to the barred iron door to see if it was locked. She'd never picked a lock before...but surely it wasn't that difficult to figure out...as you have probably already noticed friend, Abigail Jones tended to grossly underestimate how difficult things would be – but that was the reason she usually succeeded. A stubbornness that led right down to her very core, a mind that could see the mechanics behind things, and figure out the rest from there. That's what she was...that's what I hope she still is.

In the meantime the Abigail-on-the-bucket gathered her courage and made a leap for it. The door was locked, the cold iron reassuring in its lack of conductivity in the same way that the stone wall was. Further inspection told her she not only that she didn't have anything to pick the lock with, but also that she couldn't stand to be in contact with the ground for long enough to try. She hopped back onto the bucket just as the room began to sway again. She noticed that her tolerance to the spell was increasing, and then began to calculate the rate at which it did so in order to work out how long she needed to stay on the bucket for. She frowned when she figured out that it should be afternoon...the room was lit by a burning torch by the heavy wooden door and naught else. Where was she that the sun couldn't reach? Was she underground? Why would you go to the trouble of building stone walls if you were underground already? She leaned back against the wall and waited. Somebody had brought her here, she didn't know how, or where – but that somebody had brought her for a reason. All she had to do was wait, and try not to fall asleep again, and eventually they would come for her...until then she used her heartbeats to try and keep track of time.

Hours passed...or at least she assumed they were hours. It couldn't have been days because the torch still burned. She had counted 19,325 heartbeats when she dozed off...she jerked awake when her weight tipped the bucket into overturning, but when she tried sleepily to right herself she found the muscles in her thighs had seized and straightening them was a torture in itself. Worse, she was thirsty. Possibly worse still (but she wasn't sure since she was a healer) the floor was covered in blood that had gone sticky and brown and was probably full of diseases. It was getting cold between the unforgiving stone walls of the (perhaps) underground room. She quelled a stab of panic in the pit of her stomach and wondered if she should reconsider her decision not to call for help. It stood to reason that whomever had brought her here wasn't friendly...and she was caught between trying to attract attention to herself and being reluctant to do so, in case the attention was worse than the lack of it. She got off the bucket again and took a few trial steps, then she paced for ninety-three heartbeats before the room span. She hopped back on her steel shield and waited some more. After another three thousand or so beats the straw mattress began to look cosy. It was almost blood free and if she ripped it open it might even be warm. She just had to wait for the spell to wear off. It crossed her mind that perhaps the person who had summoned her was doing the same, and then it occurred to her that 'summoned' was exactly what she had been...one minute at home, the next minute in a cage. She wondered if this was what parrots felt like when they were caught. Above the door the torch still burned as her eyes drooped and her throat began to burn. She swallowed to no avail...sooner or later she was going to have to give in and lie down...but one thought alone cheered her...somewhere out there Stephen was *pissed,* and it was only a matter of time before he showed up in a rage and dragged her all the way home...for once, just this one time, she would even leave out the kicking and screaming part...if he would just show up.

Chapter 22

Marcus Lester stood outside the door to the Shadow Lord Underridge's private chambers and tried not to cringe at the sound of the man himself shouting down his friend. Aaron was taking a lashing already – an unfair reprisal. He had told them that summoning the experiments was a bad idea and they had made him do it anyway – against the teams better judgement. His father had even told them before he died – it would be years before the youngest were ready and some of the older ones would never accept the change – and here they were, not ten months later and with a breakout on their hands. The subject had been perfect: healthy, strong, able bodied and with wonderfully complex thought patterns that would have benefited them with years of study – had he chosen to stay. Marcus had stood by Aaron when he had told Mo'ash, with no trace of uncertainty, that this particular subject was a flight risk. 'Put them in cages then.' the old codger had answered. Genius. If *only* they had thought of that.

And now this; he'd been waiting all morning whilst Aaron took the heat and the others potentially wasted away in their cells. They had followed orders, and he had half a mind to march in there and say as much. Instead he closed his eyes against another wave of nausea and found a bench a little way down the hall that he could discreetly rest on. Blood magic was *hard*...but it was his families niche. It had kept them on the Convocation for generations simply because none of the other families knew its secrets, and although they might never admit it- they were terrified of its power. Everyone was. Even Aaron, now that he had seen the results for himself. Still the size of the spell had knocked him for six, even if he wasn't letting on. It took a tremendous amount of power to move one person across a distance of so many miles, let alone six people. He was tired, and starved, and he would sleep well when he eventually got the chance, but for now he borrowed from his massive reserves of power and used it mostly to stay upright. He swept a hand through his golden locks and checked his timepiece for the fourth time since five minutes ago.

Let me talk about Marcus Lester for a moment, friend, just so that you and the readers can get the full picture of the man. I mention his hair specifically, because everybody knew that Estorans had black hair...it was just the way things were. Marcus wore his blond hair like a crown resting on his perfect Romanesque face. Blond-haired and blue-eyed...a favourite with the women. Marcus, much like Aaron, came from a long, long line of Estoran nobility. They were sons of great men, and grandsons of great men, and so on. Both were of old money, both would one day sit on the Convocation themselves and ultimately have power over all others. Marcus Lester was a man whose voice held sway, who could buy and sell the whole island and who kept a wealth of slaves. Slaves. Most of the population were slaves...The powerful Estorans were literally soul stealer's, thieves of the soul. They simply...took people. They locked up the part of the soul that allowed free will...when it came to the mind; the actual awareness of consciousness, there was nothing they could not do. Flicking the off switch in a persons brain was as simple to them as striking a match or tossing a coin. They could force a soul out of a body, alter it in some way, and then put it back in. The result would walk and talk and breathe and die, if that was what was required of them. Marcus Lester and Aaron Wreather were worse than most Estorans. Could you get any worse? Yes. If you mixed research alchemy and dark science with a full blooded, gifted Estoran. If you have the imagination to foresee what sort of research might be produced when you were able to physically alter a persons being into whichever shape you desired. On an island full of demons Marcus Lester and Aaron Wreather were just about the worst. Each of them sported a resume that would make the devil himself jealous.

Aaron emerged from the doors prompting both guards to straighten their backs and look lively. Marcus scowled at the pair on the way past. One of them alone had the decency to look embarrassed. They hadn't been very lively whilst Wreather was inside. He was pretty sure he'd seen one of them yawning. He hurried to keep stride with Aaron.
'What did the old goat have to say?' he asked his companion, who pulled off his gloves as they descended the stairs a few flights.
'What we expected he would.' answered Wreather. He checked his pocket watch and sighed dramatically. 'All he has accomplished is to waste time for the others.'
'Do you think they'll find him?'

'The hunter? Absolutely not. We have five left, let's focus on the positive for now and summon him back later.' he answered. He failed to notice the sag of relief in the other man's shoulders.

They came to a stop at a doorway and entered into the lab. Mariana DeBossa looked up from the blue globe and ushered them over.

'Hello my darlings, how did it go?' she greeted them, waving a hand to two glasses of wine and a full carafe of red on the desk. Wreather ignored the wine and crossed straight to her side. Marcus scoffed and poured the drinks...Wreather was obsessed, it was just part of who he was.

'Never mind that, what's been happening?' Aaron replied. He slipped a hand around the curvaceous Mariana's waist and gracefully kissed her cheek, all the while keeping his eyes on the globe.

'Well...your mage...' she said, and waved a hand over the large, round, polished chunk of iolite. The glassy surface flicked like a screen to a little girl in a cell. The room around her was smouldering and burned. Aaron laughed outright.

'Come and see this Marcus, you were right!' he called. Marcus came over with a glass for him and he sipped it as he watched.

'Your Shaman....well, see for yourself.' said Mariana, and waved a hand again. The Shaman had gotten through the bars without any trouble and was testing the room for holes in the sealing barrier they had put up. He was a young man, late twenties, a perfect candidate...and it looked like he knew a fair bit about his craft already, certainly by comparison to the little fire mage, a girl of seven and with no idea how to control her own power.

'Hmm. Next.' said Marcus, then added 'No surprises so far.'

'The Shapeshifter.' introduced Mariana, and on the globe the world changed to a room with destroyed iron bars that lay mangled all over the floor. The older man had caught himself on one of the chunks of metal that lay strewn like streamers about the room. He was bleeding on the straw mattress.

'Is he alive?' Aaron worried, fear in his tone.

'Oh absolutely, he can bleed a lot more than that...remember that boar last year? He's just sleeping.' she answered, businesslike.

'The witch.' said Mariana, another ripple, another change of scene. The witch had made a salt circle on the floor and was curled up inside of it, asleep.

'Smart.' muttered Marcus.

'Indeed.' agreed Mariana. 'Annnnd last but not least, your healer.'

The three looked down at the globe, Mariana with an expectant smile on her face. Aaron laughed first.

'How long has she been on the bucket?' he asked.

'Since she woke up. I think there's something wrong with her, if I'm honest. She hasn't even called out for help...are you sure she's a genius?' she answered with a question.

'Is that...blood on the floor?' queried Marcus.

'Wasn't that part of the spell?' Mariana thought aloud.

'Not my spell, my lovely.' he answered, then shrugged. 'She must have brought it with her...I wonder what she was doing at the time?'

'No matter. I'll do the Shaman and the Shapeshifter tonight. The others can wait till morning...' considered Aaron, then drifted off, his gaze still on the globe.

'Aaron...what are you thinking?' Mariana questioned him after a moment or two.

'She is...different...isn't she.' he said almost to himself. Mariana smiled at his curiosity.

'She's going to be the one. I can already feel it...we're going to change the world Aaron. Thanks to you.'

'Thanks to us.' he corrected, and left his colleagues to go and introduce himself to two of the people he had spent the last eight years studying.

Chapter 23

The hunter strode the dead forest like he owned it. He was furious and, unlike Abigail Jones, he knew exactly where he was. Luckily for him he had been armed when they had plucked him right out of his life, and they probably should have considered that when they put him in a Gods-damned cage. He grunted as he shifted his grip so that his left arm took more of the strain than his right. His shoulders were beginning to ache, but it wouldn't be long now.

He had been on board *'Sweet Serenade'*, and drifting somewhere far, far north of here. The sea had been calm, blue, warm...He had drifted so far north that the seasons changed, and whilst the summers had been unbearably hot on deck the winters had been spectacular. Just right. He was in the middle of cooking the fish he'd caught that morning; Some kind of multi-coloured creature that was as common in those waters as the salmon were back home. He usually ate it raw like the natives, but that day he had wanted a cooked meal. He had landed his fishing boat in a cove for an hour or two – nobody around for miles (he made sure of that) and built a fire. He cooked up some biscuits while he was there, picked a few oranges. When he came back to the fire he was starving, and just as he was about to set down his sword- poof! Up in the air like a ball of angry smoke and dropped in the middle of an Estoran cage – for the second time in his life. When he awakened, the one thing he knew for absolute certainty was that he was not staying there. It would take more than iron bars and stone to keep him inside. A few soft words here, a dead man in a black robe there, and he was free. What sort of an idiot took a prisoner without guarding them anyway? These people were nuts...but this was not new information to him.

And so it came to be that he hung from the edge of the cliff that overhung the ocean on the islands westernmost point. He secured his grip with two daggers; one to stand on and one to cling to...and he waited for the howling, snorting, growling creatures that the bastards had set on him to follow his scent right off the damned cliff. As predicted a straggling group of the beasts burst from the bare, dead trees above him and leaped straight from the tree line and off the cliff. Only a single hound had managed to scrabble a grip on the edge whilst the rest of its group sailed, still howling and yipping frantically, to a messy death beneath. The hunter did not look at the carnage, nor flinch against the awful crunch the hellish hounds made as they smashed into the unforgiving rocks below. He focused instead on the dog that was managing to pull itself back up. The hunter knew a lot of things about the Estorans...for example, he knew that the dogs were slaves just like their human counterparts, that they probably died a long time ago, and that without an Estoran controlling them they would be no more than rabid monstrosities, as likely to turn on each other as they were to find prey. Each dog saw with the eyes of his pack, and each master saw with the eyes of his slaves. The hunter knew he could not let the dog get away, he knew because he'd had dogs of his own once, a long time ago.

He pursed his lips together and made a squeaking noise that made the hound flick panicked eyes back at him. He half pushed, half swung himself up the cliff until he got a firm grip on its back paw. He tugged, putting his full weight momentarily on the dog. The animal screeched as it fell. It sounded so scared...the hunter ignored the flicker of empathy he felt for the poor, zombified animal. In this situation it was kill or be killed...and he had no intention of becoming prey.

He pulled himself up over the cliffs edge cautiously. Peering first to make sure the coast was clear and then listening like only a hunter could. There was another pack but they had fallen for his decoy...however...when a pack goes missing questions are asked, searchers would be sent. What he needed as soon as possible was a ghost scent...and where did you get one of those in a forest that was dead? He smirked as his vision settled on the decaying forest floor. There was nothing there but the pulp of dead undergrowth, black and slimy and stinking...and perfect. A few minutes later he was used to the smell and creeping, filthy and soundlessly, through the trees to skirt the island to the south. He dared not go near the roads, you didn't have to be an expert at tracking to know they would have the tiny harbour watched day and night till they tracked him down. It was a no-go...but he had to find a way off the island before the smell of decay seeped into his pores. When he was sure he had put enough distance between himself and the dead dogs he made his way back inland. He needed a place to rest up and work on a plan. He'd been running for hours, and it was time to check supplies and see where he stood. No fire, not here...and the perpetually dark and misty island had a coldness to it that was starting to get beneath his clothes. There was bound to be a cave somewhere, on an island as rocky as this. He picked an incline at random and followed it to the summit. There was no cave this time, but another crag ahead looked promising.

By the third rocky facing the hunter had found his home for the night. It was not a deep enough cave to hide a fire and he wasn't acclimatised to this cold weather, but he was tired enough to rest with the shelter about him, despite the wind. The cave was just two yards wide and as little deep, but he propped his crossbow at one end and slept sitting upright, his hand still on the trigger and his senses turned up to volume 10. Nothing would get near in the night...or the day, it was very difficult to tell. Only his internal clock told him to sleep whilst he could, and that somewhere out there it was the middle of the night...wherever the 'Sweet Serenade' was. Rather than lament his failing water supply and lack of food he took comfort from the ten bolts in his quiver and the sword laid at his feet. If they found him whilst he slept there would be no chance of him being taken by surprise. There was no chance of him being taken anywhere, in fact. He was not prey, and there was no way he was going down without a fight.

He wakened to the accursed howling again, and they were close...too close. Run or fight...and he was fast running out of places to hide. Estora was not a large island, maybe ten miles across at its widest point, and the cover he'd gained from the putrid forest floor obviously wasn't doing a good enough job of masking his scent. He wasn't far inland, maybe a mile or so and he could find a nice cliff to repeat yesterdays effort with. He snapped his eyes open, grabbed the bow, sheathed his sword and was on his feet in seconds. A quick peek out of his hiding place showed him his position had been well chosen. The hounds were climbing the hill face towards him and on the edge of hearing were voices calling to each other...the masters of the search no doubt. He took a second to adjust his hearing and found them, a few hundred yards still further inland...
'They have him to the south!' a gruff Estoran voice teased him. He sneered at the comment. They had him? They had him? The comment incensed the hunter beyond reason, and rather than get a head start on the dogs he sought out a nook that would cover him whilst he took a few shots. He nestled down behind a rock and tried to calm himself...he had ten bolts and there were seven dogs...he was

far too far away to get a clean shot at the men controlling them. He realised he was doing nothing but wasting time and cursed. He was not wasting his precious bolts unless he had to and it was time to move. He crested the hill and swung southwards once again. It was time to face facts...There was one way off this island and, guarded or not, impossible or not, a boat was his last chance. He headed for the harbour, and hoped the dogs wouldn't catch him before he made it there.

It was just as he had expected; there were initiates in their dark brown robes everywhere. He had pelted at full speed and made it to the little town that passed for their port, the hounds yipping excitedly all the while maybe a quarter mile behind him. He had gained some time when the pack stopped to check out the place he had spent the night, but now he found himself between a rock and a hard place. Ten bolts and a sword...four initiates that he could see so far. It was fairly standard procedure: 'shoot then move, guard your thoughts, don't let them see you.' he repeated the mantra in his mind as he worked. He edged from the trees like a shadow and dropped into a silent roll as the nearest of the brown clad devotees turned unexpectedly and changed direction, coming back up the path towards him. The hunter straightened in the shadow of the sandstone building and took the shot at the back of the black-haired man's head. The initiate went down like a sack of grain being dropped. The hunter dragged his body off the path and back into the tree line with him. One down, three to go, and just a matter of time before either of them noticed their comrade was missing.

Back around the other side of the old building the hunter lined up his next shot. He re-used his bolt, just in case. The second of the four went down equally as silently as the first, unfortunately he couldn't get to the body without being seen by the other two, who were split-seconds from turning their heads a little and noticing the distinct lack of their third member. The last two stood together, facing the little wooden jetty and standing between the last two buildings. The hunter didn't have time to think any further as one of the pair turned to look for his friend and frowned. That was all the invitation he needed. He approached both just as the hounds burst from the trees in their relentless pursuit. The hunter put a bolt between the frowning Estorans eyes and drew his sword in one liquid motion to slash the other deep across his face. The man went down with a strangled cry and the hounds fifty yards behind him went into a baying frenzy with the smell of blood on the air. The hunter stopped at the jetty and swore, because after all of his efforts there was no boat. There was no boat. He shot a look over his shoulder to see the fangs of the incoming pack and, behind them and dominating the whole island, the mountain where they had carved out their Temple, lights in windows as high as his eye could see. No. He wasn't going back there. He wasn't done yet.

With the hounds all but nipping his heels he made his decision, ran at full speed and leaped from the safety of the ground into the freedom of the water. He couldn't swim...and the icy water reached out tentacles to swallow him whole...but in his experience there were some things that were a whole lot worse than drowning...and most of them lay on the island behind him. He closed his eyes, held his breath, and trusted his fate to the hands of the Gods.

Chapter 24

Abigail pricked up her ears and listened, wishing, not for the first time, that she had Greer or Siara's skill at hearing. Was that whistling? It sure sounded like a jaunty tune...however, she had been a long time without water and it was perfectly plausible that she was hallucinating.

'Hello?' she tried, but her throat was so dry nothing came out but a croak. The whistling continued, down the corridor outside the door and bouncing off along the walls away from her. Abigail thought fast, forgetting her earlier decision to not attract attention to herself in favour of the possibility of some water on the horizon. She had been here so long she had lost count of her heartbeats, and her legs were all but useless from cramp. With a sudden flash of inspiration she got off the bucket and picked it up, then rattled it up and down the iron bars a few times. The whistling outside abruptly stopped, she heard footsteps coming back towards her door...she watched the door expectantly, her forehead resting on the cool iron of her cage.

'Hey.' she tried when the door swung inwards, it came out just as rubbish as her earlier attempt had. She cleared her throat and looked towards the dark figure that stood in the open doorway. She waited, heart pounding a drumbeat in her ears, and watched the silhouette come closer. The young man whose face appeared struck her at once.

'It's you.' she said to the boy from the Golden Fox, the young man with the black hair and the clear blue eyes. He looked startled, his black hair messy, his clean-cut suit out of place when compared to the apron she had seen him in before.

'I'm sorry...you know me?' he asked, his voice confident. The man before her now shone a fine contrast between the man she had seen in Calle not a month before.

'You work in the Golden Fox.' she said flatly. Her voice still croaking but at least decipherable. 'Got any water?' she remembered, the pounding in her head reminding her of her immediate needs.

'I...did a trial shift there, to help a friend. I wasn't very good.' he answered. He took a few more steps into the room so that she could see him properly. His bright eyes took attention away from all else on what might have otherwise been a plain face. He wasn't a

particularly tall man, nor particularly striking...those eyes though.
'What are you doing in there?' he asked her. Abigail laughed.
'Don't you know? If you don't know and I don't know then how the
hell did I get here?' she replied. She took in the look of utter
confusion on his face and sighed. 'Please, do you have any water?
I've been here a long time.' she tried instead. The young man pursed
thin lips together in thought.
'I'll be back, stay there.' he said, completely oblivious to the irony of
his words. Abigail smiled the smile of a woman trying to ignore
another persons glaring stupidity and watched him dart for the open
door. There were retreating footsteps, some splashing sounds and
then the steps returning. She took the cup he offered eagerly and
nearly drank before she stopped herself. She tasted a sip...it was
dank, and had been standing a long time, but it was clean so far as
she could tell. She downed the cup and thanked the young man
profusely, he hung back from the bars and shifted from foot to foot
like he was nervous.
'So...' she began afresh now that she could speak again. She could
literally feel the water working a magic of its own into her system.
'Where is erm...where are we?' she inquired. He shifted his eyes to
the door.
'I don't know if I should be in here...' he mumbled cautiously. She
followed his gaze.
'Please. Where are we? What is this place? Honestly I know nothing
and you are the first person I have seen.' she tried...anything to stop
those nervous feet of his running out the door and leaving her alone
again.
'You're in the Temple. Where else?' the young man responded.
Abigail blinked.
'What Temple?' she persisted. He laughed, an action that lit up his
whole face and made his eyes crease round the sides.
'You say that like there are other Temples.' he spoke while still
laughing. She didn't get the joke, if there even was one.
'But there are.' she answered with a frown. 'There are hundreds of
Temples...every town has one. Which particular Temple is this?' she
clarified, following the chain of thought to the end as she spoke.
'This is Shade's Temple, and there is only one.' said the semi-
stranger. Abigail felt her mouth fall open. The man was correct,
there was only one Temple devoted to Shade.

'But that's on Estora.' she breathed softly. The man laughed again, this time maybe a little nervously.

'Of course it is.' he answered. He took another long look at the door. 'I have errands-'

'Don't leave.' she reacted quickly, before she could think. He came a little closer.

'You're not from here, are you?' he mock-realised. She tilted her head.

'That's what I've been trying to tell you. I was on Porta...and then suddenly in this cage...You have to help me, get me out or find out why I'm here or – wait!' she called as he reached the door. 'At least tell me your name?' she tried. The young man with the beautiful eyes stopped and turned to her slowly.

'It's Aaron. Aaron Wreather.' he said softly.

'I'm Abigail Jones. Will you come back Aaron, even if you can't help me?' she persisted. He shifted again, as if he was itching to leave. He turned away, and in profile she saw him give an indecisive nod. 'Thank you.' she said as he left and the door swung shut behind him. She rested her head on the iron bars again and thought about the encounter. Outside in the corridor Aaron Wreather could have clicked his heels together in glee...because during their conversation the healer had climbed down from her bucket...and she hadn't even noticed she had done it! The islands energy was working it's way into her system. From now on, it was all just a question of time.

Chapter 25

They were a day out from Salston. Nobody had wanted to
stay behind but someone had needed to. They had to have a home to
come back to once it was all over, and so Stephen had convinced
Siara to hang back in the clearing whilst he and the others threw
some things in packs and went off to go raid Estora. It wasn't going
to be that easy – of course it wasn't – but Stephen hadn't gotten past
the anger yet, and until he did it was the only outline of a plan they
had. It wasn't even really a plan, more like 'let's head in the direction
of Estora and hope we can stop Stephen taking on the island alone.'
Asa sincerely hoped that they pieced together the rest of the details
along the way, but it was starting to look more and more like they
were storming a beach. What they needed was *structure,* but what
they had was a whole lot of rage...how did a Wanderer, a Shaman, a
human and a wood elf execute a rescue mission...would there be
anything left to rescue? That question he could at least answer.
Celeste was able to place her based on her spirit, and according the
the Priestess that spirit still lived. Why they had taken her to begin
with was another matter altogether.

They had spent the better part of a day in frenzied argument.
Stephen wanted to leave straight away, Greer was for doing the
same. Asa knew the risks and wanted to seek advice from the druids,
Stephen had relented after a long discussion and Celeste's
intervention. Her elven voice had lulled a temporary calm on them,
and given her a chance to pass Asa Lupine all of the information that
she had. Abigail was alive, on Estora and the druids had no blood
magician to bring her back...even if they did have one- they didn't
have a sample of her blood...and the only other methods to get her
out of there was either the good old fashioned way- on foot... or via
Shaman.
'Get close enough, I get her out.' he had told the others. That, so far,
was all of the foresight that they had. How they were going to get to
Estora, how they were going to find her, how they were going to get
back out – all of it was up for discussion as they picked their slow
way through the forest. A whole day had gone past since she had
vanished and every minute stretched before Stephen like an eternity.
Every minute put them farther apart and Abigail in more danger.

They had camped around a large fire, protected by Asa's magic and after they had finally fought their way onto the road again. Stone walls were no problem when you had your own Shaman...although Greer had not been impressed with her introduction to rock-travel.

In the morning they set out before dawn had even broken. The sky was just lightening when they had been awakened by scratches on the other side of the wall. Liandor had been on watch and had very calmly announced that they should move. Nobody had argued, particularly not Asa, who didn't like to admit that without the plants he used in his protective circles the camp was not quite so safe as they all believed. He kept quiet and breathed a sigh of relief when they moved on, happy to have made it through the night without the weakened links of his magic being exposed. With the dawn came a thinning of the trees, and before long the smell of salt filled the air. By lunch they had walked twenty miles already and could make out the brickwork of a town on the horizon. The wall on the left gave way to beach, sloping gently out to calm blue waters that would have been idyllic had it not been mid-winter and therefore freezing. Stephen felt his heart beat heavier with every passing moment...they were so close and still so far, and he knew the panic he felt wouldn't leave him until he set eyes on his ward again. A thousand thoughts plagued him – it was all his fault, he shouldn't have taken her, he had put her in danger – she had been in nothing but danger since they had left Beeton...the same thoughts circled and circled, never leaving him and threatening to topple him from sanity. 'There is a man.' said Greer beside him, adding a blessed new thought to the whirl inside his head. She had been silent for most of the journey so far, and he couldn't even guess at what she was thinking. When he had packed to leave she had packed too, and when he had asked what she was doing the Wanderer had simply shrugged and said:
'Pack.'
And that had been enough. He followed the length of her pointed arm to the beach on their left and, sure enough, there was a man floating face down in the frothy waves. Without thinking Stephen Laurence dropped his pack and tore off the road and across the sand. He splashed into the water, gasping at the fierce coldness of it and paddling out until the water was about his waist. He grabbed the man by the back of the jacket and hauled him bodily onto the sand. By

the time he had dragged him out Liandor was with him, helping.
Between the two of them they got the fallen man up the beach
enough that the waves no longer reached him. Whilst Stephen caught
his breath Liandor rolled the man onto his back.
'He not breathing.' said the elf. Asa and Greer caught up, carrying the
others bags. Asa leaned over the man and placed a hand flat on his
chest, then he connected to the water in the man's lungs and brought
it out of him. He turned him onto his side again and relaxed when
the man began to cough it out. Liandor turned him onto his side
again until his lungs were clear.
'He is alive.' said Asa, and then double took at Stephen, who was
watching as if in shock, his hands still on his knees and his body
covered in patches of sand.
'I...think...I know him.' the butler explained. He took a step towards
his old friend and was stopped by Greer, who looked fretful.
'His heart does not beat.' she growled in a low warning. Stephen
frowned and shot a look to Asa, who checked for a pulse. The man
was moving, he was alive.
'But he's moving-' he began, but stopped when Asa shook his head.
'He is not alive?' said Asa, very confused, and straightened. When
the hunter finally opened his eyes it was to see four very suspicious
faces staring down at him. He blinked a few times...alive? He hadn't
expected that. He had become so sure that the sea would kill
him...and there, staring down at him, was something else he hadn't
expected.
'Stephen..?' he rasped carefully. The butler looked older,
rougher...less presentable...but he hadn't changed beyond
recognition.
'Cobol.' Stephen answered, and knew he was correct the second the
un-dead man had spoken. He offered a hand to help the hunter
upright. 'You don't have a heartbeat.' he stated, still wary. The hunter
gave an ironic laugh that ended with a sneer.
'That's because I'm dead.' Cobol answered, and then checked
himself at a thought he had just overheard. 'Who is Abigail? Why is
she on Estora?'
Stephen Laurence took two steps back and raised his crossbow.
'You and I need to talk.' he said simply, before anybody did anything
else...and never was a truer word spoken.

Chapter 26

The door creaking to life made Abigail sit up sleepily on her straw mattress and watch. A head appeared, blue eyes pierced the shaded room and Abigail smiled her hello. She added a yawn for effect, but cut it short when she noticed that Aaron wasn't alone. A slightly taller and awful lot older gentleman was with him. The gentleman had a beard to his knees that was clearly dyed black- there was a visible matte staining on the glossy finish of his velvet robes. It also didn't match his hair, which was streaked with more white than black. His dye was no good, the alchemist in her noted, he's obviously used it on his head and sweated streaks all over his face. 'I can make you a solid black you know, one that doesn't bleed.' she told the elderly man. For some reason he looked angry. She threw a questioning look to Aaron, whose face had gone red in his effort not to laugh. 'I'm sorry, I'm Abigail. It's very nice to meet you.' she added, remembering her manners and attributing the old man's cold glare to her lack thereof. He nodded, affirming her suspicions.
'Abigail, is it? My name is Lord Bracken.' the old man introduced himself in a voice that wobbled with age.
'This is my boss.' Aaron explained.
'Ah. Lord Bracken, do you know why I am in this cell?' she immediately got to the point. The gent frowned.
'No. Don't you?' he retorted. She let out a slow breath and then offered a pleasant smile.
'No. I don't suppose you have the key?' she tried instead. The old man patted his robes, looking for all of the world like he would topple at any minute. Aaron stepped forward to offer a steadying arm.
'It's here somewhere...' mumbled the elder. 'Ah-ha!' he exclaimed as he found a bunch of keys hanging around his belt. He placed the key in the lock in super-slow motion. Abigail held her breath as she heard it finally slide in.
'Wait...How do I know you're not here to cause trouble?' grilled the old Lord. Abigail stared at him.
'Um.' she answered. The Lord reached a surprisingly quick arm through the bars and locked eyes with her. Abigail gasped at the coldness of his touch and the unexpected speed of his elderly

reflexes, but, when she tried to pull away, found she was unable. The old ones deceptively vice-like grip had her – but worse...he had her eyes, and he was trying to...climb into her mind through them. Her skin crawled at the feeling of it; dirty and unwanted, someone pushing their way into her thoughts. She fought it, not knowing how she was fighting it, just that if she didn't her eyeballs might implode. 'It's alright Abigail, just let him look he won't hurt you.' Aaron's voice floated to her from outside her private war. She held on another few moments, pushing back against the pressure. It was like her mind was a bubble and the old man was trying to pierce it into separate pieces. She gave in because she was exhausted after twenty seconds, not because she wanted to. When her resistance shattered she felt the Lord Bracken searching through her head like it was a filing cabinet...taking notes and reading what he wanted to...he didn't change anything though, he didn't touch anything, so to speak. He stepped in, a bubble within a bubble, floated about for a bit and then left the way he had come...back out through her eyes. She stumbled back away from him and slid down the bars. She didn't know anything else after that. She slept, without dreams, and when she woke up she was a free bird, minus her cage.

She opened her eyes and stared at the ceiling, and wondered how long she had been there for. There was water and an empty bowl of (what might have been) soup on a dark-wooden side table. Someone had fed her, then. She drank the water in one go and looked for more but there was none. She lay back on her elbows and looked around. The room was enclosed, no windows but with two doors. It seemed to be carved out of stone, just like the floor in her cell had been, but it was a whole lot cosier. The bed she was in had feather pillows and a proper mattress that wasn't even lumpy. There was a dresser, a wardrobe and a full length mirror, as well as a fireplace and two huge, luxurious leather easy chairs with a coffee table between them. It was alright, it kind of reminded her of home. She was happy to find that whoever had put her to bed had not stripped her completely, and had left her shirt on. She shivered at the thought of some stranger undressing her and sent up a short prayer that it wasn't Aaron who had done so. She got out of bed and had a look in the wardrobe. There were four outfits, all of them black velvet and with a sort of 'robey' motif. She picked a random one and hoped it at least had some pockets. She pulled the garment on and looked at herself in the mirror. She looked like a drone. She tilted her head and looked at the mirror...there were little blue stones in it and they almost looked like they were...glowing.

A sharp rap on the door interrupted her thoughts. She stayed where she was.

'Come in.' she said. Nothing happened. After another few seconds the chapping came again and she smiled, puzzled. She crossed the room and opened it. There was a young woman there, with long black hair tied back from her head, dark brown eyes that were glazed over like she might be on drugs, and the same thin lips that all the other Estorans she had met seemed to have. After the woman hadn't moved or spoken for a few seconds Abigail waved a hand in front of her face.

'Hi?' she tried, optimistically. After another few heartbeats the young woman smiled.

'Mistress Abigail, Lord Wreather requests your attendance for breakfast.' said the robot.

'*Lord* Wreather?' she repeated. There were a few seconds gap in the conversation.

'Yes ma'am.' stated the woman. Abigail stared at her.

'What's your name?' she quizzed her. The girl stared straight ahead. She let a long enough pause pass that she was sure the girl wasn't going to answer. 'I'm not going anywhere with you until you tell me your name.' she decided curtly. Was she a prisoner? The girl remained silent and smiling. Abigail closed the door and went back to sit on the bed. She watched it until the chapping began again. She wondered if maybe the woman was an idiot. She also wondered what would happen if she just sat there, and didn't go to breakfast.

Her traitorous stomach growled.

'Damn it.'

...Knock, knock, knock...

She opened the door again.

'Hi.' she grumbled, annoyed.

'Hello, my name is Lorne. Lord Wreather requests your attendance for breakfast.' altered the mecha-woman. Abigail flinched as if someone had hit her.

'Let's just go.' she snapped...and followed the robogirl to a potential death-by-toast.

Chapter 27

Breakfast was served upon a round table and by a small army of Lornes, who laid out plates and cutlery, cups and bread, and then vanished out a side door. Abigail sat beside Aaron and two empty places and ate copious amounts of bread. He had greeted her warmly and showed her to her seat, and then she'd been so hungry she had laid into the bread.

'Who's coming?' she asked, finally slowing down. She hadn't eaten in days, and though the bread was a little stale it was the best damn loaf she'd ever had. Aaron didn't seem to mind her being so rude, rather he was resting on an elbow and looked amused.

'Two friends of mine. People I can trust to find your family.' he answered. She narrowed her eyes.

'My family are dead. I was...staying with friends.' she explained simply. Aaron blinked at her in shock. 'If you just send a message to Stephen he'll come get me...or just drop me off at the nearest port and I'll find my way back-'

'Your family are dead?' he repeated back to her.

'Killed by Estorans. In the riots.' Abigail stopped at the lump in her throat.

Den of snakes hissed her own voice in her head. She almost choked on her bread.

'I'm so sorry...Gods this must be the last place in the world you woul-' answered Aaron, and stopped mid-sentence.

'What?' she prompted after a substantial pause. He looked at her with a wild inspiration in his eyes, and she laughed as she recognised the same eureka moments that she sometimes had.

'What if that's why you're here? What if you had some sort of...of...unfinished business here...and the island sort of...dragged you back to finish it?' he tried enthusiastically. She looked sceptical.

'The island brought me here.' she repeated flatly. It was not a question. He shook his head so that his dark hair got even messier. 'You don't how this place works. Estora's...different.'

'Different like how?' she pried. They were interrupted by the arrival of his two 'friends', Marcus and Mariana. He stood to introduce everyone, and she followed, wiping crumbs from her face and clothes as she went. White bread crumbs really stuck into black velvet...

'This is Marcus Lester and this is the Lady Mariana DeBossa...And this is the Lady Abigail Jones.'

'Lady?' she asked. She had been quite careful not to mention that. Aaron looked a little bewildered, and she remembered something...the cold intrusion of another person inside her head, looking at things, taking notes...they knew more about her than she knew...and she still didn't know if she was a prisoner or not. The island brought her here? Yes, and tomorrow she was going to ride her seahorse to the fairy castle.

Her thoughts were cut asunder by the glittering warmth of Mariana's laugh. Abigail flicked her attention to her and pasted a smile to her face. This woman was gorgeous...not just beautiful, not just sexy...she had curves that made men blush and women jealous, a bosom that defied gravity and delicate, gentle brown waves in her hair that fell to an hourglass waist. Abigail giggled, and pretended she was laughing with her, and not in shock. Marcus was yellow haired and reminded her of the figure printed on gold coins. She didn't know who it was, but logic suggested it was the semblance of some King or Emperor or something...anyway that's what Marcus resembled to her.

'Blond.' she said, as she shook his hand and held Mariana's a moment. She was confused. She didn't know if she should shake it or kiss it. Marcus squinted at her.

'Everyone else here has dark hair...you're blond. Sorry.' she explained herself, her face a blank. 'I was just thinking out loud.' she explained. He smiled but it seemed fake, frozen somehow, just like Abigail's was.

Where are the green threads? Asked the voice in her head. Abigail pinched the bridge of her nose. Everybody sat down and the Lornes came out with breakfast. She looked over the selection, recognised some toasted bread and what she hoped was cheese, and then asked Aaron before she tasted everything else.

'What is this? And this? And is this a vegetable or..? This looks like a tomato, but tastes like mushroom...most of it tastes like mushroom...what do you mean that's meat?' and so on. Mariana laughed to cover her indiscretions and made small talk with Marcus. Aaron found the whole thing delightful, and talked her through the menu as if he had all the time in the world. Marcus was getting impatient, Marcus was always impatient. Real work took time, trust took time, and Marcus was a man for the short route rather than the long game. He kicked his comrade gently under the table when the two started talking about herbs.

'Will you be bringing Abigail this evening?' he barged into their conversation at a suitable moment. Aaron looked at him with his mouth open.

'Bringing me where?' she asked, and took a sip of the delicious coffee Lorne 3 had brought out.

'Ahaha...I hadn't thought-' he began.

'Oh but you have to! I will lend her something to wear, I insist!' persisted Mariana. Abigail looked from the Goddess to the Emperor, and then back to Aaron, who was blushing.

'There's a party tonight, for harvest, you have to come. I'll do your hair, rouge your cheeks! It'll be great fun – what size shoe are you?' she persisted.

'There are sizes?' asked Abigail, who always had a butler to do things like buy shoes. Mariana giggled and flashed a thought to Aaron:

'Genius?'

He grinned at her, ferocity behind his eyes like a hungry lion.

'Goddess.' he shot back, all internally. Mariana pursed her lips at them. Marcus and she stood as if to leave.

'Wait, I need to get home, Stephen will kill me if I'm off going to parties while he's worried about where I am.' she protested. The three stopped, and turned blank faces to her. Marcus smiled warmly, and again she caught the spark of something wrong behind the smile. It was the same smile Catherine used, she suddenly realised. It was her 'composed' smile.

'We have already sent him a message. They left whilst you were asleep. They are going to bring Stephen to the Temple, so that you can all leave together. It shouldn't take more than a day or two...we are not so far away on this island.' he smirked with the same reassurance that she already knew she didn't trust. Unfortunately for Abigail Jones she was a smart cookie, and she knew exactly where she would be going if they knew she was on to them...straight back in the cage. So she smiled, and gave a satisfied nod, and cringed on the inside because if they *had* sent someone to Stephen...it sure as hell wasn't to lead him here.

Chapter 28

In Salston the group occupied the quietest, darkest corner of the bar. Stephen had been all business since they had come across the hunter outside of town, and had hurried them here. Cobol would say nothing other than that their friend was in danger and that they needed to get to the island if they wanted to save her. The hunter had been intent on leaving after that, having no wish to return there himself...but Stephen was having none of it. He took the term 'finders keepers' to a whole new level and even threatened to break out the rope if he had to. Cobol complied...but not willingly. His conscience got the better of him in the end...the very least he owed to someone who had known him in his past life was an explanation...especially if it meant saving his ward's life.

In the bar Cobol nursed his tankard guiltily and wondered where the best place to start was. At the beginning maybe...but where was that?

'Well?' demanded Stephen as he dropped his bag on the floor.

'Well, what?' he drawled, his half-elven voice bouncing around the room and making heads turn. Stephen resisted the urge to punch him.

'Well what happened? Where the hell have you been? Why did they kidnap Abigail and how do we get her back? There's a bit of a time limit here so I'd be grateful if you started talking...' the butler answered. Cobol took a drink of his ale as if the answers were lying at the bottom of the tankard, then squinted up to Stephen, who was blocking the wane light from the door.

'OK.' he decided finally. 'OK...but you better sit down.' he began. Around him Liandor and Asa exchanged a look, Greer took a seat facing the door and Stephen grumbled, he looked like he might explode with anger any second. Cobol was keeping him from his mission, and as far as he was concerned (and glad as he was to lay eyes on the elf after all of these years) he better have a damned good reason.

'I died on Freisch, with Ger dead already at my feet and a pack of dogs on my back.' related the hunter. The others exchanged glances. The half-elf looked alive, he sounded alive and he breathed- but he had no heartbeat, no blood pumping through his veins. He sneered at their glances and looked back at his drink. Slowly, Stephen pulled out a chair and sat. After a moment Greer leaned over and filled the tankard from the jug. He watched her, brooding, before he continued.

'There was this man...this...Estoran. He found me when I was about to- well. I was on my last legs. I woke up on the island, he told me he'd saved me. I had no reason not to believe him. I stayed a few days and then I left to come home. Except when I got to the harbour they were waiting for me. They put me in a prison cell and kept me there, and he, the one that 'saved' me...he...' his voice trailed off, his eyes still on the table. No man likes to admit he has been tortured, no man likes to speak of it- of endless, painful hours sweating in the dark -let alone a once proud hunter like Cobol. 'He wasn't what he seemed.' he settled in the end. He cleared his throat. 'They took my blood, they...did something to me. They were trying to make me one of them. That's what it all comes down to. Three months in an Estoran prison with them coming and going from your mind and you don't know what's real any more. Before I knew it I was in that blasted Temple of theirs, learning how to control a pack of hounds the exact same way they do, and still dead. He didn't save me, he infected me. He put this anger in my head- this rage at all things living...an anger I refused to use. I learned enough from them to get out of there unnoticed and then I ran. They wanted me to hunt *humans*, Stephen. Other ones like me that they can...'*fix.*"

'Why didn't you come home?' said Stephen, his problems momentarily forgotten by comparison to the troubles of a friend. Cobol shook his head, the sternness on his face somehow serene, as if he had long since made peace with his past.

'That was the first place they would look for me. I had to hide. I...acquired...a fishing boat and I ran. I went north but it didn't matter. They may not have found me but everywhere I went I still had the ringing in my ears...I can *hear thoughts*, Stephen...I'm one of them. How could I come home? I couldn't even be around people. I stayed on my boat, and then the other day I blinked and somehow I'm back on the island again...Summoned I guess.' he answered. He gave a deep sigh and downed his cup again. Greer refilled it immediately. The hunter was beginning to like Stephen's furry friend. There was no sympathy in those brown eyes of hers, just curiosity.

'That sounds like what happened to Abigail...' said Liandor in Druidic. To his surprise Cobol turned to him and answered as if he'd understood. It was only much later he figured out what 'hear thoughts' meant.

'I'd be willing to bet your friend met the very same man. What is she? A mage? Another Shaman? What?' pressed the hunter. Stephen's jaw fell loose as he considered the implications.

'She's a healer. And she was missing during the riots. Her parents both died...Cobol, her mother was Isabel Delanois...' he explained, his voice trailing into nowhere.

'Then her father was the Laird...' considered Cobol, and let out a long, slow breath. 'The guy who took me? Aaron bloody Wreather? He's an alchemist.'

'They picked her.' said Asa, bleakly.

'They picked her. And if they make her one of them...an Estoran healer? That will change the world.' the hunter finished. The group sat in silence a while, all eyes on the table, all thinking. It was Stephen's chair sliding out that cracked the façade.

'What are you doing?' asked Greer as he stood. He put his pack over one shoulder and nodded without meeting her eyes.

'I'm going to get on a boat. I'm going to bring her back. Do you know what will happen to Abigail if they put her in a cage for three months? I do...and we might already be too late.' he worried aloud, swallowing at a lump in his throat. The others didn't know about Catherine and the closet, they didn't know about the coldness...the impartiality with which she treated death. To his surprise Asa Lupine cut the atmosphere with a soft laugh.

'Sit Stephen. We plan.' he said firmly. Stephen squinted at him like he had lost his mind. Asa shook his head and fished in a pocket until he found two little black stones, which he rubbed together and then placed on the table. He selected the first.

'Life.' he named it, then added 'Abigail.' in a way he hoped would explain it to him. He selected the other stone and picked it up.

'Death...mmm...magic. Estora.' he named the second stone in his palm. He tried to place the death stone on top of the life stone but the magnetic force he had caused by rubbing them together caused the life stone to slide away. He repeated the process a few times, and then looked up at Stephen, to see if he was getting it. He looked puzzled, and a little annoyed.

'He wants you to know that life magic and death magic can't exist in the same place. He thinks that means they can't make her one of them.' deciphered the hunter, still staring into his drink. Stephen sat back down.

'But that begs the question...' he started.

'What will they do to her instead?' Cobol finished for him. 'You're right. We need a boat.'

'We?' asked Greer, eyebrows raised. Cobol gave a grin that might well have been evil, in the wrong light.

'I've been meaning to pay Aaron Wreather a visit for quite some time now. It'd be a shame to let the opportunity pass me by.' he said, the gruff, half-elf back in his voice suddenly. It had been a long time since he had felt the feeling stirring now in his soul...he had been too long without it: without hope. Without allies...he had been too long hiding in the shadows...it was time to let Aaron Wreather know exactly what kind of 'hunter' he had created. It was time to get back out to sea, and show that bastard what it felt like to be the prey.

Chapter 29

Abigail sifted through the herb cupboard in absolute dismay, opening a drawer here, prodding at an unknown ingredient there, and generally tutting and shaking her head. When Aaron returned she had emptied three drawers out onto the table and was shaking her head over the contents.

'Your witch hazel has rot in its core, your comfrey is mush and your dock still has maggots in it...they get into your stock they'll munch the lot you know? Who picked these? Whoever it was they need fired.' she greeted him. He was getting used to her ability to jump straight to the middle of a conversation, without pleasantries. In a world of strict regulation and politics he found it refreshing. Also it really irritated Marcus, which he was quickly learning was a new hobby of his.

'I have to buy them from Salston. Estoran herbs are...-'

'Different?' she finished for him. She tossed him a bundle of something orange and hairy that she didn't recognise.

'Fire grass...it's the only type of grass that I can get to grow here. It has its own chlorophyll system and doesn't depend on the sun. Everything else that grows on Estora is pretty much fungus based- what are you doing?' he asked, as she pulled out a few more ingredients and sought out an alembic.

'Well look at your lab! Honestly you have no idea how lucky you are...resources like these? Just think of what I could do...' she told him as she ground charcoal with a pestle and mortar. 'I'm doing a dye for your old boy. He needs it. Don't tell him though, just...put it in his desk or whatever.' she added. Aaron smiled, he had left her for five minutes. Five minutes.

'So you were working on the blight?' she asked. A stab of fear in his chest made him look towards his own desk, a book lay open on it.

'Yes...' he mumbled, distracted. He crossed to the book and closed it, seeing as he did so that the research notes were indeed on his work with the blight...and didn't contain any of his 'other' notes. He closed his eyes and sent a silent thanks to Marcus, who had removed all the incriminating documents the night before, his friends amused acknowledgement prodded the edge of his senses in return. 'Yes. My father started work on it many years ago, and I took over his research after he died. I'm no farther forward I'm afraid. It seems that our magic is doomed to poison the world.'

'So you stay here?' she speculated, adding the charcoal to some alcohol. She lit the oil lamp and slid it beneath the bowl.

'So we stay here.' he answered.

'My father worked on a cure too.' she said conversationally, then realised what she had just said and almost bit her tongue off. He smiled, amused at her reaction.

'It's quite alright Abigail. Lord Bracken told me everything there was to tell about you. I know who you are. Who your father was...I have nothing but the utmost respect for his work.' he said gently. If it was meant to reassure her it did not, she felt her toes curl.

'And why did Lord Bracken feel the need to do...whatever it was he did?' she asked, trying and failing to keep a trace of bitterness out of her voice. She expected him to turn cold, but instead he took a breath, and approached the bench.

'You know why. Since the war there have been intruders here. People who want us to suffer for what a few of our number did. It doesn't matter to the rest of the world that the men responsible were punished with death...They look at us and they see murderers. They see the people who killed their loved ones...and they blame us.' he explained. He surprised her again with a gentle hand on her shoulder. She quelled the instinct to squirm away and tolerated it.

'Why don't you?' he pondered quietly. She froze, tongs in hand. She had never thought about it before. She hated the man who had taken her parents away – who wouldn't? But blaming a whole race of people for the actions of one man had never even crossed her mind before. It would be akin to hating all dogs in the world because of the puppy that had bitten her when she was four, or hating all the horses in the field because the big black mare had kicked her once. She frowned.

'I couldn't blame an island for something one man did. That doesn't even make any sense.' she answered. She felt her temperature rising, the urge to get out of the room and away from him growing in her feet. She took a steadying breath and focused on the dye before her, adding the thick paste to beeswax and stirring it till all was smooth and black.

'Rock salt?' she queried. He moved a few steps behind her and placed a wooden container on the bench. She measured a half cup and added it to the mixture, again smoothing it down.

'What if you found him? The man who...took them away from you. What if you could find that man whilst you were here, on the island?' he asked. She turned to him, narrowing her eyes.

'I thought you said the men responsible were dead?' she demanded fiercely. He smiled, because nothing seemed to get past her.

'Their leaders are, yes. It might not have been a leader though...it might just have been a man following orders.' he explained. She looked suspicious, and then dismissive. She started pouring her dye into a glass bottle with a funnel. He watched her hands, one of them shook.

'It wouldn't matter. I don't remember him.' she said simply. He smirked.

'What if I unlocked your memories?' he offered. She stopped what she was doing and turned to him once more. The foot of air between them buzzed with unspoken questions as she locked her clear green eyes on his. She considered the consequences, then considered whether or not she could trust him. What she didn't do was question whether or not the young man with the cerulean blue eyes was able to do what he was offering...she had already felt the power of Lord Bracken in her head...but could she trust him? She paused too long, and realised her mistake when she saw the hurt in his eyes. He turned away and walked to the desk again, where he opened the book of notes and sat in the black draped chair there. She pursed her lips together and wondered what to do next whilst he pretended he was working.

'It's not that I don't appreciate the offer, it's just-'

'That you don't trust me.' he said with a heavy sigh. He smiled, but unlike his other smiles this one was empty. She suppressed a shiver.

'I do trust you...I do.' she decided there and then. 'But there are things that are best left alone. My parents died a long time ago, and it was hard enough the first time around.' she tried. He put down his quill and pinched the bridge of his nose.

'I'm sorry. I didn't think.' he answered, and something about him seemed older somehow, much older.

'No...you should do it. I mean I'm not ready but...when am I going to be on Estora again? You should do it.' she said out loud. She had to, to drown out the voice in her head that was screaming how bad an idea it was. She thought ahead instead, if she could find the man himself, if she could ask him what he meant by leaving her alive...would she be able to stop herself killing him? Could she kill a man? Was it harder to kill an Estoran that it was a regular man? Were they like the zombies they created? Did you have to get them in the brain?

She smiled at Aaron whilst he read the stream of thoughts from her with the ease of a hardened professional.

'We'll start tomorrow.' he settled with a smile, and even dared to reach out and take her by the hand. She let him, despite the protesting in her brain. She was fun to watch, a human constantly arguing with itself...Her aura shot out green from her race, blue from the magic in the ground and with a fleck of silver here and there where the energy was seeping in. He had her trust, and half the battle was won.

'Why don't you go with Lorne and find Mariana, she wanted to spend more time with you. The poor thing, there really aren't many women around here.' he said.

'I've seen plenty of women.' she responded before thinking. She pointed to two of the many servant girls that waited by the door, she suspected one of them was Lorne: the original. Aaron laughed and turned back to his work. He waved her away. She narrowed her eyes again...what was so wrong with being friends with the servants? Every noble person she had ever met had an attitude about it, Catherine had hated her relationship with Elena and Stephen...she just didn't get it. People were people, no matter who gave birth to them.

There was a tinkle as she set the black dye on the desk beside him and turned to leave. He looked up and watched her go with a smile. The black potion bottle sat there, inconspicuous. He picked it up and turned it in the light. A black potion was an ominous creation...poison was black, always black...and in the tiny bottle the dye looked deadly, yet all it was, was colouring. He set it on the desk again, rubbed his chin and wondered what the feeling in his chest was. After a while he took a few notes and went to find Marcus. They still had a lot of work to do if they wanted to keep Abigail Jones on Estora...and the Convocation simply would not tolerate their failure in this.

Chapter 30

Mariana held the purple lace number up against Abigail's body and giggled her glee. She seemed to do that a lot.
'You have to! It's going to look divine on you!' she announced with happiness. Abigail couldn't help but smile. Mariana in her quarters was exactly like a fairytale princess in her castle. Everywhere was fur and feathers, glitz and glamour. There were powders and pots, jewels and shoes, cloaks and boas and chiffon. Abigail was introduced to a world of femininity that she hadn't experienced in a long time; and yet in the midst of it all a memory popped into mind...she and her mother used to do this, long, long ago. The afternoon passed in a swirl of make-up and hairstyles that she had no interest in, but the play in itself was familiar, and comforting to her in a way she hadn't expected it to be. After many hours of trying on everything that Mariana had brought to her she fell exhausted at her dining table and lay gratefully and gracelessly into the bowl of stewed vegetables that was set down before her. She recognised some of the food from breakfast, but guessed at the rest. They knew she was vegetarian of course, but she couldn't tell what was meat and what wasn't yet so she chewed carefully whilst Mariana picked at her meal and drank quite a lot of wine.
'So you shall have the dark purple and I shall wear the red. Together we will be the prettiest women in the room.' announced Mariana, whom Abigail suspected had drunk enough already. She reached a hand out to the jug, saw it was nearly empty, and nodded to Lorne, who brought another. She filled a half glass for herself, and topped up Mariana's glass.
'That will be lovely.' said Abigail, resigned to feigning interest for the moment. Another couple of glasses would probably do the trick though. 'It's been a long time since I danced at a ball.' she added, to keep the talk moving forward. Mariana giggled, drank, nibbled her stew.
'Well don't you worry, I will be there to look after you – just like we were sisters!' she exclaimed, and held her glass up in a cheer.
Abigail clinked it, and took a sip. The wine was warm, but not unpleasant. She grinned as she put it back. Stephen would absolutely

murder her...she remembered Aaron as she had first seen him, refusing to sell her Estoran wine in a bar. She laughed.

'Sisters.' she repeated. She sipped again. The wine was spicy, and tingled on her tongue with herbs she couldn't place.

'And this time you will have Aaron on your arm, won't that be nice?' the gorgeous Mariana persisted. She played with her long curls and pushed the plate away. She took another drink, and Abigail refilled her glass. Abigail watched, frozen. Would it be nice? The other woman laughed at her expression.

'It's good. I'm glad he found someone like you...we always thought he would grow old alone, the amount of time he spends on his work.' she continued. Abigail tilted her head in thought.

'Did he find me? Is that why I'm here?' she challenged outright. Mariana looked shocked for a moment, and when she next spoke it was with more sobriety in her voice than she'd previously had.

'Abigail.' she turned serious, and leaned across the table to pat her hand like she was a frightened animal. 'None of us knows why you are here...but for his sake I'm glad. I haven't seen him this happy in a long time...since we were children, in fact. Before he lost his parents.' she explained seriously. Abigail frowned, and would have liked to pursue the conversation had Marcus not rapped on the door.

'Mariana...I'm coming back here in one hour and you better be ready this time, you hear me?' he said as he came in. He saw Abigail and smiled his phoney smile. 'Evening, Lady Jones.' he greeted her as if he hadn't known since breakfast that she would be there. He turned back to Mariana. 'Be ready.' he told her.

'I'm always ready, my darling.' she replied curtly, but with a sexy smile attached. Marcus responded in kind.

'Yes My dear, but you're still always late.' he retorted. 'Ladies.' he said with a nod, and then left again. A nameless robot women scurried off after him and Mariana signalled to another to clear the table. She stood, clapped her hands together and said:

'That's not how you're wearing your hair, is it?'

And Abigail *just knew* that an hour would not be enough.

Two hours later Marcus knocked on the door again, apparently he knew Mariana DeBossa very well indeed. By then they were ready, excepting the glass of wine Mariana had insisted upon before they left. She placed the empty glass into the hands of a Lorne and grabbed a delicate scarf on her way to the door. She pushed the Lorne there out of the way and opened the door herself, to find Marcus and Aaron looking rather dashing behind.

'My dear one, you look wonderful as always!' Marcus greeted her with dual kisses on each of her cheeks. 'And Lady Abigail...don't you scrub up nicely?' he announced, and tried to do the same to Abigail, who froze whilst he planted air kisses on each side of her face...perhaps it was an Estoran thing, but people in the islands didn't randomly kiss on greeting. She flicked uncomfortable eyes on Aaron, who was looking at her like he had seen a ghost.

'You look...very nice.' he mumbled without meeting her eyes. She blushed because she felt silly...Mariana might be drop-dead gorgeous but Abigail had witnessed the layers of powders and paints that she wore to make her that way, she even had some on her own face. She was scared to smile too much in case it cracked. How did women live like this? She was pretty sure at least one of the creams contained lead and was poisoning her as she walked...but she resigned herself to one night as a painted lady, she would wash it off later and it had made Mariana so happy. The four of them made their way along the many carved stone corridors that made up the Temples upper levels. By the third hallway the persistent thudding noise that seemed to ring from everywhere was getting on Abigail's nerves.

'What is that noise?' she asked Aaron, who still hadn't looked her in the eye yet. He looked surprised.

'Oh the picking? I'm so used to it now I don't even hear it.' he said, looked at her and- did he just blush? 'The whole Temple is carved into the centre of a mountain. They're still carving on the upper and lower levels...they're still carving everywhere.' he explained.

They came to a solid stop at two heavy, dark-wood doors in an otherwise seemingly empty tunnel. There were two Lornes at the door, except that these two were male and therefore had short black hair instead. She wondered what their names were, then wondered if it mattered. She blatantly had no idea how things worked here, all she had done since she got there was second guess herself.

'All ready?' asked Marcus, and then signalled to the two man-Lornes, who opened the doors in unison. All at once the noise of enchanting, if a little depressing, music floated out, so loud Abigail wondered how she possibly couldn't have heard it before. Voices came with the music, laughter and accented common. The hallway burst into light around her like the sun had burst through, and she peered around the door to see a party in full swing.

The hall itself was monstrous big, there were torches all along the walls, torches in a chandelier, torches in stands all around the floor. Abigail had to squint because she had been so long in the dim, blue-lit rooms downstairs. There was a band, high up on a decorated balcony, who played a waltz that might be described as 'a little morbid'. Abigail was slowly learning that the Estorans couldn't help the morbidity, it was like it was built into their make-up. On long tables and beneath the band there were rows of chairs laid out for the halls many inhabitants...enough inhabitants to make Abigail nervous. If Estora was so tiny, why were there so many of them? Where did they all come from? Did they all live in the Temple?
'I'm supposed to introduce you,' said Aaron, as he led her by the arm to a table on a platform a level above the rest of the room. The table had twelve seats, and she recognised Lord Bracken on the end. The old gent grinned when he saw her, and stroked a silky smooth, perfectly dyed beard. She dipped her head to him and tried to listen to Aaron over the noise of the room.
'...but they insisted. Forgive me.' he finished. Woah forgive him? Forgive him for what? Someone announced she and Aaron and she was led forward to stand before the ten men and one lady that made up the Convocation of Shadows on their raised table.
'Hi.' she struggled, as all of the background noise in the room was tuned out to dull fuzz. She shifted her weight nervously...she was not the one turning down the volume.
'Abigail Jones. It is very nice to meet you.' spoke one of the Convocation of Shadows. He had a kindly caste to his eyes, and she believed he meant what he had said. She looked down at her feet because her knees were trembling. There was just her now, she and them, and Aaron's hand on her arm just a disembodied tension. She concentrated on remaining upright as their collective gaze fell on her. It was a physical pressure she felt, like their minds had barraged her all at once until she was struggling to think straight. A queer thought entered her mind; that she was the field mouse and they were the fox. The solitary Lady's voice tinkled with laughter and cut into her brain like icicles. She felt herself sway. They were waiting on her to speak.

'Thank you...f-for putting up with me.' she stammered stupidly. The laughter rang out again, like music or bells or the noise of fairy wings fluttering. She struggled to make out the features on their individual faces. The impression she got was of old age and power...lots and lots of power...enough to make her want to go lie down in a dark room for the rest of the night.

'We hope you have a pleasant stay, Lady. Do let us know if there is anything you require.' the kindly one was saying. She might have nodded, she definitely tried to curtsy, she had already given up on her legs when Aaron became a whole person again and swung her out of there and into a seat. He put her down and went off for water or something. She had to get out of there...there was what appeared to be a balcony or terrace behind some ornate windowed doors at the opposite end of the hall. She must have went there, because the next memory she had from that night was of being on the balcony and looking out over an island so small she thought that if she jumped from this high up she would land in the sea. There were pinpricks of light far, far below. Houses perhaps? Or camp fires? She leaned on the chipped stone balustrade and tried to figure out what had just happened.

When Aaron finally found her again she was feeling a little more like herself but a lot less like playing along. He looked concerned, and carried three glasses.

'Wine and water. I didn't know which.' he worried, urging her to take two of the glasses from him. Thus freed he put a hand on her forehead to check her temperature. His hand was impossibly cold and felt wonderful so she allowed it. She sniffed the wine and sipped it; again the spicy warmth on her tongue and mix of curious flavours.

'What do they put in this?' she asked, sniffing it again. Aaron cracked a smile and then went back to concerned again.

'It's a secret.' he said coyly.

'Ah. That's how the Golden Fox gets its wine.' she teased with a grin.

'Don't tell anybody. They wouldn't go if they knew actual Estorans ran the place.' he joked, laughing so that she couldn't tell if he was serious or not. 'About before. I am truly sorry, they insisted on meeting you. I knew it wouldn't be...easy for you.' he finished.

'Why's that?' she asked, sipping her new favourite drink. He smiled a puzzled smile.

'Because you, my friend, are a healer. And they – or we, more accurately – are the opposite of healers. Your life magic, and our death magic, are at opposite ends of the spectrum. You don't get Estoran healers, dear one, because the two types of magic cannot exist in the same space at the same time. That's why you feel unwell...their collective power is pretty impressive...and big enough to hurt you. I got you out of there as soon as I could.' he explained. She watched the lights below whilst her brain processed the new information.

'I'm in danger here, aren't I?' she asked honestly. He gave a soft laugh and again, she didn't know if he was genuine or not.

'No.' he answered, and the honesty in his voice struck her like a blow to the face. 'Not as long as you have me.'

'I see.' she said carefully. 'And how long will that be?' she asked though she didn't want to know the answer, not really. He laughed again, as if it were all a game, and for the first time she became aware that there was something slightly...unhinged...about him.

'As long as you want me to.' he replied. She didn't look very reassured.

'Why can't I feel-' she started, and then stopped because she had absolutely no way of explaining her connection to the earth beneath her feet. It was a healer's connection, and before she had known she was a healer she hadn't even known it was there. It was the feeling of always having roots, of always being at home in the world...it was the feeling that let her pick out the green threads that connected all things...and here it was missing, and she didn't even know how to explain herself.

'Why can't you feel what?' he asked, suddenly very interested in the conversation. She looked about her for inspiration. She gave up and shrugged instead.

'I always feel sort of...connected to other things. I don't feel it here. I feel isolated.' she tried. He looked thoughtful.

'You feel life. There isn't any here.' he said faintly.

'But you're alive.' she insisted. She stopped when she saw his expression. Slowly, slowly...she reached her hand out and laid it where his heart should be. Nothing. She moved her hand to his neck, the skin ice cold beneath her fingertips, and felt for a pulse. Nothing. Something in her brain pointed out an oh-so-obvious fact.

'Why am I alive in this place?' she asked. Why hadn't the death magic seeped into her and killed her like everything else here? She checked her own pulse just to make sure, and found it, steady and solid (if a little fast) on her wrist.

'A sealing spell. After I found you I had Bracken cast a sealing spell on our floors to protect you. We have a week...we can always get him to re-cast if your friend isn't here by then. I told you Abigail...you're safe with me. I wouldn't let them harm a hair on your head.' he said. He tried not to sound like he was reading from the script.

'But why not? Why go to all this trouble for me? Why not just kick me off your island and be done with it?' she persisted. Back on familiar territory, he smiled.

'Because perhaps you will be the Lady of Beeton one day, and when that day arrives perhaps you will remember what Estora once did for you, and tell the rest of the world that we are not all bad.' he mused, charming again. Abigail gave a half smile. It was an evasive answer and she didn't like it. He noticed. 'And maybe because there aren't many women on Estora.' he teased gently. She narrowed her eyes at him.

'I finished my wine.' she stated, because she didn't know what else to say.

'Good, you shouldn't drink that stuff it messes with your brain. Do you dance?' he asked.

'Not well.' she replied.

'Humour me.' he demanded, and held out his arm for her to take, just like she was back at home but without Catherine scowling at her from a corner. She took it because she had no excuse not to, and followed her possible captor to the dance floor.

Chapter 31

     In Salston Stephen strode towards the towns solitary merchant with purpose and demanded to know what time the next crossing was. The grizzled, grey and worn fisherman looked at him out of one eye, the other screwed tight shut, and told him what the Estorans did to trespassers.

'Las' time I took a boy over 'e was hangin' on the lamppost when I 'appen back. No passengers mate, sorry.' said the older man in a thick accent. The merchant's name was Peirs, and he was the only person in town who had any money...not to mention he owned the one boat on the jetty. He made all of his money through the trade crossing. The whole world was afraid to trade with the Estorans...not Peirs...but he drew the line at tourism.

'I need to get there anyway.' Stephen tried, the lump in his chest hadn't gone anywhere for two days now. He was getting used to talking through it, without anger bubbling over the surface. The fisherman-come-trader whistled and pursed his lips in thought.

'I can't mate. Sorry. You'll need to find someone el-' he settled in the end.

'There isn't anyone else and you know it! Look, we have six gold between us, surely that's enough to cover it?' protested Stephen. The greying merchant seemed to think for a moment, but shook his head.

'It ain't about money mate. You'll get killed.' answered the trader. He patted Stephen on the shoulder. 'I don't want that on my conscience, ya know?' the man claimed. He turned to the crates he was loading and left Stephen standing there. He put a hand to his forehead and then turned back to the others...at this stage he was not above clobbering the gentleman on the head and thieving his boat. Old habits died hard with Stephen Laurence, and he turned a look to Cobol that queried 'should I?'

'Amateur.' Cobol muttered under his breath. He approached the two men and placed a firm hand on the traders shoulder, he turned the man around so that he could see his eyes – and then he took a deep breath...because he did not like to do this. In a flash he had a dagger at the mans throat and had lifted him from his feet by the scruff of the neck so that the merchant gulped and choked.

'If you don't take me to Estora I'm going to smash your brains all over the nice cobblestones on the street there, and let the gulls eat what's left of you. Do you understand?' he asked in a monotone voice that was somehow more scary than his actions were. The frightened trader nodded and Cobol dropped him. He smoothed out the man's fine jacket and let him compose himself.

'When do we leave?' he asked. The fisherman, shaking, took a minute to reply.

'At dawn-!' he stopped when Cobol grabbed hold of him again and whisked him upwards. 'No please! It's the tide! You can only get through the rocks to the port early in the afternoon! I'm sorry!' squealed the man in his own defence. Cobol tilted his head, sensing for the truth...the fast heartbeat, the beads of sweat, the smell of fear...the man was not lying. He rested Peirs feet on the jetty once more and smoothed out his over-comb for him.

'Think I'll sleep aboard tonight...never could sleep right on land.' he said an inch from the man's eyeball. Peirs nodded, and smiled, and felt lucky that his brains were still inside his skull. Given what Stephen knew about Cobol he guessed the trader would never know exactly how lucky he was.

'I thought you would use your...you know...'powers' or whatever. I didn't think you were going to scare the poor guy half to death!' said Stephen, once Peirs had made his excuses and gotten out of there. He looked after the man, who disappeared into the inn for a stiff brandy, and wondered if he would come back, or if he would just abandon his boat.

'I don't do that.' replied Cobol, surprisingly annoyed by the idea. Stephen frowned.

'Why not use it if you have it?' he asked. His old friend was rummaging amidst the boats cargo, looking for something to sleep on. He sighed, and straightened.

'They might have infected me Stephen...but it's up to me whether or not I become what they are. Their magic is like a drug. You hear thoughts, you can look into souls, see what makes people tick and make them do pretty much what you want them to. It's not human. That's why the Gods gave them their own island...so they didn't infect everyone else. The more they use the power the worse they become, the more...corrupt, I guess. The more I used it the more I wanted to use it. So I stopped.' he tried to explain. The truth was that there was a void in his head, and the more he borrowed from it the more he fell into it. The longer he lived the worse it got, the less he felt, the more he overheard. When he had walked into a bar to get a drink in Calle and found himself silencing the whole place just to get a drink in peace he had known it was time to get away from other people. He had taken the boat and left. He wasn't human any more, or elven. He didn't fit in with his own kind. He didn't fit in with those who had tried to mould him. Maybe he fit here though...with other people who wanted to fight it instead of turning a blind eye like the rest of the species.

'Sorry. I never even thought of it like that. And...you don't have to do this. This is my problem, not yours.' said Stephen. They had come up with a plan, all they needed was the boat and enough time to get there. And for Abigail to still be alive of course, but if what Cobol had reported was true then they had no interest in killing her...Asa had added another note of urgency to the matter. He was sure that if Abigail was on the island for too long she would run out of earth energy...the way he had explained it to Stephen that meant that she might die. Healers needed a constant connection or something, their bodies were only able to hold so much and once that was gone, boom. Instant death. The real reason there were no healers on Estora. 'Don't worry about it. You take the others back inside. I've got this.' he told Stephen. The muscled hunter yanked out a dusty cloth that would pass for a blanket and tossed it onto the deck of the small boat. Stephen took a step and then frowned again.

'You think he'll come back?' he asked, and pointed after the fisherman. Cobol gave a loose shrug.

'Doesn't matter. Boats are easy...It's the people inside them you have to worry about.' he said dismissively, and climbed aboard. Stephen went back to the inn to spend an uneasy night awaiting the sunrise. He was getting closer...all she had to do was hang on.

Chapter 32

Abigail lay awake in the endless night and thought till her head ached. Why bring her here? Why keep her here? Why not send her away? Aaron made out like it wasn't safe for her to be here...so why not just send her away. And then there was that. Aaron. Nobody else had stepped forward to capture her or torture her, nobody else even seemed to acknowledge her. She was beginning to wonder if the island really had brought her here somehow, because so far as she knew there didn't seem to be any threat. Tonight she had made comments that she was sure should have gotten her put back in the cage...if she were really a prisoner. Tomorrow (or later in the eternal night, at least) Aaron was going to help her remember a killer...and it wasn't something she necessarily wanted to go through with...but the lure of it. The temptation. And what if he still lived? She was almost certain they wouldn't be happy if she lost her control and killed the man. But could she look him in the eye and *not* kill him? Then there was Stephen...nearly two days and no word. Shouldn't their messengers have come back by now? Something was not right, and she still hadn't figured it out, and that was making her very frustrated indeed. Two hours before dawn she rose, dressed, and had Lorne show her to the lab. If she wasn't sleeping she might as well be working...maybe she would have a look and see what the unsolvable problem was with curing the blight...and maybe she would make something capable of blowing the whole place up...just to be safe.

When Aaron appeared mid-morning she had accrued a small wealth of work, read all about iolite and its qualities and had two or three potion bottles hidden in the many folds of her oversized robe. She hadn't traced her own clothes yet. She didn't suppose she was getting them back, they tended to frown on individuality here, hence all the waves of black and brown cloth.

'Morning.' she said, sipping the tea Lorne had brought. The tea was chamomile. She ranked camomile up there with lavender and geranium as her three least favourite teas.

'You shouldn't walk around here alone.' he admonished. He didn't look like he had slept either and he sounded more than a little grumpy.

'Why? Is it dangerous without you to protect me?' she teased. He scowled, and drank from another cup. He made a face, which made her laugh, and eventually so did he.

'What have you been doing in here anyway?' he challenged. He crossed to the bench and looked at where she was in the notes. He looked from the iolite chunks on the table to the hammer in her hands.

'What are you doing with those?' he asked, suddenly worried.

'Well...I figured if your iolite could hold death magic and store it, then why couldn't it do the same with life?' she explained. She selected a chunk of the blue stone and set it in a metal bowl. He gripped her wrist before she managed to summon any energy and locked eyes with her, a warning all over his face.

'Don't do that. The crystal will reject it and you will explode. It's been tried before.' he warned. She frowned at the real concern in his tone, and then shrugged.

'Oh well, I'll just heal the damage...you should probably leave though.' she considered, not comprehending how mad she sounded. He guided her physically away from the experiment and turned a few pages in the notes, he let her read, and watched the light of understanding dawn on her features.

'Wow.' she breathed faintly. 'A whole wing of the Alchemists Guild...' she looked down at the page, which described in great detail how her own father, one Dr S H Jones, had been responsible for the loss of part of the Alchemist Guild laboratories in Calle. She smiled. He had been trying the exact same thing she just had.

'It's a shame...if you could heal the stone it could transmit or store...you'd have a- a healing stone you could pull out and use whenever you wanted to.' she contemplated thoughtfully. Aaron grinned on impulse. Sometimes, with Abigail, he forgot himself.

'That's the chain of thought he was following...if it had worked we could have planted stones everywhere that protected the land from us...We would have been able to travel, to go anywhere, to live anywhere we wanted to...but it didn't. And we are still here, twenty-five years later. Still looking at the same problem.' he said, turning the pages idly.

'I suppose it stands to reason...I mean if iolite can hold death magic then why would it hold life? It would have to be something different, wouldn't it...it would have to be opposite...whatever the opposite of iolite is.' she thought out loud. Aaron was deep in thought beside her. She was thinking a few weeks back to the time that Stephen had been bitten by the creature in the forest. You must be able to heal the infection that they passed on, as long as the wound wasn't fatal, or you got to it in time...but once a person was dead they were dead...and no amount of life energy would change that. Was it the same with the land? With the dead forests and empty rivers that the Estorans caused wherever they went? She shook her head.

'I need a break.' she mumbled quietly, rubbing her eyes. She was getting tired...missing her night of sleep might not have been such a good idea after all.

'We should start...if you still want to. Your memories, I mean.' he reminded her. She took a deep breath and nodded slowly.

'I don't know if 'want' is the right word, but let's get it over with.' she answered. In her head, her own voice *huffed*.

She sat facing Aaron across the desk. He didn't do anything, didn't say anything, he just took his seat once she was comfortable, and then peered at her over the desk in a way he hadn't before. She frowned into his eyes until he reached out and touched her face.

'Go to sleep.' he said on the edge of the world, and she fell gently away into darkness.

The darkness shifted into shadows, changed as if a torch was being directed at her in the night. Immediately ahead of her a blue orb floated at eye height. She blinked at in shock, it had tiny little wings, tiny little arms and hands, tiny little legs and a tiny little face.

'Wha-' she tried to say...but in this place she was not in control of her actions or her voice. She just went along for the ride and watched. Her child self followed the blue fairy through the trees as it wound and wove, playfully. She chased it, laughing, because, she remembered, she thought this was all a game.

'I'm right here.' came Aaron's voice from close behind her. She couldn't turn to look, so she fought her own fear of lack of control of her body and waited it out. It was just a dream after all, just a memory.

'The trees...' she remembered to herself. The sound arose about her like the gentle pitter-patter of rain. The branches whispered together above her. Somewhere amidst the delicate thrum came the sound of someone calling her name. She followed the fairy, all too aware of what would come next.

They came out onto a cliffs edge where the forest dropped back behind her and the sea crashed beneath, not thirty yards ahead. The fairy reached the edge of the cliff, hovered a moment, and then plunged to its apparent death. The young version of herself screamed and chased after it, telling it to come back or it would die. It was that scream, she now theorised, that must have attracted her parents. She stopped at the edge of the cliff and tried to see through the tears she was crying. The fairy was gone...intricate and as intriguing now as it had been then. Who the hell saw fairies anyway? Only crazy people. She was suddenly too aware of Aaron's presence, and of how personal a memory this was. She really hadn't thought this through. Somewhere, back in the lab, her face was burning red, she was sure of it. In the memory strong arms scooped her up and carried her away from the danger. She wished she was looking at her father, but instead she faced over his shoulder, back towards the figure rising over the cliff. Whilst the child raged and screamed the woman took a deep breath. Her father always smelled of alcohol...not the type you drink, the purest kind. She had forgotten that one detail...it explained why she found comfort at a workbench.

'Stop there.' said Aaron, and suddenly she could move again. She stepped out of the image like it was a picture, and joined him on the outside of it all. 'He spoke to you, what did he say?' he asked.

Abigail felt herself blush again, she didn't know if it was possible to blush in her own mental image of herself but she certainly felt like she did. She locked eyes on her father, his sandy hair and square jaw frozen in a shocked expression.

'He said 'mine.' ' she admitted, embarrassed by it but not sure why.

Aaron didn't laugh, and for that she was eternally thankful. He stepped up to the picture and looked at the figure on the cliff. He was shadowed, and cloaked, and wrapped in the darkness of Estora. Aaron waved his hands over the image as if he were pulling apart the shadows, and sure enough the darkness began to fall away and a face slowly became visible. Abigail held her breath whilst an outline appeared, then a jawline, then a cheekbone...blue eyes like every other Estoran, black hair...the man might as well have been Lorne.

'Greaton.' said Aaron purposefully. He stepped back from the picture to cup her face in his hands. It was a strange gesture and it gave her pause.

'You alright?' he asked almost tenderly. She felt her shoulders go rigid.

'Fine. You know him?' she asked, an unexplained quaver in her voice.

'I knew him. In fact...I was there when they caught him. They hung him from the Temple arch until there was nothing left but bones. It was a slow death. You were not his only victim, I'm afraid.' he said delicately, letting her go to turn back to the image. Abigail felt numb. Revenge had never been high on her list of priorities – she was too busy trying to stay alive – but now that the opportunity for it had been snatched finally away from her she felt the loss of it like a hole in her heart.

'It's for the best. I don't know what I would have done to him, if he were still on this island.' she answered. Her left hand was shaking so she planted it in a pocket. Too late though, he had noticed it...again.

'Do you want to continue?' he asked. She looked at the scene in front of her and resisted the urge to say no.

'Can I stay out here this time, and watch?' she asked. His gaze turned inward for a moment, and he nodded. The whole scene before her played out like she was in a theatre. She watched from the audience, using the barrier like a shield. It could be anyone's story playing out, it didn't have to be her own.

'The clearing.' she gasped, when the little family stopped running. She watched the dogs circle, heard her fathers final confession of love and wept silently as he made a run for her child self. The dogs leap.

'St-' started Aaron, but she placed a finger over his lips and kept watching. Her fathers death was horrific. Gore and blood spilled over his torn up body whilst miniature Abigail trembled and her mother screamed continuously in the background. The man came into the picture, hushing Abigail with the same gesture she had just given Aaron. Like he was playing? He placed a hand on her mother and the child turned away. The teenage Abigail watched the man suck the life out of her mother behind her...literally steal all of the green threads from her body so that they disappeared up into his hand to be folded away into the darkness.

'What was that...what did he do?' she asked Aaron, whilst Greaton knelt before her younger self and murmured to her.

'He...stole her soul. He took it away with him. Probably to use as a slave...there's something else you should know. Only the most powerful of us can do this...and only if the soul in question is...' he couldn't say it. Not when her mind thronged emotional and dangerous around him like a tornado.

'Is what?' she persisted, not letting him away with it.

'Is...already damaged. Already gone bad. Corrupt. I'm sorry.' he tried, without meeting her eyes. He felt the fury of her gaze anyway as the picture before them went dark.

'My mother was a healer. The most corrupt thing about her was her love for high heeled shoes.' she said crisply. He said nothing. The picture was still dark and she was about to leave when she remembered something...something she had always wondered about. 'Wait...there must be more...can you fast forward where I'm sleeping?' she asked. Aaron looked at her a long moment, as if considering how much farther it was safe to go in terms of her mental health, and then gave another nod. The picture before them started to swirl and change. Red and orange leaped from the image to twist and turn and dance in a vision of flames. There was Abigail on the ground, dirty and covered in (what could only be) her fathers blood. There was a circle of flames, and Greaton chanting. There was a corpse that she understood with slow disgust must be her mothers. There was an arm on the floor. Her younger self blinked at it in lack of understanding, all cried-out. The man picked up the arm and admired the fingers. He cut something off and put it in a pocket.

'There.' she pointed, as Greaton tossed her fathers arm into the flames. 'The ring.' she breathed in confusion. She felt under her robes and pulled out her necklace. The same ring from the memory hung on a leather thread next to a strange orange stone. Aaron examined the ring and gave a soft smile, even though he didn't understand.

'I never knew how I got it. He must have given it back to me. Why would he do that, do you think?' she asked Aaron. The voice in her head answered very pointedly.

Because he knew *who you* were.

She swallowed.

'I don't know. He wasn't a predictable man. He obviously meant to come back at some point and...'

'Turn me into one of your slaves?' she asked without thinking. Aaron's face remained carefully blank. Her thoughts caught up with her tongue and she cursed herself.

'They work for us and we protect them from the dangers of the night. We give them shelter and food. They are here through choice.' he lied smoothly. He even managed to look hurt. He was learning though, he was learning a lot. He was mostly learning that there was almost no way in hell Abigail Jones was going to stay on this island of her own free will. He was going to have to arrange for plan B...which involved forgetting all about trust and murdering her friends until she agreed to their demands. Against all of his own expectations he did actually care about her. It would be a terrible waste of a wonderful mind if they couldn't win her over with charm and enticement over violence. She looked ashamed, like she genuinely cared that she had upset him. Human emotion was a useful thing.

'Let's get out of here, we've both had enough for one day.' he sighed wearily. He took both of her hands and guided her smoothly towards the lab.

Abigail blinked a few times and tried to get the hang of being in control of a body again. When she finally sat back upright Aaron was gone, but she still heard his voice, talking quietly to a slave woman. She peeked over the desk to see them both crouched on the rug by the fire, a young girl with flame red hair between them and cuddling into a dolly. It struck her that the child was the first she had seen on Estora, it also struck her that children should not be dressed in black robes three sizes too large. The woman led the child through the door and Aaron came back to her, grinning reassuringly.

'Alright? Take it easy.' he said. She squinted up at him and yawned.

'Sorry.' she apologised, appalled at how terrible her manners had become since she had been living in a cave. He gestured to a waiting woman who brought coffee. Abigail thanked the blank faced girl and sipped slowly. The hot liquid burned but she let it, it was bringing her back to reality, piece by piece.

'So...' she started. She let her voice fall away as her thoughts did. All she could think of was the man in her memory, of his face and his hands. Of the ring around her neck that reminded her every day that she was an orphan. Why had the universe guided her here and shown her this? To learn her mother was evil? It didn't make any sense. In fact in made about as much sense as an island summoning her here of its own accord. This whole thing stank. She met Aaron's eyes and wished she could trust him like she said she did. She wanted to- Gods but she wanted to...but every time he came near her she felt...she felt lost.

'Let's get some food.' he suggested, rubbing his tired eyes. She nodded, and followed him once more further into the Temple.

Chapter 33

And on a cold and dreary Salston morning Stephen, Asa, Greer, Liandor, Cobol and one very wary trader named Peirs had climbed aboard 'the Honeydew' and were on their way across the sea. The wind speed was good, in spite of the rain, and it looked a whole lot like they would be in range of the harbour in Peat on the other side before the tide was high enough to ride in. Peirs took his time and relied on the sail. She was sitting a little low with all the passengers aboard, but she had carried heavier loads. It was coming into the hard months, where the wind became unpredictable and the waves tended to rise high. Sometimes the trade route was impassable, like in the deep winter, where snow storms reduced the visibility to nothing. Estora and Porta were both rocky islands, and it didn't do to loose ones way in the mists...particularly on the other side. There was more than one reason why Peirs was the only trader in these parts. He was good at what he did...and despite his want to run in the night he couldn't abandon 'the Honeydew', she was, and always would be, the only woman he had any time for.

Above the roar of the wind and the flapping of the sails were two sounds. The obvious sloshing of the waves as the little boat skipped the water and the steady slink, slink, slink of Cobol running a sharpening stone down his newly acquired blade. He had borrowed Stephen's mini-crossbow. It wasn't nearly as powerful as the one he had lost when he threw himself into the sea- but it was better to have some power at range over having none. Getting in would be easy. They weren't expecting it and they weren't looking for him...at least not here. Wreather would be a problem...he would know when they got too close. He stopped sharpening and looked at the scar on his wrist where the Estoran had once shared his blood...back when he wanted to 'save' him. He grunted, and looked at the edge on the short sword. The balance was bad, it was chinked in three places and it didn't have a hand guard, so he was likely to lose a finger if he fought with it...again...better than nothing. Luckily for him the Estorans weren't big on security. Estora – for the most part – was unguarded. Why wouldn't it be? No bugger ever wanted to go there. He chuckled to himself and slid the weapon through his belt loop.

'You all set?' asked Stephen. The man was all but wringing his hands together.

'All good.' he replied in his gruff voice. He was careful about his voice nowadays. The elven lull had never been fun for him, but now it was too close to the other thing...the mind control. It was too similar, too easy to slip from enchanting to controlling. Stephen still looked worried so he stood and stretched his legs. 'It'll be easy. I go in, mug an initiate, steal a robe. After that I walk into the Temple and kill Wreather, grab the girl and get out. Piece of cake.' he said light-heartedly, or about as light-hearted as Cobol got, at least. At this point the butler was past reassurances though. His whole body shook, whether from the bite of the wind or the adrenaline – or even from lack of sleep, who knew? But he was in a bad state, so far as Cobol could see.

'I want to come with you-'

'Not a chance.' he cut him off. There were a hundred, thousand reasons why. 'I told you, your soul glows like a beacon to them. You all stay on the boat – and I mean *all* of you. I'll get your friend back or she'll walk out on her own, but if you go in there you're dead. There's no need for that, not when one of us is dead already.' he continued. Stephen looked out across the water, almost like he wasn't listening. 'Don't make me have to knock you out and tie you up OK? Just stay on the damned boat and stay alive. Don't let him come closer than a couple hundred yards. If I'm gone more than three hours: leave.' he said steadily. Stephen ground his teeth but nodded his agreement, or at least his understanding.

'Don't die this time, eh?' he asked his oldest friend. The hunter gave a half-laugh and hefted his tiny crossbow.

'How can I not win with this?' he grinned his retort.

Three hours later and the sky turned stormy, but whilst most of the passengers worried over the weather the old trader smiled and turned into the darkened clouds. They had never been to the island before, never seen its misty shores nor encountered it's permanent night. Cobol too, was fairly comfortable. He was getting restless though. Another hour and it would be time for Peirs to make his trades as usual, and then they would get into position and wait while Cobol rowed in to pick up Abigail...if all went well, that was. The problems would be had in the escape, particularly if they hadn't killed her. On an island full of dead things a human aura attracted more moths than a flame, and a straight run for the door would get them both killed. Above them the sky darkened further, past stormy grey and into stormy black, and then from heavy black clouds to dense mist and a sunless sky. The group huddled together on the boat subconsciously, herding together for protection. Even Greer did it, now that there was nothing in her stomach to bring up. An eerie silence fell about them with the mists, as the flapping of the sails and the winds lessened. The waves were unnaturally calm here, unnaturally dark...and relentless.

'W-what happened to the sun?' asked Greer, whose inner wolf was urging her to make a swim for it.

'There is no sun here. No moon either. No stars.' answered Cobol, his voice low and quiet.

'It is just like the legend.' gasped Liandor equally faintly. Cobol snorted.

'You think Shade really scorched the sky to give his people a paradise? Kids stories.' dismissed the hunter. The druid shook his head.

'You should respect.' he warned. 'Shade made the people, Shade scorched the sky, Shade walks amongst us.' the druid recited in broken common. The last was quoted from a holy text. Cobol shook his head. He didn't need to be worrying about the Gods right now, he was too busy worrying about himself. 'Peirs, skirt to the north east, I'll go in level with the mountain.' he called to the trader. The older man nodded and angled in towards the port...before he could obey the hunters orders he had a trade agreement to follow through on, and he hoped his acting skills were up to par. The little boat crept its steady way calmly northwards, and Cobol put the adrenaline rush on hold and thought about the prize at the end. Aaron Wreather had wanted him to hunt people? He should have been more careful what he had wished for.

Chapter 34

After they had eaten Aaron let Lorne take her back to her room. The child she had seen belonged to a friend who was away on business, or so he had told her, and he needed to tend to her. She was left to her own devices for a while, but she was dozy from food and lack of sleep and she curled up on top of the soft covers and drifted off. She wakened with a headache and severe thirst, found Lorne again (the actual, original one) and got something to drink. She sat by the fire for a while, then she plaited her hair all up again. She liked it that way. It stayed out of her face. She considered the iolite shards around the mirror for a while.
They're watching us.
'They'll be bored then.' she answered under her breath. After a half hour of nothing she firmed her purpose. The potion bottles she had taken from the lab earlier rested reassuringly, one on either hip so they didn't clink. It was time to use them. Tonight. And then it was time to go home.

There wasn't any way to sneak food or water out without them knowing, not whilst they watched her. She had to wait until she was alone with Aaron and then slip it into his tea. She would go late in the night, whilst the initiates rested from their training and after Aaron had finished his chores for the day. With luck nobody would know to look for her until morning, and by then she would be gone...one way or another. There were still issues though. Whoever summoned her the first time might be able to do it again, in which case escape would be futile...The Lord Wreather was the one with all of the answers...and tonight he was going to give her them, because she was going to ask *really* nicely. She got bored of waiting, and thinking. Her thoughts were circling and she craved company – not dead company, company like Stephen or Greer. Like Asa. Company she missed. In the end she decided to go to the lab again, and went to find Aaron to tell him. It was still too early to make her move, but if she had to sit on her hands any longer she knew she wouldn't make it through the day.

In the hallway outside Aaron's study she heard raised voices. Lorne raised her hand to knock but Abigail took her wrist and lowered it. She shook her head.

'Go back to the room, Lorne.' she commanded with as much authority in her voice as she could muster. The girl turned glassy eyes on her, stared at her for four seconds and then lost interest. She did as she was told, and headed back to the room at a lurching pace. Abigail shook her head at the poor creature's departure and then jumped back from the door as it rattled in its hinges. The raised voices ceased. Abigail caught her breath. Something really bad was on the other side of that door...she sensed it, and was currently reconsidering her earlier wish to be able to sense like a hunter did. For a few more beats all was still, but then came the ominous, unmistakeable sound of something heavy and reluctant being dragged across the floor. She swore quietly, looked around for inspiration and settled her eyes on a candle lighting stick. The device was used to light the wall candles that were too high to reach. She didn't think to question what it was doing in a hallway lit only by iolite, she just picked it up and spun it, trying to get a feel for the weight. Thus armed, she placed her hand on the handle and turned.

Marcus was across the room and facing her. He was trying to drag Aaron into an easy chair. There was blood on his hands, and up his arms, and if she had to guess she'd say it was all over his robes too, even though the black negated the stain. Aaron was slumped half on the floor and half in the chair. He'd been stabbed...three times, her brain informed her. The stink of blood floated up to her nose and she hated that. Whenever she smelled Aaron's scent from now on she would be able to smell his blood.
'What are you doing?' she asked blankly. She did not understand this. Did Estorans kill their friends often? She corrected her own thoughts. He wasn't dead yet, just bleeding out. He didn't have long.
'You shouldn't be here.' Marcus all but hissed at her. He dropped Aaron's body and took the five strides that separated them. In shock, Abigail simply watched Aaron's pallor fade to ice-white over Marcus' shoulder as he grabbed her by the lapels and raised her off the ground. He slammed her back into the door, closing it in the process and knocking the wind from her lungs. She turned her attention to him as he rattled her again and her head slammed against the wood with a crunch. In spite of her complete lack of understanding and inability to breathe her brain danced merrily in her skull and informed her that she was carrying a weapon. She brought the staff up in her right hand and surprised him by using it as

a wedge between his arms. It was either let her go or break an arm, so he relented and dropped her. Before he recovered she whipped the pole round and hit him with the end, as hard as she could, and right in the spot where Liandor had shown her not a week before. It was like she had hit an off button...and Marcus Lester crumpled to the ground before the fight had even really started. She calmed herself with a deep breath and looked about her, shaking. Circumstances, it seemed, had changed...and there was no time like the present. Unfortunately for Abigail Jones if she wanted to drug Aaron Wreather then she was going to have to heal him first. You couldn't heal an Estoran, of course. It was impossible. And maybe if someone had told Abigail Jones that beforehand, she wouldn't have gone and done it anyway.

Chapter 35

The first thing that she did was lock the door. She didn't need a Lorne appearing and foiling her plans. As an afterthought she slid a chair up under the handle to jam it in case someone came along with a key. She needed some time...and the green potion would buy her that. She held both up to the light and put the red one away. She pried the cork off the green and slipped its neck between Marcus' lips. He probably wouldn't wake up for a while, but the Valerian would make sure she was long gone by the time he did. Working quickly and ever conscious of Aaron being no more than a hardly breathing heap on the floor, she sought a length of cord or rope and found two strips of black leather within grasping distance. She didn't stop to think about her remarkable good luck at the find, she didn't question it...she was too busy. She tied Marcus' hands and feet together and sprung to her feet. She got a grip under Aaron's arms and heaved, pulled and struggled until he was nearly upright in the chair, then she puzzled over whether or not to tie him up too. She settled for not, because she didn't want him to be suspicious of her intentions. There was water on a table with some fruit and a teapot. She didn't have time for the tea, so she emptied the potion into water and poured it into a china cup. It was obviously red. It didn't matter. He'd be so groggy when he wakened that he'd drink whatever she gave him. Thus ready she took a last look about herself. It was simply a matter of the heal itself. She leaned over him and slowed her breathing into deep, slow breaths, the way Asa had shown her. Once she was approaching the trance state between sleep and wakefulness she reached a hand out and touched him.

She wakened across the room and on her back. She sat up slowly, rubbing a pain in the back of her head. She looked at Aaron, who was still slumped over in the chair, then to her hand, which was covered in rapidly fading blisters, as if she had just stuck her hand in a fire. She shook her head and tried to ignore the stars in her vision as she straightened. At this point her brain gave her a kick, a little jolt of memory about the lecture Aaron had given her on their two opposite types of magic. Maybe, she reasoned, it wasn't possible...but that just wasn't good enough. She crossed to the curtain and took the tie-back from the hook on the wall. She turned, steeled herself, and looped his wrist around her own. It burned, and sent electric jolts up the length of her arm...but she held on long enough to tie a double knot in the join, and then she had no choice *but* to hold on. She focused on her breathing, in the vain hope that it would help her to ignore the pain she was in. In and out, in and out, slow as you can...She felt her eyelids close through the fuzzy connection to her body, and when she forced them open again she was watching her ten year old self help Elena in the kitchen at home. They were making lunches for the farmers. It was a harvest time tradition and it was all hands on deck, all day long. She smiled at the memory. She hadn't had a good time of it when she had lived with Catherine...but all life was just a series of moments. And this one before her had been a happy moment, in spite of all that had been going on at the time. She remembered that morning and waited, watching her little fingers butter bread, until she knocked over the blueberry jam and Elena first taught her how to swear. In her minds eye she laughed, because she had forgotten that day. She noticed she was alone all of a sudden. She shouldn't be alone here, not in this place. Where was Aaron to take her to the next memory? He wasn't in the vision, and it played out and faded before her like it had never existed to begin with. She was in darkness, and before she even had time to think the ground fell away beneath her like a trap door had been opened beneath her feet. She screamed but it was from instinct alone. She quickly learned that screaming would not stop her from falling, but *would* make her descent noisier. Besides, she was in the in-between place, in her own mind or in Aaron's, and she wasn't convinced that she *could* die here. So she stopped screaming and decided to make her own demands.

'Aaron Wreather you show yourself right now or I swear to Prudence I will leave you here to die!' she swore, using the Goddesses name to reinforce her intent, and maybe to ask for help...even if she would never admit it. She promptly stopped falling and landed on her backside. 'Very funny.' she grumbled angrily. She stood, brushed herself off, and looked at the scene around her. She was in a forest, in the night. There was no moon, and there were no stars, and she was not herself, but Aaron. She looked down at her hands and then up into the clearing before her...where *she* was. She blinked at seven year old Abigail, at her mother screaming, at her fathers torn and destroyed body on the ground at her feet...at the little smear of blood on her own cheek where she wiped a tear away and stared at herself. The child before her took a step and a dog growled. She felt the man whose mind she occupied laugh, and put a finger over his mouth. She might have fallen to her knees had the power of his memory not held her upright. She could only stare at the betrayal, open mouthed and without comprehension. How could this man that had helped her be the same man from back then? She had seen Greaton's face- but not until after Aaron himself had put it there. She felt the urge to cry. Wow. That hadn't happened in a while. She thought of Stephen suddenly, and felt the desire to run to him and hide, wherever he was...if they hadn't killed him yet...and all the time she had been eating with him, drinking with him...dancing with him...and he?

She was in the bog again. Half-swamp, half-marsh. The ground beneath her feet sucked at her shoes. She watched herself sink for a while.

Kill him.

She told herself, but she disagreed intensely. Now more than ever she needed the answers, and now more than ever she knew that he had them. Get the answers, get out of there, try not to get killed in the process.

Kill him.

Not yet, she couldn't yet. She needed to know.

No good will come of this.

'What the hell do you know?' she questioned out loud.

'..Abigail?' the voice, his voice, sound sucked out of it as if he were yelling in a vacuum. She turned her head towards its source, spied the Estoran sinking, like she was but faster, and only a few yards away. Without considering the consequences she launched herself at him, hitting, kicking, scratching, clawing...all the while unaware that her touch would heal him, and blast them both out of there and back into the room.

Chapter 36

Cobol dragged the rowing boat ashore and waved to '*the Honeydew*'. He couldn't see it over the distance but he knew Stephen would be watching through the eye piece he had borrowed from Peirs. He felt a twang at his earlier treatment of the trader...mostly because the man had showed up this morning to see them here safely. It was a rocky passage, their path marred by outcrops of jagged island and heavy mists, and he doubted (now that he had experienced the crossing above water, and awake) that he could have piloted the journey for himself and still brought them here in one piece. The trader was alright, just scared...understandably so.

He dragged the boat up the rock strewn beach and into the undergrowth...such as it was. In the end he broke a few bare tree branches and tried to camouflage the little wooden boat at least a little. There was nowhere better to hide it in the barren forest, so he left the little rowing boat to hope and got his bearings. He was to the east, and you couldn't miss the mountain, not with his preternatural vision and the fact that the dense black tower could be seen from anywhere on the island. It towered over all and disappeared up into the clouds – or it would if the mists ever cleared long enough for a person to spot it. It was easier to be here without the hunting parties, but that didn't mean that there wouldn't be people around in the few villages that spotted the island. For that purpose alone he would stay in the cover of the trees for as long as he could. There were a few houses around the Temple entrance that he would need to be careful of. After that it was just a case of purloining some clothing...sounded easy enough, but these things rarely were.

A half hour of jogging later he slowed to a walk and allowed his breath to catch up with him. The damp brick of the first house loomed into view. He stopped in his tracks and dropped into a crouch. There he stayed, still breathing hard, and pushing his senses ahead of himself...What did he hear from the house? No heartbeats, but that was no indication of occupation here, where nothing lived. He listened, smelled: nothing. Nothing unusual anyway...the settling of a floorboard in an empty room, the smell of ages-old wax and dust...the smell of rot. It was all but abandoned, so far as he could tell. Once satisfied that the house was definitely empty he approached from the gable end. The trees providing cover up until the last seconds and the Temple looming over all, the stairs to its entrance just a handful of yards away. He placed a hand on the gate of the little walled off garden and quickly changed his mind when he spied the rusting on the hinges. He jumped the little gate instead and cautiously stalked the length of the path. There were other houses behind this one, but he had been lucky, and none of them provided a view of this garden. He eyed the windows as he walked...all were closed in safeguard to the pervasive damp. A good sign.

At the door he tried the handle to find it open, just as he had expected. On an island like this every person knew their neighbour, and there was almost zero crime, given the harsh punishments the Estoran masters were likely to dish out. He let the door swing inwards and raised the mini-crossbow in readiness. It might be tiny, but within the confines of a hallway it would be deadly enough. He crept from the doorway and followed it. There was a stairway on his left and an open entrance-way at the end. The clothing he needed would be upstairs, but his first priority was to ensure the house was clear. He bypassed the stairs and went on to the end, swinging the crossbow around to cover the open archway. There was a room beyond, a reception room. It was sparsely but luxuriously decorated, with a few dusty leather couches, an abandoned fireplace with a huge, dirt-coated mirror and a separate section at the back containing a dining table and chairs. He relaxed a little, no self respecting person would live in a house this uncared for. The most he had to worry about would be squatters upstairs. He turned to leave and something twinged his senses, something all-too-familiar to him. Blood. He turned back to the room and sniffed, letting his senses elongate once again. He crossed to the fireplace, then followed the smell to the table. One of the chairs was squint, as if someone had been sitting here. He leaned over the table and inhaled. There were lots of different bloods ingrained into the wood...as if many people had bled here. He straightened and looked around the room again. There was nothing odd about it, nothing unusual save for the dust. He wrote the curiosity off as something he did not have time for right now. It may have been that the table once belonged to a physician...it could be that simple. The smells were faint and old. A door he hadn't seen from his previous angle caught his attention, but when he opened it there was nothing there but a kitchen. He screwed his nose up at the smell of stale food and reeled his senses back in again. He closed the door and headed for the staircase...there was only so much one hunter could take.

Upstairs were three rooms, all empty. He found a wardrobe in the largest, and opened it to find his prize. There were a half-dozen robes hanging on hooks, dusty and abandoned. He pulled out the first and shook it out. When he was satisfied it wasn't going to fall apart in his hands he shouldered the crossbow and pulled the velvet over his head. The robe restricted his access to his weapons, but if he wore them outright he wouldn't get very far without being caught. He resigned himself to hiding them under the robes many folds and took the trusty dagger from his ankle loop...it was the only weapon of his own he still possessed, having survived the sea as well as Stephen's pat down. From now on he would be working at close range, but that suited him fine. If they were close enough for him to shiv then they were too close to begin with, and had probably already figured out that he wasn't one of them. Besides, if he was caught the first thing he would do would be to take the damned robe off, and then the dagger wouldn't matter any more...he pursed his lips together. He would quite like to keep a hold of the weapon, since loosing them was becoming expensive.

Back outside he turned his attention to the towering mountain. A wide stairway swept up off the road and led to its heavy stone doors. The doors lay perpetually open and unguarded – again, security. He let out a deep breath and stilled the trembling in his hands. It was just adrenaline, because this was the hard part...getting in and out minus the side helping of death. Well...not his death anyway. Searching for Stephens lost friend amongst all the soulless ones the Temple contained wouldn't be easy...but finding Aaron Wreather would, and it was a good place to start. He climbed the stairs, composed and calm, hands clasped in front of him like he belonged there and hood draped down over his eyes. He had counted fifteen floors the last time he had escaped...now all he had to do was find the damned stairs again.

And on the boat Stephen paced and fretted, asking Asa every five minutes how much time had passed. By now it had already been forty-five minutes, but in the absence of a sun or moon in the sky the only way to tell the time was to ask Asa, who hummed and clicked to the spirits for an answer. Even the trader didn't have a time-piece. He didn't need one; he told time by the tide.

'What's taking so long?' Stephen groaned in despair. Greer squeezed his shoulder gently.

'It is a big mountain.' she answered, and had he not been quite so strung out he might have spared a laugh.

'I want to go in.' he confessed, hoping that she did too. The woman frowned sympathetically.

'We would die.' she said simply. She shrugged, then turned back to watch the distant shore.

'He is good yes? This...other hunter?' she asked. Stephen ran a hand over his roughened chin and thought back through the years.

'He used to be.' he answered.

'Tell me.' she demanded. She watched him with brown and orange tinged eyes until he spoke.

'Well...He once sacrificed himself to save the whole town...but it was more than that. He was the chief before Illion you know, before he went missing in the war. Before that he made the best leathers on Freisch. He used to make the others bring their best catch up to the manor. He always said the first pickings went to the landowner...and the Laird loved pheasant...I never knew a house to have so many feather mattresses.' he reminisced. He stopped, remembering another time and smiling. 'He helped birth the White stallion. Abby's favourite horse. None of us knew what to do and they didn't keep a stable master in those days. We thought the women had it covered but they came out yelling that it was 'breach'. The Laird sent me down to fetch Cobol and then there he was, up to his elbows in mare and pulling the creature out with his bare hands. The most disgusting, beautiful thing I ever saw.' He joined her in turning back to the island and tried not to think about all of the things Cobol was not. He was not an assassin, for example. He was not a ninja, nor a master of illusion. He was just a hunter. One man in a pot of vipers. Apparently he wasn't even an Estoran, just like he wasn't really an elf, either. He grinned to himself and watched for signs of life – any life – on that barren shore. If anyone could do it, it was the man they had just sent it there. All he had to do was have faith. He didn't ask Asa the time again after that, because both Cobol and Abigail were coming back...regardless of how long it took them to get there.

Chapter 37

Aaron came to with a start to see black robes moving away from him and the traces of some kind of powder in the air. He choked for breath as his lungs filled with a drying, rot-fumed substance. He reached out gladly for the cup that appeared before his eyes and downed it in one go. He sank back into the chair, letting the cup slide from his grip.

'Don't go back to sleep.' urged Abigail's voice from somewhere in the room. His head swam, his vision blurred...but most of all there was an overwhelming sense of ungodliness, of wrongness, and of...death...and it hung in the air about him so obviously thickly that it almost looked like darkness. He blinked a few times, and wondered why he had never noticed it before.

'Abigail?' he tried. His voice hardly obeyed. She handed him another cup of water and he drank. 'Why is this water red?' he asked, or seemed to. She let out a deep breath and then he heard footsteps. She dropped into the opposite chair and folded her legs up beneath her. He looked over her shoulder to the reclining body of Marcus on the floor by the door.

'Because I made a truth potion, and put it in your drink.' she said simply. Her face was completely blank, no emotion whatsoever. It made him feel cold.

'Oh.' he realised. A whistling came from the fire and she leaped out of the chair again.

'I didn't trust what was in the teapot so I used the fruit pulps instead. I think I'll call it...'fruit mix tea.' What do you think?' she asked as she retrieved the pot with a hook and set it on the table next to the decimated fruit bowl. All was still and quiet bar from the crackling of the fire and her pouring the tea.

'I think you are terrible at naming things.' he responded, then wondered why he had said it. She smiled, coldly, the way a lioness smiles just before it eats you. 'What did you do to Marcus?' he asked, dazed by the change in her.

'Oh he'll be alright. He just needs to sleep it off. You should worry about yourself, not him. I haven't decided what to do with you yet.

Marcus is safe by comparison.' she said in that same, strange monotone.

'I don-' he started, but stopped when she turned without warning and slammed his silver letter opener into the space on the couches arm and right between his fingers. He swallowed. Her aura burned briefly blue, and then shifted back to calming green.

'I'll be doing the asking. You'll be doing the answering.' she purported, and then passed him a china cup of tea. He wondered if she had any other weapons that he couldn't see. She took her seat again and sipped daintily.

'So why did you kill my parents?' she asked, as if discussing the weather. He blinked.

'They told me to. I respected your father. I had no wish to do it. It was an order.' he answered and cursed his own, traitorous tongue. She pinched the bridge of her nose and hung her head a little. She was upset, confused...volatile.

'Why were you ordered to kill him?' she asked.

'Not just him. Your mother, you. I assume because of their experiments.' he answered. A bead of sweat on his brow. He had no control of his tongue, it was like she had somehow accessed his brain without the rest of him being present...with a potion. It was exactly like what a Soulstealer would do, minus the drugs. He'd have been proud if he wasn't so scared.

'What experiments?' she asked, her eyes snapping back to him. If looks could kill...

'They were trying to cure the blight, they said. There were fifty-nine of us unaccounted for. The Alchemist Guild sanctioned the experimentation...on live subjects. We went to war to stop them. The riot was a cover story for a planned assassination. It wasn't just your family. There were others.' he explained. He wondered if he had the guts to cut out his own tongue with the letter opener, but almost as if she heard him thinking it she leaned over and pulled it from the leather. He watched her, half-wary, half in love.

'Why didn't you kill me?' she asked, almost sadly...like maybe she regretted the fact. He frowned.

'I couldn't. You were just a kid. You didn't even know what was happening. I convinced my superiors to let you join the program instead.' he replied quietly, trying to stifle out the sound of his own voice. It didn't matter now anyway, she was halfway to transformed and she could probably hear his thoughts...she had healed him for goodness sake. The process was unchangeable regardless of whether or not she left the island...he had just wanted so badly for her to stay. 'What program?' she inevitably asked. He gave a mental sigh as his lips betrayed him yet again.

'Our own experiments. Mixing the magic's. Changing the course of history...Mixing the blood.'

'Mixing the blood.' she repeated. She pulled up the sleeve of her forever trembling left hand, where a scar ran the length of her wrist. 'You cut too deep. You caught the nerve.' she mumbled, mostly to herself.

'I was in a hurry. There were others to find.' he answered.

'Others? How many others?' she asked, fear ringing out in her voice. More than one like her? More than one that could heal a dead thing and keep their species from dying off like it was meant to?

'There are six of you. We lost the hunter. There's a mage, a Shaman, a witch, you and a Shapeshifter.' he said, looking at his feet. 'The others are here. They're two floors down. That child you saw is the mage.' he explained. For a while she didn't say anything. Then she finished her tea and set it aside.

'And how could you possibly be old enough to do all of this?' she asked, already suspecting the answer. He chuckled, mirthlessly.

'I'm dead remember. I've been dead a very long time. I look like this because this is how I looked at the time that they killed me.' he explained. She squinted at him, her bad humour forgotten over her curiosity. 'One only achieves true power after death.' he recited. She looked at him, her face sinking back to unreadable.

'You were going to kill me.' she concluded in realisation.

'Only once we knew you would heal us.' he affirmed. She suddenly understood what had happened, and gave a humourless laugh of her own...'you're not supposed to be here.' Marcus had said.

'I was supposed to find you and heal you, that's why Marcus attacked you. Godsdammit but that's the stupidest thing I ever heard. If it had failed you would be dead.' she pointed out.

'Aren't I dead anyway?' he asked, pessimistically. She seemed to consider for a moment. The woman inside growled her anger behind her eyes...but on the surface she didn't want his blood on her hands...not when she wanted to do a few 'experiments' of her own.

'How did you summon me here?' she asked, turning the silver letter opener in her hands. Without realising she had cut into the tip of her finger. She didn't even flinch, just kept spinning the little blade. He gulped.

'Marcus is a master of blood magic. I have samples of your blood from back then. They are in the desk drawer over there. Take them with you when you go and he won't be able to bring you back.' he said. She narrowed her eyes. The potion she had fed him was designed to make him tell the truth, not to make him help her.

'Why are you helping me?' she asked, dubiously. He raised an eyebrow.

'Because...' he started, and then wondered what his tongue was going to say. 'I care about you. You are the single good thing I ever did with my life. I want you to live. Also if you turn right at the end of the corridor you'll get to the servants stairs...and there's something else you should know Abby-' he blurted.

'You don't get to call me that.' she snapped at him. He looked up from his shoes to catch her wipe a tear away. This was it, wasn't it. The culmination of nearly ten years worth of work...about to kill him and walk out the door.

'There never was a sealing spell...it's in you. The magic I mean. It's already in your aura.' he whispered, afraid of what she might do next. She stood suddenly, and whirled on him, the blade in her hands. He didn't move. Whatever she was going to do he probably deserved it.

'It's alright, Abby- Abigail.' he told her gently, as she brought the little knife up to his throat and rested it there. 'I forgive you.' he said gracefully, and covered her hand with his own. He pulled her towards him until the blade bit into his skin, and closed his eyes, keeping his breathing steady, waiting for her to finish the job. Instead, she let go of her grip and backed away from him, leaving the letter opener in his hands.

'Keep the truth potion in the jug there, you'll need it to prove your innocence.' she said in a voice that he could hardly even hear. She crossed to the desk, opened the top drawer and gaped at the contents. Then she took the whole thing out and emptied it roughly into the fire. The bottles of blood hissed and spat, sizzling into oblivion on the hot wood. She stared at him a solid second and then turned abruptly and headed towards the door. She was going to leave him there.

'Two floors down?' she asked him as her foot brushed Marcus. He nodded.

'And seventeen total to get out of here. Don't get caught.' he urged, struggling because of the lump in his throat. He watched her walk away, open the door and close it, without even a backwards glance. He closed his eyes and listened to the sound of her soul retreating. Good luck to her, she would need it to get out of here. He knew he should send for help but instead he held his silence, and quietly poured himself another cup of tea. When they arrived he would feign innocence, pretend he was sleeping...nobody would think to doubt the word of Lord Wreather...except himself perhaps. Why had he helped her? Why was he helping her now? Why did he care? Why did the thought of her lying cold and dead on his slab turn his stomach? Where had the desperate need to possess her soul, to being her here to be with him...where had that gone? What had she done to him? He sipped his fresh cup of un-tainted tea and watched the flames rise, having recovered from their dose of blood. After a while he felt she was safely on the stairs and descending, and he reached out a silent, final command to Lorne.

'Go with her. Get her off the island, and you will be freed.' he told her urgently. Somewhere in the building his slave pricked back her ears and went about his command. He paused at the thought...he had *slaves*?...

...What the *hell* did she do?

And deep down, in the darkest recesses of Aaron Wreather's chest...his dusty, aged heart gave a single, solitary beat.

Chapter 38

Abigail took the stairs two at a time, slowed to pass a black robed Lord and then hurried on again. At the corner she stopped dead. Why was there a Lord on the servants stairs? She turned slowly, very slowly, aware that there was someone breathing behind her.

The Lord looked at Abigail and Abigail looked at the Lord. He was unkempt, unshaven and sweating profusely in his heavy black robes. They both knew the other shouldn't be there, the question was...what did they do about it? Abigail blinked, then opened her eyes to a dagger in her shoulder and the pain of a thousand hot needles up and down her arm. Her attacker closed in. Abigail stifled a cry and stumbled back the three steps to slide down the wall. There were footsteps approaching – a woman's pale face. 'Lorne run!' she breathed.

'Lady Abigail?' asked Lorne, and leaned over her. The world made an interesting pattern of blue and yellow spots as she tried to see the man over her shoulder. He had paused, a tiny crossbow drawn and aimed at the back of Lorne's head.

'Don't...' she struggled to say. Then, when the Lord behind the servant lowered the tiny crossbow, she tried unsuccessfully to pull the dagger out. She coughed, tasted blood in her mouth and swooned as her strength faded.

'She's a healer, isn't she?' queried an unfamiliar male voice. Her brain niggled at her.

That's Stephen's crossbow.

He gripped the dagger and pulled and she bit through her tongue to stop herself crying out. There had been enough noise out here already...they were going to be coming for them. She lunged for the Lord whilst he was still gripping the dagger and she should be screaming.

'What did you do to him..?' she croaked, her hand instinctively covering the wound in her shoulder. It was already healing, now that the blade had been removed, but it still hurt while it closed...though the pain was more of a relieved one than an acute one. The stars started fading back into the night-time colours of the hallways that she had become accustomed to.

'I didn't do anything to anybody, not yet. You're Abigail Jones. We met once a long time ago, when you were very little. My name is Cobol. Perhaps you remember me?' he tried. He ran a hand over his face to wipe away the perspiration from climbing fifteen flights and assaulting a teenager. 'Sorry about that.' he apologised genuinely, and hefted the dagger.

'And where is Stephen?' she asked, looking at the man's hunter leathers and wondering at his disguise whilst Lorne fussed around her fast diminishing wound. She locked eyes on the man. She was ready to fight if she had to.

'He's about a mile offshore with Asa, Greer and your druid friend. He's waiting.' he said quickly. She looked from the crossbow to the man's eyes.

'Shit.' she swore softly.

'Excuses me?' he asked, not sure he had heard properly.

'You're the hunter. You're the hunter. ha. Of course you are. Did you know there are others?' she asked. He looked confused.

'Other what?' he asked. She pulled up her sleeve and showed him a scar on her wrist that was almost identical to his own.

'Others.' she gestured, her clear green eyes locking his feet to the spot.

'He made more.' he stated. She gave a nod. She picked herself slowly off the ground and tried to arrange her robes so that there wasn't an obvious, bloody. tare in them. 'Put your robe back on. We're going to get them and get out of here.' she commanded, speaking with the air of a woman who was born to give orders. He tilted his head at her.

'Can't.' he responded. 'Not while he's still alive.' He turned his back and headed up the stairway, wiping the blood from the dagger on his leg as he went.

'No.' Abigail said – no – demanded. Cobol stopped, turned back to her and regarded her squarely.

'He took my life from me.' he asserted.

'No he didn't. You're still walking and talking.' she replied without missing a beat. The hunter screwed up angry eyes.

'Why defend him? He got to you too.' he argued. 'What do you know? You're still alive.' and turned again.

'The Lord Aaron Wreather murdered both of my parents and left me to die in the dirt. You think I don't hate him? You think I didn't want

him dead?' she snapped. She climbed the few stairs between them and all but spat in his face. 'I just healed the man. They fucking tricked me into it and I did exactly what they wanted like an absolute fool – but I healed that man. And that man? The Lord Aaron Wreather? He does not exist any longer. He stopped existing the second his heart started beating again. And if you want me to do the same for you, Cobol, I suggest you take your are down those stairs and help me get the others out of here...because if I managed to control myself long enough to not kill the sorry bastard then there is absolutely no chance I am letting you undo all of my good work.' she finished, an inch from his face and white with fury. He felt his mouth fall open...she had...healed him...and his heart was beating? 'He's alive? Like, properly alive?' he questioned in disbelief.
'We don't have time for this.' she said. 'But yes. And can we go please? If Lorne gets caught with us she'll be murdered.' she added, giving the servant a worried glance. The girl stood off to the side and with a straight back, now that there seemed to be no danger – exactly as she had seen her a hundred times in Aaron's employ.
'We can't take her, he can use her eyes.' argued the hunter.
'She's coming.' said Abigail. 'As soon as we are off the island he will free her.'
'You think.' corrected Cobol.
'I know.' she retorted with a heavy sigh. She didn't know if she liked this hunter. He was sharp, and quite good looking in a rugged sort of way, but he was arrogant, and she was too comfortable being the arrogant one in any given relationship.
        They descended the next flight in silence once Cobol was back in his disguise. He tried to give her the crossbow but she refused.
'Here.' she said, and pushed open a door. A brown robed initiate looked up, startled. Abigail had a lie ready, but unfortunately the light of recognition dawned in the man's eyes...he obviously knew her from her time on the bucket. Before he could exclaim Cobol shot out with the dagger once again, and the man clutched at it, as it dug home into his throat.
'Wow. I'm glad you didn't do that to me.' she said coldly.
'You're a lady...I think.' he answered. Blood poured from the man's clasped hands to cascade all over the stone floor. It was a whole ten seconds before he fell to his knees and thus forward, until he lay in a

growing pool of his own gore. Abigail crossed to his body and twisted the dagger free with a bit of a struggle. She wiped it on her robes and tossed it to Cobol, who watched her with hard eyes. There was something...irreverent in her treatment of the body. She turned him onto his back and patted his pockets until she pulled out a set of keys. She held them up like they were a prize and smiled enthusiastically. Then she turned and walked away up the hall. The other two hurried to catch her, skirting the body as they went.

The first door they came to she would see in her nightmares for evermore. She passed it without comment, but Cobol peeked in to see an empty cell in a guards room, a steel bucket discarded, upturned, in the cage. Lorne followed the other two quietly as they walked on. Before they reached the second room the air thickened with smoke. Abigail screwed up her eyes whilst Cobol stepped in front of her, and sensed.

'Magic.' he uttered. Unsurprised, Abigail approached the door. She couldn't see anything through the little eye hole and so she chapped delicately.

'I'm going to come in. Don't be frightened. We're here to help you.' she called through the opening. She listened. She didn't need Cobol to tell her that the little girl was sobbing on the other side of the door. She pushed it inwards and ducked as what looked like a flaming arrow shot over her head and singed Cobol's hair on the way past. He tried to get past Abigail and into the room to fight whatever the threat was but she stopped him, her arm solidly across the door.

'It's alright. You remember me? I'm here to let you out and take you home...you want to go home? Then please don't hurt us...we're friends.' she soothed the child that Cobol couldn't see. He hung back with Lorne whilst Abigail stepped timidly into the room. There were a few clicks, the sound of a door creaking on its hinges, and then Abigail appeared, holding the hand of a very young girl.

'This is Amber. Amber this is Cobol, and this is Lorne. And we are playing a game to see who can be the quietest, OK?' she asked softly. The girl wiped at tears and gave a brave, exhausted smile. Cobol grimaced, he had a sudden image of himself fireman's-lifting a small child through a dark forest.

'We need to go.' Lorne suddenly announced. 'They are trying to get into the room.' she turned pale blue eyes to Abigail and spoke in a monotone voice. 'Marcus is blocking the door.' she finished. Abigail gave a deep breath.

'One more.' she pleaded.

'You must leave.' said Lorne in her strange, possessed voice. Abigail looked at the two of them, and then bolted down the corridor. They had no option but to follow her. The next room had no air of magic to it, and she hurried with the door and then entered to see an old man, grey and bleeding out all over the floor. She swore, then dived into the room and fiddled with the lock until it clicked. She swung the door wide.

'Here to help, go with him.' she addressed the man, and then she ran off again.

'Abigail!' Cobol hissed as she passed. She ran out of the door and further along the corridor. There was magic in the air, magic that sealed out her power as she approached. It was an odd feeling, like your blood pressure suddenly hitting rock bottom or the ground beneath you falling suddenly away. She was cut off from her ability completely. She reached the door and put her hands on the barred window there.

'Hey. I don't have time to free you, you should get out while they are chasing us.' she stage-whispered to the back of the old woman's head. She turned bright eyes inside her protective circle and watched as Abigail squeezed her hand through the bars and threw the keys so that they clattered against the bars of her cage. 'I'm sorry.' she added. The witch turned her silvery head of long hair back towards the opposite wall, but otherwise did not move. She hadn't reached the Shaman but she was out of time. Cobol and Lorne were helping the Shapeshifter through the open door and she bolted ahead of them, grabbed the girl and scooped her up and ran ahead to get the next door for them. Without any further trouble they were back out on the staircase and hobbling downwards....one flight, three flights, ten flights. At fourteen flights Lorne glossed over again.

'They're in.' she said to Abigail, who nodded and set the girl down.

'They're going to come soon.' she told Cobol.

'Yeah I got that,' he answered, out of breath. 'We're a half hour away if we keep up the pace. We should be able to outrun them.'

'I have to heal him.' she forewarned, and pointed to the still-bleeding Shapeshifter.

'Just...leave...me.' the old man panted.

'Oh hell no.' said Cobol and Abigail simultaneously. They exchanged a glance but didn't stop.
'Wait till we get to the trees then.' Cobol told her, and she nodded her agreement.
'No...' groaned the older man.
'Shut up.' growled the hunter, and Abigail grinned...because maybe she did like him after all.

Chapter 39

Once they reached the tree line they stopped, not far from the house Cobol had visited earlier. They lowered the stricken man to the ground and Abigail got to work. Cobol struggled out of the heavy black robe and curled it into a ball, then he launched it as far into the trees as his arm would let him. The healer was on the ground, glowing green from the hands and in some sort of trance where her eyes flickered but no-one was home. As a horn blasted loud from the higher regions of the Temple he knew they were out of time. He drew his crossbow instinctively, sneered at the size of it and stalked to the edge of the trees, where he peered back towards the steps nervously.
'Hurry up.' he hissed over his shoulder. He checked the bow was loaded and ready, and then fixed his gaze on the stairs.
'Oh...' came Abigail's voice from behind. He risked a glance to see her stumble backwards a little, holding her head.
'You OK?' he asked, a little concerned about how many people he was going to have to carry out of there.
'Yeah...dizzy.' she answered. Lorne was splashing water in the Shapeshifter's face, trying to wake him. Amber gave a frightened little sob and clung to the healer's legs. She patted her flame red hair with one hand and pinched the bridge of her nose with the other.
'Right, get him up, we're going.' urged Cobol. The bad feeling in his stomach was rising. Five people couldn't escape a pack of hounds as easily as a solitary hunter. Could the rowing boat hold five? They were going to find out soon enough. He grabbed the old man by the lapels and pulled him upright, Abigail passed the kid to Lorne and helped her heave him up by the shoulders.
'We're jogging.' he told her, and she laughed. She had very little strength left after that heal and he knew it...but she wasn't saying anything, and that told him everything he needed to know. With a grunt they had the man suspended between them, and were back off on their way again.

They hadn't gone five minutes when the healer stumbled. Cobol stopped abruptly and stared at her.

'You, what's your name? Yeah you. Take her place.' he addressed Lorne. The still-a-slave did as she was ordered despite Abigail's protests.

'I can do it.' she pleaded, but relinquished her share of the weight to the other woman. The Shapeshifter was skinny, and didn't weigh that much...but she was tired, and weak, and it had been the second longest day of her life. She took Amber by the hand in exchange and the mad pace resumed. After another five minutes the hunter himself slowed a little, and then quickened to the extreme. A few minutes later Abigail heard what he had. There was a howling on the wind. She gasped, and would have frozen to the spot had Amber not turned innocent eyes up at her in question. She didn't want to scare her, so in spite of the images of gore and blood and death in the night that flooded her mind, she smiled her most reassuring smile, and patted the girls hand.

'Not long now.' she chirped to the girl in a light voice. Amber smiled happily and skipped along beside her, the only one of them who had any energy left. She ignored the reproachful look that Cobol shot her. She had to keep the girl happy or she started shooting fire arrows...it might be interesting if the hounds caught up but she didn't fancy taking the chance with an untamed mage. The girl was a project for Asa if ever she saw it...and until they reached him she was taking no chances.

After fifteen full minutes had passed Cobol grunted and pushed forward with renewed effort. They were still a good way off, but they were making better time than he had on his own...probably on account of the speed. They were tired, and breathing hard, and even Amber had started to suffer, her exhaustion from earlier plain on her face. He redoubled his efforts because the hounds had entered the trees, and his senses prickled up and down his spine like someone had poured cold water on him. It was simply a matter of time now, and whether or not they had enough of it. He hoped, but as the minutes passed the hope started to fade. They weren't close enough...but they could still try...and if the worst came to the worst they would fight. He would fight. He was not going back to their cages...never, ever again.

Chapter 40

Howard Willis opened his eyes and wondered at the fact that he was moving. Someone was dragging him- two 'someone's'...What mattered was that he was out of the damned cell and they were taking him off the island. As soon as his feet started working again he tried to carry his own weight.

'Hey.' greeted a girl with red brown hair off to his left. She had the little girl with her, the one that stank of smoke. 'You awake?' she asked . He screwed up his forehead as he identified her as the woman who had been flicking in and out of his dreams.

He cleared his throat to tell them that he was, and that they could stop carrying him, when he caught the smell on the wind. Hounds. They had set the dogs on them. Slowly, his memory returned. Howard Willis shrugged his two helpers free and slowed to a stop. He turned an ear towards the howl...two hundred yards and closing...seven of them, one man...

'Go.' he told the others, and did not stop to watch their reaction, because he did not have time. He turned to wolf, regardless of his clothing, and bounded off into the trees. Abigail stared after him, her knees weak. She had never seen Greer shift before, not like that, and the contracting and reshaping of body parts had frightened her more than Estora had. Cobol's hand on her shoulder, giving her a rough push, knocked her back to herself.

'We need to keep going.' he told her. She nodded and followed him towards the shore. After a moment she dashed back and scooped up the remnants of the old mans clothes, because Greer always complained about having no clothes left, and then followed the annoyed Cobol and the others at a run. Another ten minutes and they would be safe on board and on their way out of here...That was if Stephen had hung around.

A hundred yards behind them the huge, dark shape that cut a path through the dead foliage edged closer to the pack. They were blue eyed, all. Sick and sniffling and feeling their way around the island with their blind eyes. They were disgusting, and they were pathetic. Any fool knows that a dog hunts with its sense of smell. What use was a pack under your control if you tried to hunt using their eyes? The Soulstealers were a stubborn race, forever refusing to bend to any other species' parameters. That's why nobody wanted to ally with them. That's why they had to steal people right out of their own homes in the middle of the night. Howard Willis had a wife out there in the lands beyond. He'd had a pack, and a family, and he had belonged. And then they had brought him here, to this place of death and darkness and hopelessness. He burned with a fury that could only be satiated with blood, and in that moment he believed with all of his heart that he would kill them all if he had to, but he was getting back to his mate alive. There was no question in his mind, not with his newly healed body and the seemingly boundless energy he felt. He hadn't felt this good in a long time, in fact, and he was desperate to unleash himself in the fray.

  The black wolf landed in the middle of the pack and gnashed his teeth in sheer joy. The one he landed on died as he tore its throat free and shook it ragged so that it flew from his grip to land across the clearing somewhere. He had the next by the back leg and yanked until he felt flesh tare. The third nipped his hind quarters as he reared on his back legs and flattened the forth, and the second limped away slowly on three legs. He went in for the killing blow, a quick rip in the throat, and then spun on the third. He was not quite quick enough, and had to spin again to avoid the fifth hound, who had seen the opportunity and taken it. The wolf was outnumbered, and so he ran towards the sloping tree he had leaped from once already and landed behind them. The third and fifth were not as fast as he after all, and they went down beneath his claws and teeth and in a shower of blood droplets. By the time he had finished with those two the remaining two dogs had witnessed their fate and chased the second dog into the woods to hide. Howard panted. He could go after them, but there might be more danger lurking in the shadows. He had been careless enough for one night...too careless, he realised, as the snap of twigs behind him was the only alert he got before the sharp pain burst all around his strong hip muscles. The wolf whined, and turned to get a whiff of man scent. He had forgotten about the man. He gave a yelp as he limped off into the trees towards the others, the dagger still lodged in his haunches. The man came after him, he heard his indelicate, crunching steps on the slippery forest floor.

  In the cold, misty darkness of an Estoran night the wolf nipped at his hindquarters in an effort to free the blade. He fought not to pass out from the pain as he wrenched it out, spitting his own blood away as he did so. The crunching noises came closer, closing on him, one man without his pack. One wolf without his pack either. Run or fight, run or die. He picked himself up and limped ever onwards towards the shore and the smell of friends...knowing in his soul that today would be the day that he died.

Chapter 41

K'rella La Marquette; fortune teller, herbalist, tarot reader, hedge-witch and part-time pickpocket, gripped the metal in her hand until it pierced the skin and her palm began to bleed. Excellent. The dragonroot was wearing off and she was done here...she had found what she had come for, and she didn't like it one bit. It was time to go home.

For a woman like K'rella life wasn't just difficult...it was straight up confusing. When she had been eighteen she had finished her apprenticeship and gone on to find her own village, with her own hut and her own group of terrified children who threw stones at the local 'witch'. But that wasn't difficult, no, that was just part of the job. What was difficult was dealing with the time lapse. The problem was, you see, that time was one solid block on the outside, but fluid and moving on the inside...just like K'rella. She had floated in the Other worlds, she had seen the whole of time as a concept, and she had gotten permanently scrambled as to where she fitted into it all in her physical self. Effectively, she was 'all there'...just in different places.

Right now she was in a whole lot of trouble. The smell of blood floated to her, everywhere was shouting and noise...the smell of smoke, at least, was fading. A stranger had come to check on her, and found her sitting in her circle, as always. When she was in the circle she was chained to her body, she couldn't float free and get lost in the past, she couldn't spend so long in the Other worlds that she forgot to feed her physical self...but someone had broken the bubbled. Someone had wakened her. There was a young girl who was still alive in this place...and she had broken the spell long enough to pull K'rella back into her body, only to find that she was still on this Gods-forsaken island. Ah well, time to do something about that...now that she couldn't feel the cursed blood link any longer. She opened one eye and peered about her, just to double check. No, she was still in the circle. She was definitely too early this time around. Which meant she still had to-wait. She was getting confused again. She needed more dragonroot. She would get some from the Shaman...maybe. Unless she was late.

K'rella splashed the welled pool of blood across her salt barrier and felt an astral version of herself peel away. Good. Whilst the barrier was broken the sealing spell on the rest of the room went down, and then she had just a few seconds to work. She let the blood run down her finger until it threatened to drip off the tip, and then used it to mark the sacred symbol of teleportation on the floor. The men outside must have felt her spell weaken, since one of them was rattling the key in the lock in an effort to get in. K'rella grimaced because she hated this part. While grasping the keys firmly in one hand she reached her other out and touched the symbol. She focused her thoughts, thinking only of mountaintops, open plains and freedom, and then she pushed her thoughts downwards and into the symbol. Her stomach lurched, she heard the door open, she heard a man shout incomprehensibly – and when she opened her eyes she knelt in water on a rocky beach. The voices were gone, the man was gone, the iron bars were gone. She smiled the smile of a witch well satisfied and toddled off towards the trees. The boat was here somewhere...it was just a question of memory.

After he had been gone for approximately two hours the smell of salt filled the air and the noise of the waves drifted to them through the stillness of the mists. Cobol took his bearings and then swerved north. He sought the tree-stump he had used as a marker for his hiding place, sighted it after a few more panicked minutes of exhausted jogging, and tore off towards the little boat's hiding place, leaving the others struggling to catch up. Abigail reached the hunter first, free of the child-shaped encumbrance that Lorne had, and found him pacing frantically whilst carrying a broken and bare tree branch. She caught her breath, her hands on her knees. She was at the end of her strength...the very end. She didn't even think she had enough left to drag the boat to the water. They were so close she could taste it...her freedom was out on the waves and edging as near as they dared in the dark, treacherous waters...all they had to do was reach them.

'The Godsdamned boats gone! The boats gone!' he fumed. He threw the branch so that it smacked hard off a tree and shattered into three pieces.

'So we swim.' she gulped, suddenly sure they were all going to die. He looked at her accusingly, as if he had overheard her thoughts...she would have gulped had she not been so parched.

'Do you always say one thing and think another?' he asked, his aggression momentarily turned to her. She pointedly thought about all of the reasons why he shouldn't blame her just because *he* had lost the boat. He scowled. 'Besides, I can't swim.' he admitted, a little colour touching his cheeks.

'Neither can I.' said Lorne.

'Me either.' added Amber.

'*Seriously?*'asked Abigail. 'You own a boat! And *you* live on an island!' she exclaimed, pointing at the hunter and Lorne. Amber was ten, and therefore excused. If they made it out of here alive *everyone* was getting lessons.

There was a cackling. An actual cackling. Louder than the waves and cutting the night to bounce off the bare branches of the doomed forest and echo around in the night. As one, the group stopped, and looked at each other.

'What...was...that..?' asked Abigail slowly, and in no more than a whisper.

'I think it came from the beach...' said Lorne. Cobol had already closed his eyes and was sensing outwards, reaching with his sense of smell and hearing...there was howling behind, a stranger in front...water lapping on wood...he weighed threats. He snapped back to himself and grabbed Abigail by the arm.

'This way, someone is stealing our ride!' he called out as he dragged her, running yet again, towards the beach.

Chapter 42

Stephen watched, his jaw on the floor, as the old woman dragged the boat, an inch at a time, down the cobbled beach. He lowered the eyeglass.
'I don't know what to say.' he contributed, and passed it to Greer. She looked, lowered it and passed it wordlessly to Liandor, who in turn gave it back to Asa. At least Asa gave a chuckle.
'Is she...stealing my raft?' asked Peirs, wondering if his day could get any worse.
'I go?' asked Liandor, ready to swim it to stop her. Asa shook his head and gave a belly laugh.
'She too small for oars.' he pointed out, and indeed she was. The little old lady had no chance of piloting the craft anywhere; she wouldn't have the strength to paddle both oars at once and she would end up lost at sea or limping in a circle.
'Wait.' said Asa, putting a hand on Liandor's arm. The wood elf was already halfway over the railings and almost ready to jump in. Stephen frowned at him, and turned to the old lady. What did they do about her? It's not like they could go over there and fight her...across the waves the woman had reached the water, and he watched her drag the little boat until its nose rested in the water and then climb inside. There she waited, patiently, hands folded on her lap, as if she were about to be taxied over on magical winds. She stayed in the boat, and Stephen stayed confused. It was a further full ten minutes before another figure emerged from the trees at high speed. He was dragging someone- he grabbed the eyepiece out of Peirs disgruntled hands and held it up.
'It's them! It's them!' he declared, and hugged Greer only to be immediately embarrassed by the act. He all but jumped up and down on the spot. 'It's them.' he told her, and she gave him a toothy grin that told him not to do that again. An unfamiliar mix of scents floated to her on the wind before Lorne and Amber came into view. And she frowned towards the beach.
'Can you take us any closer?' she asked the trader, already knowing they had come as close as they could get. The man confirmed her suspicions and went back to brooding silence. He was just waiting to get caught and lose his trading rights here...or perhaps, judging by

the noise of the battle horns in the distance, they would skip banning him from their shores and go straight to death.

'Hounds!' proclaimed Stephen, and sure enough they were through the trees and scrabbling over the stones towards the little group, which weren't quite halfway to the boat. Stephen swore and cursed his helplessness. Again, Asa grabbed Liandor to stop him jumping. 'Wait.' he demanded again, this time adding the dominance of a man not to be argued with. They watched, helpless, as their friends turned as one to face their foes.

Abigail wrestled the crossbow from Cobol whilst he was still furiously trying to wrap his mind around the old lady, who appeared to be sitting in the boat and waiting for them.

'It's the witch!' she shouted to him as she spun and fired. A dog went down under the bolt. 'If I ever needed this to work it was now...' she said to herself and between gritted teeth. She lined up another shot and took it, and sure as rain falls an unloaded bolt slammed into another hound, taking it in the leg at a run and sending it tumbling over to trip up a third. There were still four incoming, and she was still terrified. She lined up a third shot and closed her eyes on her target. The snorting, the fangs, the drool...the sheer size. Nightmare dogs, just like from her nightmare memories. Behind her Lorne, Amber and Cobol had reached the boat and were loading in so she started to step back. She fired again, this time getting a good look at the bolt. It was dark wood, so dark it looked black in the already poor light. It seemed to smoke a little, and left a trail through the air as it flew. She filed the information away for later...she was too busy to panic and it was probably something to do with her infected blood. The thought of Aaron Wreather gave her a renewed vigour, and she sent another dog tumbling before she risked a glance over her shoulder. Cobol was pushing the boat the last of the way into the water, and she had about five seconds to get there. The last of the hounds were limping in circles, backless, or nuzzling at their dead friends. She turned and took two steps before the howl from behind froze her to the spot. The howl was long, high-pitched and drawn out under the moonless sky. She trembled, because she had *felt* it...accompanied by a sharp, tearing pain in her hip. The fear, the knowledge that she was going to die, the anger and pain – all wrapped up in one long, drawn out heartbeat. Cobol and she locked eyes for the briefest of moments, and then she turned and ran for the trees, past the milling hounds and off into the direction of the danger. On the boat Cobol glanced towards the ship in the distance, grunted at the others to wait, and then followed.

Twenty yards into the dead forest Abigail swung the bow up and took another shot at a single hound. She kept alert, kept moving, kept looking...he was here somewhere. In pain and bleeding out on the floor. She didn't know where, she just kept firing her imaginary (but deadly) arrows and moving forward, not stopping to consider the noise of shouting ahead, nor the baying on the breeze. She focused only on the pain, and before long came to a stop and turned in a circle. There – behind a fallen, decaying log and not moving – a solitary, dirty foot stuck out. She ran to it and had no time to be embarrassed at the Shapeshifter's nakedness. There was a gaping wound oozing on his hip, and she suddenly realised she didn't have the energy to heal him again, let alone drag him back to the boat. 'Lift his arms.' growled the hunter behind her. She jumped, having not heard a single step he had taken, and then gathered herself enough to do as she was told. Cobol didn't have to ask, the dark circles under her eyes told him all he needed to know. There two options were leave him like he had asked or carry him...and despite his instincts Cobol lifted the man by the bare legs and between them they manhandled him back through the trees. Both of them limping on imaginary hip wounds. Each step they took brought them closer to freedom, but it also brought the hunters closer. There were yet more dogs – every damned Lord on this island must keep dogs – but worse, there were people...or Estorans anyway, and they were getting closer every second. All there was left to do was hope and run...and damned the running...when they got out of there he was going to sit on his ass for a week.

Cobol was the one that stopped. He hadn't been paying close enough attention, he had been too distracted by measuring the distance of the howling and he had missed the obvious...It was hard to detect dead things in a dead forest, even for a hunter. Abigail almost dragged the man from his grip in her effort to keep going. 'Put him down.' he ordered.
'This is no time to be stopping-'
'This is exactly the time to be stopping, miss Jones.' came an unfamiliar voice from the darkness around them. She turned her head frantically but could not see the source of the voice.

'Who-'

'That is of no consequence.' conferred the voice. It was a man, but beyond that she was at a loss. It did not seem to be anyone she knew. 'Put down the Shapeshifter and put your hands in the air.' said the disembodied voice. She looked at Cobol, who gave a wary nod and lowered the man slowly to the ground.

'Good...My Lord Lester will be exceedingly pleased to see you again- and you can lower your weapon, miss Jones, we have you in a pentagram. There is no 'fighting your way out'. ' said the voice. A face appeared, black haired and blue eyed like the rest of Estora and unrecognisable in any other way. She raised an eyebrow.

'Do I know you?' she asked.

'I told you that is irrelevant.' the man replied. There were others now, another four of them, closing in from all sides.

'Well that's just rude.' she answered, curtly.

'What is he doing?' asked the first of the faceless ones. Abigail looked back at Cobol, who was still kneeling on the ground and seemed to be sensing, one hand pressed tight to the dirt. 'Stop doing that!' the man shouted, poison in his voice. He tried to cross to the hunter but Abigail, seeing his intention, moved to block his path. She looked at him, surprised by her own actions, and crossed her arms in front of her chest. The man hit her, moving like a blur to knock her to the forest floor. She stayed where she was and shook her head. The dizziness descended as her body went into auto-heal mode even though it had no more energy to heal itself with. She wondered what would happen to her but could only watch in a daze as the man closed in on Cobol. She swooned, fought it, and struggled but failed to get back on her feet. The man reached the hunter, pulled him up by the scruff of the neck and dragged him to eye level.

'I told you to-' the man thundered, and then stopped short. Abigail gasped at the silver sheen from the hunters eyes, then felt the spell even although it was not directed at her. Cobol had turned the fear, the pain, the rage from the Shapeshifter around and fired it back at them, like some kind of inverse sensing. She swallowed to no effect, her mouth drier than bone, and before she recovered from the shock wave the hunter was dragging her to her feet and pushing her, tripping all the way, back towards the beach. When she came to her reeling senses long enough to look back he had the Shapeshifter lifted over one shoulder, was sweating like a long distance runner and swearing like a trooper.

On the beach the hounds had regrouped, some of them limped but for the most part they bounded from the trees to cut them off. The ground was rocky, and Abigail stumbled every other step. Again she picked herself back up, again she shot a look to Cobol, who was carrying a body and yet somehow still managing to outrun her. She clawed back onto her feet again and felt the hot pain of something hitting her on the back of the head. She pitched forward, not knowing what was happening...did something just shoot her? There was something on her back, something that drooled and slavered and had its teeth resting too deeply into her neck. She froze...finally immobilised by fear or the creature and lack of energy. A rush of wind above her and the pressure ceased...a hound whined and tumbled away like a bowling ball. She watched it with one eye pressed against the stony beach and yelped herself as someone lifted her shoulders and dragged her to her feet. Arrows flew, the boat was close and, as a final, solid goodbye, Asa was in the water. He made a pattern in the air with his hands and then slammed a fist into the earth. Over her shoulder and towards the trees the beach fell away into a hole in the ground, swallowing rocks, trees, dogs and initiates indiscriminately, and then leaking in water from the sea that would inevitably drown them all down there, if they had survived the fall. She gaped in disbelief as strong hands carried her towards the boat. 'Lee?' she breathed, recognising the smell of leaves and wood rather than being able to see his face.

'I have you.' whispered the druid. She leaned her head on his sea-soaked shoulder and regarded her feet abstractly, wondering how they were still moving. Suddenly she was being lifted off them, and Asa's beaming face was smacking her shoulder and squeezing into the boat beside her. She tried to tell them that there wasn't enough room for them all in the little raft, but she didn't suppose it mattered any more, not with most of their hunters under the level of the holy mess Asa had made of their beach.

'She told me later that she had no memory of getting from the raft to the sail boat, nor of getting from the boat to Salston...only of Asa's arm around her shoulder and her certainty that the elf was keeping her alive with his magic somehow. She said it wasn't until she stepped foot on dry, untainted land again that she felt relief...That she came back to herself and knew she was still alive. It was the life energy you see? She had none left, she couldn't even heal herself. Salston meant earth, fresh, nearly clean earth...earth not fully tainted with death like Estora was. Only after she set her feet on dirt again did she start to recover. We nearly lost her that day, but it got us to thinking. What if she did die? Would she? Would she become like Cobol? It was a question none of us ever wanted to know the answer to. Even then, in those days, I was somehow certain that I was going to find out.'

Chapter 43

Abigail heated the mixture in Asa's good copper bowl, she mixed it slowly, stirring with a metal spoon because she wasn't sure a wooden one would survive. Four weeks had gone past since Estora. Four full weeks of questioning, soul searching, accommodating the new arrivals and explaining things to Stephen. Four long weeks, where every day she imagined she was living on borrowed time. They had come back to the caves to an overjoyed Siara and Celeste, complete with small child, old woman and a mercifully free Lorne. The Shapeshifter had chosen to return to the mainland. He had a clan far to the north, and had said goodbye to them in Salston. They had been a full week in the small port, Abigail healing where she had too and spending the rest of the time asleep or in the grip of a strange illness brought on by the energy shift beneath her feet. Things had gone past in a bit of a blur whilst she suffered from the magical equivalent of jet lag, but the end result was the same. They all went home, back to Asa's, where the elf tried to stop Amber burning down his clearing and the old woman clucked from a seemingly happy dragonroot inspired trance. Asa said she'd had too much over the years, and now she was sort of addicted to it. Without it she looked all shrivelled and old, with it she had light in her eyes, and sometimes argued with you about things that hadn't happened yet. The extra's were no problem...the problem was all around her. Inside of her, even. It was in her blood. The same blood, she reasoned, that connected all of them. Blood that had come from Aaron Wreather, that had attached itself to their souls and made them into permanent targets. No matter how hard she tried she could think of no way to sever the link. She would have to take all the blood out of her body, boil it clean or exchange it, and then put it all back in again. Healer or not she would die. Besides, where would she get the resources? She'd gone to discuss the situation with Cobol and found that there was no need. The hunter was well aware of Wreather's grip on them all and bluntly informed her that there was nothing they could do about it...after all, he had been trying for ten years. The good news was that she had destroyed the blood samples and therefore they couldn't summon them again, the bad news was that Aaron Wreather did, and would always, know exactly where they were. The hunter had run far enough, and for long enough, and Abigail had no doubt in mind that he might still hunt the Estoran down just for the revenge of it – but she had other plans. She had made him live again, she had done something new and unheard of...and she needed to maintain a link with him, to see her experiment through to the end. All she had to do was keep Cobol from killing him until then. Another thought had occurred to her late one night, when she had been throwing herself into her work all day to avoid thinking about anything else – that if Estorans could trap their death magic inside a crystal – why couldn't she do the same but with life? Isn't that how Asa made the edelweiss glow? By infusing it with extra earth energy? Except the two were opposites, so it wouldn't be a crystal...hence the potion mix in front of her now. ..all that was left to do was to try and infuse the edelweiss with life, and then grind it down to powder and add it to the mixture. She took the mix off the heat and set it aside for now. It was a herbal suspension, designed to allow the powder she would be left with to dissolve. She had to move quickly though, because the plant matter would melt like candy floss if the suspension was still warm. She put the few stems she had gathered on the work mat and let herself go into what was becoming her regular healing stance, took a few deep breaths and healed. In front of her very eyes the plant stems grew roots and shot out buds on silvery-green stalks that bloomed into icy white, snowflake shaped flowers. Just when she was marvelling at how amazing it was the plant exploded in her face, sending silvery dust into the air all around her. She sneezed, then she took her gloves off and called it a night...because there was such a thing as going too far.

She tried to scrub the powder off of her face and neck in the stream, but she scrub as she might the plant wouldn't come out of her hair. Eventually she resigned herself to having a silver splash in her hair for a while and wondered if Asa was still awake. It was past midnight already, but he hadn't come to say goodnight. She found him around the side of the house, tending to the herbs that still grew in spite of the snow that settled in the branches of the trees. He chuckled when he saw her, the characteristic belly laugh she had grown so fond of so quickly.

'I had an accident with some edelweiss.' she explained. He gave an amused nod and straightened his back out, clicking it back into place and holding it like it hurt him. She had looked at his back, there was nothing wrong with him. She had the sneaking suspicion that he wasn't so old as he made out. He said he was 75, but since (according to Liandor) elves lived twice as long as humans that would make him approximately in his late thirties. She tried not to think about it to much, since by the same approximation that would mean Lee was only about thirteen...and he didn't look like any thirteen year old she'd ever met. She waited for her master to hobble back to the fire with her, where he took a seat and she put the kettle on.

'Elderflower?' she asked, he gave a satisfied shrug, pleased with her progress in the tea department. A true alchemist could be judged by their ability to make tea...it was in the ingenuity, and the patience, and it was a rule Asa lived by. Once the water was on the boil and the teapot ready she waited beside him almost reverentially. It had become a custom of theirs, passed on from Asa's knowledge of the old ways. Whilst the kettle boiled nobody spoke, they would talk only once the tea was made. It was a mark of respect paid from student to teacher, but more than that, it was a chance for guests to gather their thoughts before they spoke. It prevented words cast in anger, it prevented thoughtlessness...and ninety-nine percent of Shamanism was ritual and thoughtfulness. If there is one thing that Asa Lupine did for Abigail Jones, other than the alchemy, other than the magic...it was to teach her a modicum of restraint that nobody, not even Catherine with her beatings and punishments, had thus far been able to drum into her. He taught her patience, and for that the rest of us were eternally grateful.

'What is mmmm problem?' asked Asa, once they were finally settled and happily sipping. The tea was too sweet for his liking, but Abigail always made it too sweet. One day she would have no teeth and the world would have no honey left. She leaned back on the upturned tree stump and sighed.

'The Estorans have a crystal, the iolite. They use it to store energy, and I want to do the same, but with life...only I can't find the right conductor. It doesn't work with earth, or water, I can't get it into any of the plants with them withering, I can't get it into sandstone, or gold, or silver, or steel- what am I doing wrong?' she asked, more to the sky than to Asa. The large elf sipped from his worn clay cup and then produced his pipe, because he tended to smoke when he was thoughtful. Abigail breathed in the scent of spent match and whatever delicate mix of herbal tobacco he was using today and felt the tension go out of her. Elderflower had been the correct choice. After a long while of silent speculation Asa grunted.

'You try the iolite?' he asked her. She shook her head.

'Aaron-' she began and stopped herself. 'He said I would explode. I wanted to try it.'

'hmmm.' pondered Asa, but it wasn't his usual hum, it was more of a concerned sound. He said nothing, but wondered how long it would be before she talked about her time on the island. All of the information they had about her time there had come from Lorne, who seemed to hero worship Abigail as if she were some sort of Goddess...the woman had her freedom now, and there was a happy one...feasting eyes upon blue skies and wondering what, in this beautiful new world, that she could become. The entire expedition had been worth it just to see the power of her oppressors leave her once they reached untainted earth. The smile she had given to the weary party had been worth a thousand words, and it hadn't left her since.

'Opposites.' concluded Asa solemnly.

'That's what I was thinking...but what is the opposite of a crystal?' she asked, lost again. Asa smirked. He leaned over with his pipe in hand and gestured her to come closer. She sat by his feet as he carved a circle in the trodden down earth. He stabbed the circle and wrote a little 'N'

'Is north yes, North is earth. East here, east is air. South is fire, West is water.' he explained whilst she watched, completely in the dark as to where he was going with this.

'mmm Stone, is crystal, is earth....cooked? With fire? So...' he pushed her and waited for an answer.

'So...I want something wet and windy?' she asked. He grinned and slapped her shoulder, nodding.

'No plants.' he said, and shook his head at her as if she were being silly. He picked out the silver bit of her hair and dropped it again, chuckling.

'So...I need something wet, conductive and possibly involving air.' she summarised. She sipped at her tea and thought hard. So it had to conduct, what if she took a metal and heated it into liquid form- no, because that would involve fire again. It was a shame there weren't any fluid metals-

'Asa...do you have a thermometer?' she asked slowly. The Shaman was off in thought, thinking about Ambers lessons the following day and how he couldn't get her to get the hang of commanding her magic at will, and not just sporadically burning down his forest. 'Yes.' he nodded, once he had rejoined the conversation. Abigail thought for a second.

'Do you have more than one? I...think I need to break it.' she explained. He beamed at her and gave a happy nod.

Quicksilver...now why hadn't he thought of that? Oh yes, because it was horribly poisonous...and he wasn't a healer. He had a chuckle to himself as she dashed back to the makeshift lab on her second wind.

In the calm, freezing depths of the Portan night Abigail used the last of her energy to reheat the herbal solution over the open flame. She sat cross legged on the floor by the box-laboratory and laid her forehead, silver hair and all, in her hands. She tried not to fall asleep. Gradually, like dozing on the edge of her dreams, she started to notice a tingling up and down her spine, She looked around her, and thought she was alone until she noticed her own green threads dance and stretch upwards, towards the desk. She narrowed her eyes, squinted into the darkness and saw nothing...she went back to her work, then looked back towards the desk and pulled a face, crossing her eyes and sticking out her tongue. There was a burst of laughter in her head. Not in the room, just in her head. It was Aaron's laughter and she physically forced herself not to sneer. She had assumed it was Amber dreaming again, hence the funny face. She took a deep breath and went back to stirring the mixture. She tried not to look up again, and for a while they stayed in silence. She thought about tea, and what not to say, and he wondered why he had come. He had been sleeping...and here he was.

'How are you feeling?' she asked eventually. He gave a half-hearted laugh.

'Very much alive. Thanks for that.' he answered. She struggled to keep the satisfied grin from her face.

'No symptoms, no pain, nothing like that?' she asked again. When in doubt, fall back to professional. She couldn't outright dismiss him, not when displeasing him risked her entire family...such as it was.

'No pain...' he said carefully. She heard the implication behind the ghost of the words in her ear.

'But?'

'I...Feel.' he tried after a long moment, then cleared his throat. He hadn't confessed it to any of his comrades yet.' Marcus says...' he started, then paused to find the difficult words. 'That there's green in my aura. He said it looked like the soul of a child.'

She had stopped, and was looking in his astral direction, her face unreadable like she so often tried to keep it. Out of courtesy he refrained from skimming through her thoughts. In truth she was in shock, he was reaching out because he was alone on that island, just like he had made her.

'And what do you feel?' she asked eventually. There was another long pause, so long that she sought out the thermometer and shattered it on one end, letting the mercury inside drip free into a copper bowl.

'Lost.' he answered, after an age. He was a little shocked when she let out a laugh.

'Yes, I know that feeling well.' she laughed softly. She put the mercury down and took the mixture from the heat. She felt his presence move around the room until he was behind her, watching her hands.

'Are you doing what I think you're doing?' his ghost voice asked. She nodded her response, she was trying to go into her trance state, but he was making her nervous watching over her shoulder like that. 'Ohhh that's clever.' he breathed. She ignored him and focused her breathing and mind. After a few moments she felt the strength of the earth move through her, up from her roots, deep down in the ground, up through her body and out through her hands. There were no memories held in the stone, no life to heal...just an endless blank canvas that needed painted in green...and the longer she stayed there the greener it became...like grass growing in spring, lush meadow grass that was greener than green.

Aaron pulled her mind back from the empty void with what would have been a slap if he hadn't been ethereal at the time. 'That's more than enough.' he said. His voice was warm, his troubles forgotten, his tone full of awe. She swayed a little and wondered what she was looking at, as if waking from a deep, confusing, sleep. The mercury before her thrummed softly with magic.

'Get a bottle right now, you need to seal it in a vacuum or you'll lose the potency. Abby snap out of it, come on!' Aaron was saying. She followed his instructions in a panicky daze, knowing she was doing something important but not quite sure what it was. She filled the little bottle with the warm mix through a funnel. Once it was full she dropped in a small amount of the mercury and then stopped, realising she had more than enough for two or three potions. She stoppered the first with a wax seal and moved on to the next. She got three in the end, of varying colours. One darker than the rest. She held up the darker potion to the light and marvelled over her creation. A round, perfect droplet of mercury floated in the water, glowing a beautiful silver-green in the dim candlelight of the room. She sat the three bottles on the desk for Asa to look at and started to pack away for the night.

'Abigail. There's going to be a war. You have to get out of there. Take your potion to the Guild.' Aaron whispered gently in her ear, only the haunting of a voice. She frowned.

'What do you mean by war?' she asked, frightened by the fear in his voice. Before he answered there was an acute pain in her forehead, closely followed by the full fury of Cobol's soul crashing into her with all of the delicacy of a grizzly bear. Aaron vanished...or perhaps was kicked out, she wasn't sure which, and was replaced with Cobol's anger in her head until the man himself followed it through the door and into the room.

'What the hell is the matter with you?!' he started...and from there on the night descended into madness.

Epilogue

'There is one last thing I shall tell you, stranger, before the night around us gets any colder.' The old man piped up after he'd been silent and stock still for a full twenty minutes. I had finished scratching quill to paper long since, and was flexing my aching wrist. The sun had gone down hours before, and a cool breeze came with the moon. There were mosquitoes everywhere, and the pair of us huddled closer and closer to the fire as his tale had worn on. By now we were almost eye to eye, and his sudden announcement had jolted my wits. He took a deep, reluctant breath.

'The story continues with Elena Whitbrack, back in Beeton and in the sanctity of her own kitchen.' he continued. I picked up the quill again, and hoped I had enough ink left...and then he went on.

Elena baked the most fabulous, beautiful, dazzling black forest gateaux cake she'd ever made in her life. Catherine had given her carte blanch on the menu, and she had gone all out, not hesitating to spend the bosses gold on imported berries and fresh churned cream.

'Nothing but the best!' the mistress had ordered...and she had been glad to comply. She had a spiced pumpkin soup, a starter of fresh, hand-dived scallop and aged, smoked bacon. She had a full side of bream for the fish platter, charred beef with a honeyed crust for the meat and a half a roast pig for the third option. There were vegetables that the garden couldn't grow in this weather, there were buttered mounds of mash potato, steamed rice sent from the warmer climes (she'd had to read how that one got cooked) and every kind of fruit to be found in the Bay's market at this time of the year. The reason? Royalty was coming to Freisch. Royalty was coming, apparently, right to her very own dining room.

Servants scattered when she finished putting the alcohol-soaked cherries on the masterpiece that lay in front of her and stepped back with a flourish. Everywhere maids applauded, but a heartbeat later people scurried to work and busyness ensued. The single exception was Eric, the kitchen boy. At eleven years old he was learning to be cheeky as they came. He was the son of a farmer in the town, and he only helped her out when it was busiest. With a spit out back and the oven on full blast she needed all the help she could get. He gaped at the cake with hungry, longing eyes and watched her every move until she crossed to the larder. She covered the cake with a silver tin and smiled slyly to herself. She was not a stupid woman. She knew that as soon as her attention was elsewhere the boy would stick his fingers in there, just for a taste. But Catherine wanted perfection, and she couldn't risk it...so just this one time...

She sat the mini-version of the cake she had made down for the boy and beamed at the glee on his face as he swung his legs and tucked in. She laughed as he screwed up his face and spat out a half-chewed, alcoholic cherry, but happily munched on the rest. She made the last of her preparations in peace from the boy, and welcomed the final, eventual arrival of the Royal Prince.

Royalty arrived late and with a large entourage, it also arrived with a letter of regret on Prince Marius behalf and a request to house his associates and some of their cargo for a few days. Chests were brought forth, two gilded ones for Catherine to spend at her leisure and another twenty wooden ones to be stored in the cellar. The cargo was nothing but salt chips taken from one of the royal mines nearby, and would be shipped as soon as the Prince established a trade route. He was very sorry, the letter said, but urgent affairs in the Capital required his attention. He hoped they could enjoy another meeting soon. The letter was enough to set Catherine's cheeks ablush and to make her usher the entourage inside, where rooms were freshened hastily and fires were lit in long empty fireplaces. There were three Lords left after a very, very successful meal. The others dissipated into carriages and merged with the night outside. In the night the servants came, a small army of glassy-eyed, black haired and silent figures, who lifted the heavy salt chests into the long since disused cellar. Elena watched all from the kitchen, the maids, stable hands and even Hugh Clarence in tow. 'What do you suppose is in them?' asked Eric from apron height. She cuffed him into silence.

'They said it was salt...' contributed Clarence, although he didn't believe it either.

'Maisie said it was blue, blue crystals. Salt ain't blue. Salt's white.' pointed out Rachel, the ladies maid. 'She saw it when they opened it for Catherine. Gave her all that gold too, most like to shut her up.' she finished. Elena rolled her eyes at the idle gossip and kicked everyone out of her kitchen for the night. It had been a late one, and there wasn't an individual amongst them that wasn't supposed to be up before dawn the next day. They retired in the grip of imagination, and went to troubled dreams.

After her usual four hours of sleep Elena made her way to the kitchen. She spent an hour sorting bread and breakfast in the morning, and then she was free again for a few hours. She came in the back door, open already. Eric would come in even earlier than she and heat the stove for her arrival. It was the single job he had at this time of the morning, and then he had some free time too. She put her belongings away in the cloakroom and strapped on her apron. She found the dough nicely risen from the night before and made a start.

There was a clatter from downstairs.

Now Elena knew there were guests in the manner, and she knew there were probably servants taking shelter somewhere in the building...but really, the cellar? They'd be better off sleeping in the carriages they'd arrived in. She slammed the mass of sticky dough onto her floured board and stopped again at a choking noise. It had come from the cellar. And where was Eric? She had a sudden image of the boy in the cellar, trying to steal what he had got into his head were diamonds, and not lumps of salt. She wiped her hands on her apron, gave a heavy, world-weary sigh, and followed her instincts to the open cellar door that lay just outside her kitchen. There was a candle flickering below, and the light bounced off the walls and danced around the room. She followed it down the stone steps and towards its source. There was a wall of boxes, a flattened length of iron and three drops of blood, leading away from the candle and into the darkness. She watched her breath rise in puffs about her face and knew she was not alone. She swallowed, and rather than turn to follow the trail of blood into the unknown she uttered the words that ultimately saved her life.

'Wonder what fool left a candle burning down here?' she said out loud, to the wall of boxes ahead. She made a show of shrugging her fairly broad shoulders and bending her aged back to pick up the candle. Then she took a deep breath, hoping it wasn't her last, turned slowly, and ascended the steps again carefully, calmly, and very deliberately. In the safety of her kitchen she boiled the teapot and sat heavily at the servants table. Her eyes fell on a scraped plate containing three cherries, each with teeth-marks still evident on their preserved flesh. What would she tell the boy's father? How would she look his mother in the eye? What sort of men had Catherine brought amongst them? What sort of men stole away the lives of children in the dead of night? There was only one type of man who could accomplish such deeds. The men from horror fables, from ghost stories and camp-fire tales...the shadow men.

And if they had come this far without anyone else noticing it was already over. So in the temporary, feigned safety of her kitchen, Elena Whitbrack drank green tea, and waited for the world to end.

{B, print it...J}

17156121R00126

Printed in Great Britain
by Amazon